BY WILLIAM MELVIN KELLEY

DEM

A Drop of Patience

Dunfords Travels Everywheres

Dancers on the Shore (short stories)

A DIFFERENT DRUMMER

ANCHOR BOOKS
A DIVISION OF RANDOM HOUSE, INC.
New York

A DIFFERENT DRUMMER

WILLIAM MELVIN KELLEY

FOREWORD BY
DAVID BRADLEY

ANCHOR BOOKS EDITIONS, 1969, 1989

Copyright © 1959, 1962 by William Melvin Kelley
Foreword copyright © 1989 by David Bradley

Library of Congress Cataloging-in-Publication Data
Kelley, William Melvin.
    A different drummer / William Melvin Kelley ; with an introduction
by David Bradley.
      p.   cm.
    I. Title.
PS3561.E392D5   1989
813'.54—dc20   89-18441
                                                            CIP

ISBN 978-0-385-41390-9

www.anchorbooks.com

PRINTED IN THE UNITED STATES OF AMERICA
20

*T*he trouble with writing a book, especially the first one, is that by the time you are twenty-three years old, you feel indebted to so many people that you cannot decide to whom you will dedicate it. You must weigh and eliminate. And that is painful because a great many were kind and it is hard to say that one person was more kind than another.

And so, although this book is dedicated to three people in particular, I would like to thank all of the others, who, over the years and especially since I started this book, were concerned enough about me to give me an opinion, either literary or personal, though I did not always take it.

And all of those who have said to me, at one time or another:

"Why don't you come to dinner tonight?"

"You can spend a couple of nights at my place."

"Would you like me to type a couple of pages for you?"

"Here. You can pay me back when you get some money."

Thank you all again. I hope some day I will get around to you all individually.

And the dedications:

To my mother, Narcissa, 1906–1957, who, in the quietly courageous way that she went about everything, challenged death so I could be born, and won.

To my father, William Melvin, Senior, 1894–1958, who, when I was too young to realize it, sacrificed so much for me that it is improbable he was ever again truly happy.

To MSL, who, when I needed it most, gave me enough love and kindness and encouragement to start me writing seriously.

The greater part of what my neighbors call good
I believe in my soul to be bad,
and if I repent of anything,
it is very likely to be my good behavior.
What demon possessed me that I behaved so well?

* * *

If a man does not keep pace with his companions,
perhaps it is because he hears a different drummer.
Let him step to the music which he hears,
however measured or far away.

HENRY DAVID THOREAU

CONTENTS

FOREWORD

BY DAVID BRADLEY

The pond rises and falls, but whether regularly or not, and within what period, nobody knows, though as usual, many pretend to know.[1]

—*Henry David Thoreau*
Walden, *"The Ponds"*

"There is a tide in the affairs of men," wrote William Shakespeare. But as the characters in *Julius Caesar* learn, the only true tide is the ebb and flow of history—the affairs of men are mere currents. Which is not to say currents cannot be powerful; they are. They can also be enduring. Believing that prosperous passage can be had only by going with a prevailing current, some men and women will chart its flow, sound its bottom, define its contours and proclaim its precedence—thus is born the "mainstream." To follow it is not evil. Simply human. And often, for a time, quite correct.

But there is a tide. Tides turn, affecting inexorably, when they do, the dominant currents. One such turn in history's tide took place in the middle of the twentieth century—one cannot put it precisely, for tides are gradual. It is possible, however, to state with more precision the date when the underlying tide visibly affected the current called the American Literary

FOREWORD

Mainstream: June, 1962. And one can say with total precision the name of he who first drew the new chart: William Melvin Kelley.

> *a tide rises and falls behind every man which can float the British Empire like a chip.*[2]

> —*Henry David Thoreau*
> Walden, *"Conclusion"*

William Melvin Kelley was born in New York City on November 1, 1937.[3,4,5] His father, William Melvin, Sr., was a prominent figure in Harlem,[6] for a time editor of the *Amsterdam News*[7] and a resident of the aristocratic Sugar Hill.[8] The young Kelley, however, was not raised in Harlem but in the mostly white North Bronx.

Some might assume that to grow up (as Kelley wrote in *Esquire* in 1963) as "the only Negro boy on a predominantly Italian-American block"[9] would inevitably be traumatic. Such is the conclusion of critic Valerie Babb, for example, who wrote in the *Dictionary of Literary Biography* that Kelley was "forced to play Tonto or the 'friendly native' "[10] in childhood games. But this was a distortion. Kelley's actual statement was: "You must not immediately assume that I was always unhappy. You must not assume I was always fighting my way to school; this was not the case. On the contrary, being the only Negro gave me a wonderful advantage: I was always a very important part of the games my white friends and I played. When we played the Lone Ranger, I was always Tonto. When we fought the Japs, I was always the Friendly Native . . . second only to General MacArthur, and since the good general was continually being captured, drugged, wounded, beaten, or shot, it was the Friendly Native who took command of Allied Operations in the Pacific Theater . . . If it is important for a child to be part of a group of boys his age in his neighborhood, then I was content and secure."[11]

There are, of course, factors which account for Kelley's lack of trauma. For one thing, these games were played at a time in the nation's history —then in the midst of World War II—when the nation's cultural racism was directed outward, at "the Japs." But there was another factor: Kelley's grandmother, Jessie Garcia.

Mrs. Garcia was important to Kelley in several ways. For one, she told him stories—and if there is a constant in the biographies of writers, it is that someone told them stories. But beyond that she had a profound effect on the young Kelley's concept of race. "My grandmother was white; at least she looked white," Kelley wrote.[12] She was, he added, "like an old Italian woman who sat, on spring and summer afternoons, in a red beach chair on the sidewalk across the street."[13] This connection between his family and his neighbors no doubt obviated any sense of isolation he might otherwise have felt. But eventually Kelley asked his grandmother a question which, if answered fully, could have made him feel isolated: "Why did she look white when I looked Negro?"[14]

At the time, however, Mrs. Garcia avoided the intricacies (and ironies) with a partial answer. She told him that her grandfather had been a general in the Confederate Army. It was a bit of an exaggeration, the man was only a colonel, but Kelley immediately flaunted this military connection to his playmates, who at the time—1944—"were actively engaged in fighting the Japanese in the vacant lot"[15] next door. He expected them to be "impressed to their very sneakers. Instead, they did not at all believe me. 'That's a lie. And besides, who ever heard of a colored general?' " they asked. Kelley responded: "But he wasn't colored. He was white." His friends asked: "Then how can he be your relative?"[16] Kelley had no real response, and thus, it seems, his earlier sense of contentment and security was damaged.

Some might cluck their tongues here, in the belief that Kelley should have been schooled in "Negro History" so that he could counter this assault. But one must note that neither Kelley nor his friends had ever heard of a Negro general because there had never *been* a Negro general; this incident probably took place before October of 1944, when Benjamin O. Davis, Sr., became the regular Army's first black general.[17] Nor can the army of the North Bronx be criticized for failing to enlist Kelley as a regular soldier, as it was then "not U.S. policy to mingle colored and white enlisted personnel in the same regiment."[18]—this was surely evident in newsreels Kelley and his friends saw.

Ironically, this may have reduced Kelley's trauma to where he "only knew that something had happened a long time before that had returned to make me seem a liar to my friends."[19] Some might say this was trauma enough. But not Kelley. Although he later understood that, "To other Negro children, growing up in other places, the awareness of difference grew into bitterness and hatred—or resignation and despair,"[20] that was other children.

In adolescence Kelley was exempted from the more physical manifestations of working-class racism; he was not always fighting his way to school because he attended a different one—the private, white Fieldston School.[21] There he was a self-described "golden boy"[22]—academic achiever, president of the student council, a captain of the track team.[23] Track taught him great lessons; it was, he recalled, "the first time I ever worked hard at something." Eventually, though, he not only excelled in it but grew to love his chosen event so much that he claimed to have started writing because he was "looking for something that would give me as much satisfaction as the shot-put."[24]

In 1957 he graduated from Fieldston and matriculated at Harvard, steering toward a "secure and respectable occupation"[25] in law.[26] But within two years he drifted from the course.[27] Why he drifted is hard to say. Perhaps the death of his mother, Narcissa, and his father in 1957 and 1958 unmoored him. But drift he did, changing his major from economics to architecture to government to English,[28] doing a little painting, a little acting, and finally, in the spring of 1959, a little fiction writing.[29] He made rapid progress and his work was quickly recognized; in 1959 his story "Spring Planting" was published in *Accent*[30] and he was mentioned in an article on "New Creative Writers" in *Library Journal*.[31] In 1960 he won the Dana Reed Prize for best writing in an Harvard undergraduate publication.[32] He also failed every course but fiction writing.[33] He also dropped out of school.

Some would call all that more drifting. One might argue, however, that it was an essential course correction; certainly Kelley did not settle onto a new heading without soul searching nor set out without guidance. "I had just decided I would try to write," he recalled. "Since most everyone I knew had expected me to choose a more secure and respectable occupation . . . I felt called upon to give some explanation to someone. I also felt that if my grandmother, who was the only family I had, understood, I could stand up to the others when they asked me why I did not have a decent job."[34] Mrs. Garcia's reaction was simple: "I know. I couldn't have made dresses for seventy years unless I loved it."[35]

This was an important moment for Kelley, but it was also a decisive moment for American Literature. With his very first book William Melvin Kelley, not through choice or even chance, but through the ineluctable works of the tides of history, would alter charts of the American Literary Mainstream.

FOREWORD

What does Africa—what does the West stand for? Is not our own interior white on the chart? black though it may prove, like the coast, when discovered. Is it the source of the Nile, or the Niger, or the Mississippi, or a North-West Passage around this continent that we would find?[36]

—*Henry David Thoreau*
Walden, *"Conclusion"*

Writers know that experience is the wellspring of literature. As William Stafford put it: "My life in writing, or my life as a writer, comes to me as two parts, like two rivers that blend. One part is easy to tell: the times, the places, events, people. The other part is mysterious; it is my thoughts, the flow of my inner life . . . My writings are current manifestations of that blending."[37] Henry David Thoreau put it more strongly: "We commonly do not remember that it is, after all, always the first person that is speaking. I should not talk so much about myself if there were anybody else whom I knew as well. Unfortunately I am confined to this theme by the narrowness of my experience."[38]

The importance of experience is one of the few things about which writers and modern critics agree. (Thus composition teachers, be they writers or English professors, are ever exhorting students to "write what you know"—or at least to begin there.) It is also one of the few things about which critics agree among themselves. Although for the better part of the twentieth century they have argued about how literature is and/or should be read, they have ever assumed that the source was the experience of the author. For some the assumption went deeper; according to Terry Eagleton, it was the belief of some British critics "that words are somehow healthiest when they approach the condition of things . . . Language is alienated or degenerate unless it is crammed with the physical textures of actual experience, plumped with the rank juices of real life."[39] American "New Criticism" grew out of this same notion and held fast to the idea that, though the facts of the author's life or the social context were irrelevant to reading, they were vital to writing. John Crowe Ransom, from whose 1941 book *The New Criticism* the doctrine not only derived but took its name[40] and who was himself one of the "Fugitive" poets, insisted that writers be literary regionalists, emphasizing in their work the history and customs of their region. In the case of the Fugitives, the region was the South.[41]

FOREWORD

Many contemporary critics now find authorial experience of importance even to reading. Sensitized to the fact that the experiential realities of many people have been systematically ignored by history, they seek expressions of that reality in literary texts. Today, literature is often read, taught—and judged—as much for its experiential content as for its literary quality.

But the literature produced by American blacks (or Negroes, or Afro-Americans, or African-Americans, depending on the date and the politics) has always been read this way. In 1923, for example, Claude Barnett, a black newspaper editor, wrote to Jean Toomer, author of *Cane*, on behalf of "a group of three friends, the other two of whom are literary men, one colored and one white,"[42] demanding to know "who and what you are."[43] The reason for this blunt, almost impolite query was that the literary men contended that "your style and finish are not negroid, while I . . . felt certain that you were—for how else could you interpret 'us' as you do?"[44] In 1925 Alain Locke, in *The New Negro*, the seminal anthology of the Harlem Renaissance, would say that the artistic works were able "to document the New Negro culturally and socially, to register the transformations of the inner and outer life of the Negro in America that have so significantly taken place in the last few years" and contained "elements of truest social portraiture."[45]

Similarly, in 1941 Dorothy Canfield described Richard Wright's *Native Son* as "the first report in fiction we have had . . . from those whose behavior patterns give evidence of the same bewildered, senseless tangle of abnormal nerve-reactions studied in animals by psychologists in laboratory experiments."[46] Though in 1943 John T. Frederick claimed that "no longer is a book the object of interest because a Negro wrote it,"[47] at that precise time Wright's agent was pressing Wright for autobiography. And in 1955 James Baldwin's publisher requested that Baldwin "give some account" of himself to introduce *Notes of a Native Son*. Today most critics see authorial experience as even more crucial to understanding the full scope of a literary work, not only because of the laudable liberal impulse to learn from literature that which history did not record, but because American criticism today remains both segregationist and racist.

Some are no doubt squealing with outrage at this point. Yet it should be obvious to all that works produced by black writers are segregated from works produced by white writers. A glance at a few college catalogs, or at the shelves of bookstores, or a browse in the reference sections of libraries will suffice to demonstrate. Rare is the English Department that does not have at least one course in "Black (Afro-American or African-American, but probably not Negro) Literature"; even the large chain stores, let alone specialty and university bookstores, have sections for books of "Black (Afro-American or African-American) Interest." In the library, standard reference works like the *Dictionary of Literary Biography* segregate the biographies and bibliographies of blacks from those of "American" authors. And everywhere there is the implicitly segregationist terminology: "Black (or Negro, or Afro-American, or African-American) Literature"; modified genres—the "black novel."

Separation is not necessarily segregation, of course. And separating one set of works from another is part of what criticism is about. What is expected from critical separations, however, is not just distinction, but difference; if one set is spoken of as distinct from another, it is assumed that there is some characteristic or combination of characteristics common to all the works within the set and possessed by no works outside the set—a formal definition, in other words. No such formal definition has ever been made for Black Literature. "Negro literature is literature created by Negroes,"[48] wrote Frederick in 1943, and although some have added to that definition, none have altered it, and thirty years later Arthur P. Davis assumed it when he additionally defined "a major Negro writer as one whose work deals largely with black experience, measures up to appropriate aesthetic standards, and influences to some extent his contemporaries and/or those who come after him."[49] Today, when even a layperson speaks of "Black Literature," he or she means that the book was written by black; a benign statement, perhaps, but racial segregation by definition.

This literary segregation, like all American racial segregation, was originally supported by perfectly legitimate nineteenth-century beliefs: the scientific doctrine of polygeny, prevalent at Harvard in the 1850s and '60s, held that races of man were distinct species with different psychological as well as physiological traits, and allowed, indeed, led the best educated persons to think blacks incapable of artistic expression;[50] the legal doctrine of "separate-but-equal" set down in 1893 by the Supreme Court; the prevalent social custom called "Jim Crow." Indeed, one must insist that early literary segregation came about quite naturally, as an expression of what was then the American reality. One can hardly condemn the New

FOREWORD

Critics for not mingling colored and white poets in the same essay in 1941 when President Roosevelt would not "mingle colored and white enlisted personnel in the same regiment" in 1944.[51]

But, in fact, proponents of the New Criticism did not speak of colored poets at all. The reason they did not is suggested by the fact that although concentrated at Eastern universities, many were transplanted Southerners.[52] The reason is made explicit by the fact that between Fugitive poets and "New Critics" many—including Ransom—were political Agrarians, the collective authors of a 1930 anthology entitled *I'll Take My Stand*, which can, without exaggeration, be called an apologia for racism.

This bias was concealed as long as segregation was as American as cherry (or pecan) pie. But beginning in 1948, when President Truman issued Executive Orders 9980 and 9981, ending segregation in the federal service and the armed forces,[53] the segregation of literature began to lose the support of the social context. By 1953, when the Supreme Court struck down the separate-but-equal doctrine in *Brown* v. *Board of Education*,[54] the legal basis was lost. Soon the scientific basis too was gone; in 1958 Ralph Ellison could write sarcastically, "I know of no valid demonstration that culture is transmitted through the genes."[55] Thus, between 1948 and 1958 those who sought to treat works by Negroes as a distinct category were caught between the Scylla of social progress and the Charybdis of logic. To insist that race made a difference was becoming socially unacceptable; but if it made no difference, how could there be a "Negro Literature"?

Some might ask—perhaps innocently—why the critical community did not accept the idea of an integrated American Literature and eagerly apply the principles of New Criticism to the material suddenly made available; surely the blatant racism of the Fugitive-Agrarian-New Critics was not characteristic of the entire Modern Language Association. (Although the MLA did have its own tradition of racial segregation.) One less sinister, or at least less racist, explanation is that the integration of American Literature would have entailed not only the addition of a new set of works, but a reconsideration of the existing canon. To put it another way, a massive recharting of the American Literary Mainstream.

Along that course lay . . . madness. A shifting of course descriptions and syllabi. New specialties, perhaps, or equal employment opportunities for those who knew most about the writing of Negroes—in particular, those Negro scholars who had formed the College Language Association, the separate-but-equal MLA. And beyond such political shiftings there would have been shiftings in the canon itself. What would happen if works by blacks were stripped of social context? The answer was known; Baldwin, in 1955, in "Everybody's Protest Novel"—which everybody protested—had eloquently excoriated the critics for failing to apply their own New Critical standards to works like *Native Son:* "It is, indeed, considered the sign of a frivolity so intense as to approach decadence to suggest that these books are badly written and wildly improbable," Baldwin had charged. "One is told to put first things first, the good of society coming before niceties of style or characterization."[56]

Worse than that, it seemed criticism itself was at risk. For by this time, as Eagleton writes, New Criticism "seem[ed] the most natural thing in the literary critical world; indeed it was difficult to imagine there had ever been anything else."[57] But the works of blacks carried with them the critical methods that had been previously applied to them; the scholarship attached to them proved New Criticism was not the only natural thing. Which raised the question of what would happen to the works of the existing Mainstream if they were judged according to these other standards?

The answer to that too was known: in 1953 Ellison had condemned American Literature—with emphasis on Faulkner—by saying: "The Negroes of fiction are so consistently false to human life that we must question just what they truly represent, both in the literary work and in the inner world of the white American . . . these Negroes of fiction are counterfeits. They are projected aspects of an internal symbolic process."[58]

And so critics sought what would be, in effect, a gene for culture—something that, although apparently nonracial, would be characteristic of all works written by blacks but characteristic of no works written by whites. One candidate was the intention of social protest. The notion had historical basis, for some of the earliest and most powerful examples of prose writing by blacks was to be found in the documents of the Abolition movement. It also had contemporary example in the awesome success of *Native Son*, which was clearly intended to inspire readers to outrage and social action. And it also seemed that a lot of Negroes had indeed written works of protest, for during most of American history the conditions of blacks had been so horrific that a sensitive reader could hardly help but be outraged by any accurate portrayal. If the author of the portrayal were black, it was reasonable to assume that outrage was an intended reader response.

Writers—specifically Baldwin and Ellison—denied emphatically that all writing done by blacks was protest literature. Few listened. In 1964

FOREWORD

Kelley, after reading the reviews of his first novel (one of which said the novel "could only increase, rather than diminish racial misunderstanding if it were taken seriously"),[59] would publicly lament that "an American writer who happens to have brown skin faces this unique problem: Solutions and answers to The Negro Problem are very often read into his work,"[60] and insist, "for the record, that I am not a sociologist or a politician or a spokesman."[61] But by 1964 critics had come up with something better than protest; they had charted a mythical sandbar called the Black Experience.

It is remarkable how long men will believe in the bottomlessness of a pond without taking the trouble to sound it.[62]

—*Henry David Thoreau*
Walden, *"The Pond in Winter"*

Just as no one has ever fathomed the deeper reality of Black Literature, so has the black experience gone unsounded. It is obvious that, historically speaking, the experience of blacks in American has been fundamentally different from that of whites—one need only point out (as Kelley eventually did) that whites came to America as immigrants, blacks as imports. It is a bit more difficult to show that the experience of all blacks has been the same, for whatever the general rule of black life at any given time, there have always been exceptions—freedmen living next door to slaves, indeed, in some cases, owning slaves themselves. Moreover, even the "general rule" has changed profoundly on several occasions. One could argue that Emancipation fractured the Black Experience, creating a generation that had never known bondage, or that the Great Migration resulted in a triple fracture—some blacks experienced only the rural South, others only the urban North, and others both, having made the journey between. One could even argue that there is a serious difference between those who made that trek from South to North—Wright, Ellison, Zora Neale Hurston—and those who did not, whose Southern experience was secondary—Toomer, Nella Larsen, Baldwin. No matter how many possible fractures, however, all these blacks continued to share one awful, fundamental commonality: they were set apart by American society—segregated, in a word.

The objection might be made that segregation was not a universal custom. Although it was more widespread than most Americans like to believe—it was practiced not only in Alabama and the District of Columbia, but in Manhattan, in Harlem itself—custom is never universal. But federal law is. And the "separate-but-equal" doctrine was not the law of Alabama, but the law of the land. And thus, wherever blacks lived, whoever they were, they shared a crucial experience. Some were segregated by practice; all were segregated by theory—until May of 1953, when the Supreme Court struck down the "separate-but-equal" doctrine.

Not that the Brown Decision changed the lives of black folk overnight. It meant nothing in practical terms immediately, and very little for a long time; a lot of black people would die before it could mean anything concrete to them at all. Nor did the Brown Decision itself fracture the Black Experience, for if theoretical segregation was a common experience, theoretical desegregation was also.

But to some blacks, particularly young blacks, its meaning was great. To those who were living under practical segregation, its theoretical repudiation meant that they could look into the future and see only practical rather than inherent barricades between themselves and full citizenship. Those barriers were real—local laws, court challenges, mobs, terrorism—but finite. To these young blacks it must have seemed that at least the final battle for equality was at long last joined.

But to some young blacks it must have seemed that that final battle was not simply joined, but over, that it had, in fact, been won. These were the few who had always lived in a world where segregation was only theoretical. One such was William Melvin Kelley, whose background, Valerie Babb wrote, "could be said to represent the culmination of the integrationist dream."[63] For those whose experience had already distanced them from those who had grown up under practical segregation, the Brown Decision cut them apart entirely.

Some would argue that these young blacks were naive and found out the truth quickly. True. But, even so, for them there was a moment of idyllic innocence—a moment other blacks never knew—as can be seen in the following two very different descriptions of the first day of school.

On September 4, 1957, nine young blacks, handpicked as the best and the brightest, attempted to enroll at Central High School in Little Rock, Arkansas. By sad accident, one girl, Elizabeth Eckford, found herself alone. She saw "a large crowd of people standing across the street from the soldiers guarding Central. As I walked on, the crowd suddenly got very quiet . . .

FOREWORD

I walked across the street conscious of the crowd that stood there, but they moved away from me. For a moment all I could hear was the shuffling of their feet. Then someone shouted, 'Here she comes, get ready!' . . . The crowd moved in close and then began to follow me, calling me names . . . I stood looking at the school. It looked so big! Just then the guards let some white students go through . . . I walked up to the guard who had let the white students in. He didn't move. When I tried to squeeze past him, he raised his bayonet and then the other guards closed in and they raised their bayonets . . . I turned around and the crowd came toward me. They moved closer and closer. Somebody started yelling, 'Lynch her! Lynch her!' . . . They came closer, shouting, 'No nigger bitch is going to get into our school. Get out of here!' "[64]

In the same month, William Melvin Kelley entered Harvard Yard. "The empty Yard opened in front of me. The leaves on the trees were dark green; the grass too was green and I remember thinking that it looked like the view in an Easter egg . . . 'This is the place,' I whispered to myself. 'This is the place I've been looking for.' "[65]

Was there a fracture in the unity of the Black Experience on that day? Some will argue no, some yes. But most would accept this logic: if experience is fundamental to literature, it would be expected that, at least in the short term of, say, five years from these events, a book written by Elizabeth Eckford would have a somewhat different viewpoint than a book written by William Melvin Kelley. One cannot test this proposition directly: Elizabeth Eckford never wrote a book. But Kelley did; his first novel was published in the month of June, 1962. It was entitled *A Different Drummer*.

> *But I can assure my readers that Walden has a reasonably tight bottom at a not unreasonable, though at an unusual depth.*[66]
> —*Henry David Thoreau*
> Walden, *"The Pond in Winter"*

A Different Drummer is an elegant book, thin but rich, presenting highly dramatic and colorful events in undramatic tones and straightforward descriptions. Although it makes use of modernistic techniques—flashbacks, multiple points-of-view—its structure is traditional. The plot is singular: events develop not from each other but from a single, primary event like ripples spreading from a rock dropped into a pool. But the plot was also fantastic: the primary event—the exodus of the entire Negro population from a mythical Gulf Coast state—has neither historical precedent nor contemporary comparison. Yet there is sufficient correspondence between Kelley's fantasy, historical facts—slavery, segregation, the Great Migration—and contemporary events—the Montgomery Bus Boycott, the mass marches of the Civil Rights Movement—to make the fantasy seem less like pure imagination than like an expansion and purification of reality; history writ clearer, the daily news in broader headlines. Some might say that the title is ironic, for the massive March on Washington followed by only fourteen months; and that, since the future would seem to march to "a different drummer," the book was in that sense prophetic.

One begs to differ. Kelley's fantasy does not address the future or even the present; the basic information concerning the exodus is presented not as a hot news flash but as, literally, an encyclopedia entry. The events of the novel are therefore fixed in the past—in 1957, to be precise. *A Different Drummer* is, then, a historical fantasy—a myth. But because the historical events were then still recent, it was a special kind of myth. The poet Archibald MacLeish described it in a dust-jacket blurb, "not a myth of time gone, but a myth of time going—a myth for now."[67]

The "myth for now" makes clear and conscious connections with the literary past. The title and epigraphs are taken from Thoreau's *Walden*, while the name of the main character is surnamed after Caliban, the "poisonous slave, got by the devil himself," in Shakespeare's *The Tempest*. Like Shakespeare's Caliban, Kelley's Calibans have been deprived of their birthright and enslaved. Tucker Caliban, the hero, had the physical form of Shakespeare's Caliban—or at least the form assigned him by the slavemaster Prospero. But where Shakespeare's Caliban was embittered and soured, reduced to cursing, Tucker reclaims his birthright and his freedom in a series of revolutionary acts. First, he insists on having his own land. Then, after a time as a yeoman, he destroys his farm and departs for a destination unknown. And though he offers no public explanation of these actions, they make so much sense to other blacks of the region that they too depart, leaving behind only possessions which they do not value and a population of mystified whites.

Since Black Literature is not a formal concept, one cannot directly demonstrate that *A Different Drummer* is outside of the recognized literary tradition. Indeed, Arthur Davis, although he praised Kelley for "making use of fantasy, symbol, and other modern devices and techniques"[68] and for creating in Tucker "a new type of Negro character,"[69] insists that *A Different Drummer* is only "a new, bitter, and effective type of protest novel."[70]

At a time when the dominant mode of activity among blacks was protest, it was natural for Davis to discuss *A Different Drummer* in terms of protest fiction. But, in fact, one of the most striking things about *A Different Drummer* is that it could not, by definition, be considered a protest novel for the simple reason that it presents no description of horrorific conditions. The circumstances from which Kelley's blacks remove themselves could have been described in retrospect (as was Tucker's departure) but they were not, at least not in an inflammatory way. By 1962 such conditions as Kelley portrayed were known and accepted, and had not half the shock value of events daily described in newspaper accounts or television broadcasts. The only fictional act that could inspire outrage, the lynching, occurs at the end; it is catharsis, not instigation.

But Davis was correct in seeing Tucker as a new kind of black hero, a transformation of the hero as seen in Wright's work or in Ellison's *Invisible Man*, or in any number of other stories and novels written by blacks. Typically, black characters who triumphed had been comedic figures who, using guile and deception, ran away or went underground, but who never went head-on against the forces of oppression. If they did go head-on, they were tragic, fatalistic figures, who ended up dead. But Tucker liberates himself in a perfectly straightforward manner and lives to go on. He not only succeeds but survives.

And he succeeds not by accident, but through the application of an intellectual process—another transformation in the literary mainstream. Not that the heroes in fiction by blacks were all stupid—although one would argue that Bigger Thomas's elevator stopped short of the top—but they did tend to be innocent, achieving true understanding of their situation through a process of discovery—which is to say by getting kicked around. Ellison's *Invisible Man*, for example, wanders through the world like a colored Candide. But Tucker is never innocent. At fourteen he is a teacher, and although he does move toward enlightenment, he always knows what the next step on the path must be.

And he takes each next step in his own good time. Unlike many black male characters—especially in Wright's work—who are pursued by a mob,

FOREWORD

Tucker has done no wrong *even in the eyes of the whites*. He destroys no white property, defies no white man, is "fresh" to no white woman. And so he walks.

And he walks in silence. Although in keeping with the title, as well as the traditions of Black Literature, such a stance was not in keeping with contemporary black life. In 1962 blacks were not only protesting, but protesting loudly; speeches and singing were as much a hallmark of mass marches as was marching itself. But Tucker makes no sound—makes not even a public statement.

Tucker issues no manifesto because he has no ideology—another transformation, for every black reformer, it seemed, had *some* kind of ideology—Du Bois, Paul Robeson, and Wright had communism, Martin Luther King had Christianity, Malcolm X had Islam. But Tucker is not guided by the teachings of Mohammed or Jesus or Karl Marx; he is guided by no external authority at all. Some would argue that the title indicates he is responding to the principles articulated by Thoreau in "Civil Disobedience." Tucker does, as Thoreau suggests, "withdraw . . . both in person and property,"[71] but Tucker never read Thoreau; Kelley did, but that only means that there was an ideology *behind* Tucker, not guiding him.

Nor does Tucker guide anyone. People follow him, but without his knowledge, certainly without his instigation. Tucker, like Thoreau, seems to feel that there is but little virtue in the masses of men; he forms no organization, and refuses to join one. Another transformation, for the history of black agitation is virtually a chronicle of organizations—the Niagra Movement, the Urban League, the Universal Negro Improvement Association. By 1962 the movement had more "alphabet agencies"— NAACP, CORE, SCLC, SNCC—than the New Deal. Nor would such organizations have recognized Tucker as a leader, for he is not a part of the Talented Tenth.

But the most striking difference between Tucker Caliban and actual political leaders is this: he is violent. Nonviolence was obviously King's hallmark, and even Malcolm X never counseled violent actions, only "appropriate" reactions. But Tucker does not react, he acts. And though he kills no person and destroys no one else's property, he does destroy his own property and slaughters his animals and, moreover, he begins the sequence by salting the earth—Tucker wages the Third Punic War in reverse.

FOREWORD

These radical transformations of long-standing traditions in both literature and social action would seem to demonstrate that Kelley's vision was different from that of blacks who came before him. One is therefore tempted to agree with Davis and declare that *A Different Drummer* represents a new direction simply in *Black* Literature. One is saved from that error by the tide of history, which in June of 1962 swept another novel ashore.

> *The rise and fall of Walden at long intervals serves this use at least; the water standing at this great height for a year or more . . . kills the shrubs and trees which have sprung up about its edge since the last rise . . . By this fluctuation the pond asserts its title to the shore . . . the trees cannot hold it by right of possession.*[72]

—Henry David Thoreau
Walden, "The Ponds"

Even those who navigate only the tried and true channels know that June, 1962, marked a change in the Mainstream, for it dates the publication of William Faulkner's last work, *The Reivers*.[73] One of Faulkner's slightest works—he himself called it "a reminiscence"—*The Reivers* is notable because it gives readers one last glimpse of Yoknapatawpha County, one last reminder of the passionate, bloody, and complex interactions between the Old South's self-made (or self-imagined) aristocracy, the ambitious yeomanry —what some would call poor white trash—and the usually patient blacks.

But, in fact, *The Reivers* is remarkably mute with respect to actual interactions. At a time when Southern conflicts were so much a part of the national consciousness, Faulkner was drawing material from the early years of the century—the years of his own childhood—a time when contemporary conflicts were beyond prediction, indeed, beyond fantasy. *The Reivers* is less a reminiscence than an avoidance. Some would say that Faulkner had said all he needed to say on the matter of race in *Sartoris* or *Absalom, Absalom!* or in the powerful novels of the Snopes Trilogy: *The Hamlet*, *The Town*, and *The Mansion*, the last of which was completed in 1959.[74] Others would say that this kind of avoidance is typical of Faulkner, whose personal views on race relations were not only ante-Brown Decision, but antebellum—one might add, antediluvian.

In any case, few readers would have spoken of *A Different Drummer* and *The Reivers* in the same breath; the sandbar of the Black Experience isolated

FOREWORD

Faulkner, a creature of the Mainstream, from the flow of Black Literature. And yet if one is willing to step across the bar, one finds remarkable similarities between Kelley's first novel and Faulkner's last.

Both writers create, as a background for their tales, mythical areas in the American South, complete with local history and geography. The only difference is that, while Faulkner places his mythical Yoknapatawpha County in the *actual* state of Mississippi, Kelley creates a mythical state as well. To embody his invented history, Faulkner creates legendary characters like slaveholder Thomas Sutpen and Confederate Colonel John Sartoris. Kelley similarly creates Colonel Willson and the African.

Their minor characters compare also. Kelley recapitulates the class types that figure in Faulkner's greatest fictions. The old Southern aristocracy—the Sartorises and Compsons in Faulkner—are Kelley's Willsons; the poor whites—Faulkner's Snopeses—are Kelley's Lelands; and the other "men on the porch"—Faulkner's blacks—are Kelley's clan of Caliban. And if some would say that, with regard to the black characters, Kelley and Faulkner parted company, one must insist that, although Faulkner never created a black man remotely similar to Tucker, neither did most black writers.

Nevertheless, Kelley uses precisely the same techniques that Faulkner uses—shifting narrators, time frames, and points of view—and to precisely the same end: to humanize and sympathize characters whose points of view readers might have ignored. One striking similarity between *A Different Drummer* and *The Reivers* is the use of a child's uncomplicated, uncomprehending—and nonracist—point of view.

Perhaps all this is to be expected. Young writers are expected to emulate the masters and were (until recently) uniformly proud of their success in doing so. Four years and two books after the publication of *A Different Drummer* Kelley would suggest that he was "trying to follow the Faulknerian pattern . . . I'd like to be eighty years old and look up at the shelf and see that all of my books are really one big book."[75] But Kelley is able to do both what Faulkner could and what Faulkner could not. He creates Faulknerian characters as sympathetically as Faulkner himself, and at the same time creates a powerful black character—so powerful that (unlike Faulkner's blacks) he can liberate himself and other blacks without white intervention. Indeed, so powerful that he can liberate white people too: Tucker, in liberating himself, rejuvenates the Willson's marriage, revi- ✗

talizes the troubled relationship between father and son, inspires the imagination of Mister Leland. Kelley thus offers a cure for all the agony and guilt that weighs down Faulkner's characters, driving them to fatalism, alcoholism, and suicide.

Is this proof positive that *A Different Drummer* is black literature? Maybe, but there is this problem: Kelley, like Faulkner, chooses to portray the actions of blacks through exclusively Caucasian eyes. This vantage point has caused a great many troublesome questions for contemporary critics. Why, some wonder, would he write this way? Why did he not tell us of a black sharecropper hearing of Tucker's action, of black folk gathering, debating, wondering, struggling with the awful existential questions of what to take and what to leave behind. He could have done these things instead. He could also have done them in addition. The possibilities are myriad and so easy to imagine that one can almost argue that Kelley had to consciously and intentionally reject them as he moved from the basic conception of *A Different Drummer*—an exodus of Negroes—to the novel's full expression. Which is to say that he specifically rejects critics like Davis who would define "a major Negro writer as one whose work deals largely with black experience."[76]

Some, perhaps even most, may suspect that Kelley was a victim of an identity problem. Certainly such problems are not unknown, especially to blacks like Kelley, pioneers of the intellectual, social, and emotional boundary between blackness and whiteness. Perhaps Kelley chose to write from a white point of view because he had been brainwashed at Fieldston and Harvard and was uncomfortable with a black one. Perhaps in "trying to follow the Faulknerian pattern" he was actually trying to avoid a Negro pattern. Which might explain why two decades later Professor Babb would assume that Kelley's childhood must have been traumatic; because to explain the shape of *A Different Drummer*, *something* had to be wrong.

One could respond. One does not wish to. One wishes merely to point out that just as Faulkner's Southern Colonel is based on his real-life ancestor, so is Kelley's. Additionally, just as an elderly female of another race told Kelley stories when he was a child, so did an elderly female of another race—a black nanny named Caroline Barr—tell Faulkner stories. It may very well be that there was nothing wrong, no traumatic reason for Kelley's choice of perspective, and that, on the contrary, something was finally exactly as it should be.

FOREWORD

What if all ponds were shallow? Would it not react on the minds of men? I am thankful that this pond was made deep and pure for a symbol. While some men believe in the infinite some ponds will be thought to be bottomless.[77]

—*Henry David Thoreau*
Walden, *"The Pond in Winter"*

A Different Drummer was a relatively small ripple on the rising tide of change in June, 1962. Far more significant was the awesome opportunity, for the first time in history, to envision an American reality identical with American ideals. One need not belabor the obvious; the opportunity was lost. So was this incredible, visionary novel which, sadly, was never really *seen*, was perhaps never really understood, and soon went out of print.

Though the tide may never rise so high again, one can see its working against the currents of prejudice, for now it brings *A Different Drummer* drifting back to us like a bottle long ago cast upon the waters. One hopes you will reach out, grasp that bottle, open it. There is, one can assure you, something important inside. A new chart of the American Literary Mainstream.

1. Thoreau, Henry David, *Walden*, "The Ponds," 1854.
2. Thoreau, Henry David, *Walden*, "Conclusion," 1854.
3. Kelley, William M., *Dancers on the Shore* (Washington, D.C.: Howard University Press, 1984).
4. Babb, Valerie, *Dictionary of Literary Biography, Afro-American Fiction Writers After 1955*, Vol. XXXIII, Thadious Davis and Trudier Harris, eds. (Detroit: Gale Research, 1984), pp. 135–43.
5. Borden, William, *Contemporary Novelists*, 4th ed. (Chicago: St. James Press, date unknown), p. 490.
6. Anderson, Jervis, *This Was Harlem* (New York: Farrar, Straus & Giroux, 1982), p. 62.
7. ibid., pp. 62, 343.
8. loc. cit.
9. Kelley, William M., "The Ivy League Negro," *Esquire*, August 1963, p. 54.
10. Babb, op. cit., pp. 135–43.
11. Kelley, William M., "The Ivy League Negro," *Esquire*, August 1963, p. 54.

12. loc. cit.
13. loc. cit.
14. loc. cit.
15. loc. cit.
16. loc. cit.
17. Bennett, Lerone, Jr., *Before the Mayflower: A History of Black America* (Chicago: Johnson Publishing Company, 1962), p. 533.
18. ibid., p. 634.
19. Kelley, William M., "The Ivy League Negro," *Esquire*, April 1963, p. 54.
20. loc. cit.
21. Babb, op. cit., pp. 135–43.
22. loc. cit.
23. loc. cit.
24. Newquist, Roy, *Conversations* (Chicago: Rand McNally, 1967), p. 208.
25. Kelley, William M., *Dancers on the Shore* (Garden City, N.Y.: Doubleday, 1964), dedication.
26. Babb, op. cit., pp. 135–43.
27. Kelley, William M., *Dancers on the Shore*, op. cit., dedication.
28. Newquist, op. cit., p. 206.
29. Babb, op. cit., pp. 135–43.
30. loc. cit.
31. Rush, Theressa, Carol Myers, and Esther Arate, *Black American Writers Past and Present: A Biographical and Bibliographical Dictionary*, Vol. II (Metuchen, N.J.: Scarecrow Press, 1975), p. 454.
32. Babb, op. cit., pp. 135–43.
33. loc. cit.
34. Kelley, William M., *Dancers on the Shore*, op. cit., dedication.
35. loc. cit.
36. Thoreau, Henry David, *Walden*, "Conclusion," 1854.
37. Stafford, William, *You Must Revise Your Life* (Ann Arbor, Mich.: University of Michigan Press, 1983), p. 3.
38. Thoreau, Henry David, *Walden*, "Economy," 1854.
39. Eagleton, Terry, *Literary Theory: An Introduction* (Minneapolis: University of Minnesota Press, 1983), p. 27.
40. *Encyclopaedia Britannica*, 15th ed., Vol. 9, p. 939.
41. *Encyclopaedia Britannica*, 15th ed., Vol. 5, p. 35.

FOREWORD

Benson, Joseph Brian and Mabel Mayle Dillard, *Jean Toomer* (New York: Twayne, 1980), p. 33.

loc. cit.

loc. cit.

Locke, Alain, *The New Negro* (New York: Albert and Charles Boni, 1925), p. ix.

Fisher, Dorothy Canfield, Introduction to *Native Son*, by Richard Wright (New York: Harper and Row, 1940), p. xi.

Frederick, John T. *Anthology of American Negro Literature*, Sylvestre C. Watkins, ed. (New York: Modern Library, 1944), Introduction.

loc. cit.

Davis, Arthur P., *From the Dark Tower: Afro-American Writers, 1900–1960* (Washington, D.C.: Howard University Press, 1981), p. xiv.

Gould, Stephen Jay, *The Mismeasure of Man* (New York: W. W. Norton, 1981), p. 44.

Bennett, op. cit., p. 634.

Eagleton, op. cit., pp. 49–50.

Wilkins, Roy, *Standing Fast: The Autobiography of Roy Wilkins* (New York: Viking Press, 1982), pp. 201–2.

Warren, Earl, Decision of the Supreme Court of the United States in *Brown* v. *Board of Education of Topeka*, *The Civil Rights Reader: Basic Documents of the Civil Rights Movement*, Leon Friedman, ed. (New York: Walker and Company, 1968), p. 31.

Ellison, Ralph, "Some Questions and Some Answers," from *Shadow & Act* (New York: New American Library, 1953, 1964), pp. 253–55.

Baldwin, James, "Everybody's Protest Novel," from *Notes of a Native Son* (Boston: Beacon Press, 1955), p. 18.

Eagleton, op. cit., pp. 49–50.

Ellison, Ralph, "Twentieth Century Fiction and the Black Mask of Humanity," from *Shadow & Act* (New York: New American Library, 1964), p. 42.

Lyell, F. H., *New York Times Book Review*, June 24, 1962, p. 24.

Kelley, William M., *Dancers on the Shore*, op. cit., preface.

loc. cit.

Thoreau, Henry David, *Walden*, "The Pond in Winter," 1854.

Babb, op. cit., pp. 135–43.

FOREWORD

64. Bates, Daisy, *The Long Shadow of Little Rock: A Memoir* (Fayetteville, Ark.: University of Arkansas Press, 1957), pp. 73–75.

65. Kelley, William M., "The Ivy League Negro," *Esquire*, August 1963, p. 54.

66. Thoreau, Henry David, *Walden*, "The Pond in Winter," 1854.

67. Kelley, William M., *A Different Drummer* (Garden City, N.Y.: Doubleday, 1963), dust jacket, first ed.

68. Davis, op. cit., pp. 142–43.

69. loc. cit.

70. loc. cit.

71. Thoreau, Henry David, *Civil Disobedience* (New York: Modern Library, 1937, 1965), p. 645.

72. Thoreau, Henry David, *Walden*, "The Pond in Winter," 1854.

73. Grun, Bernard, *The Timetables of History* (New York: Simon & Schuster, 1975).

74. loc. cit.

75. Newquist, op. cit., p. 208.

76. Davis, op. cit., p. xiv.

77. Thoreau, Henry David, *Walden*, "The Pond in Winter," 1854.

A DIFFERENT DRUMMER

THE
STATE

An excerpt from THE THUMB-NAIL ALMANAC, 1961 . . . page 643:

An East South Central state in the Deep South, it is bounded on the north by Tennessee; east by Alabama; south by the Gulf of Mexico; west by Mississippi.

CAPITAL: *Willson City.* AREA: *50,163 square miles.* POPULATION: *(1960 Census, preliminary) 1,802,268.* MOTTO: *With Honor and Arms We Dare Defend Our Rights.* ADMITTED TO UNION: *1818*

EARLY HISTORY—DEWEY WILSON:

Although the state's history is a rich and varied one, it is known predominately as the home of Confederate General Dewey Willson, who, in 1825, was born in Sutton, a small town 27 miles north of the Gulfport city of New Marsails. Willson matriculated at the United States Military Academy at West Point (class of 1842), rose to the rank of colonel in the

Federal Army before the outbreak of the Civil War. Upon the state's secession in 1861, he resigned his commission and was given the rank of General of the Confederate Army. He was the chief architect of the two well-known southern victories at Bull's Horn Creek and at Harmon's Draw, the latter fought less than 3 miles from his birthplace. His victory at Harmon's Draw permanently frustrated northern attempts to reach and capture New Marsails.

In 1870, with the state's re-admittance to the Union, Willson became its governor. Shortly thereafter, he chose the site, initiated construction, and, in large part, designed the new state capital which now bears his name. Upon his retirement from public life in 1878, he returned to Sutton. On April 5, 1889, having just returned from the dedication of a ten-foot bronze likeness of himself which the townspeople of Sutton had erected in their Square, he was stricken and died. He is considered by most historians to have been, after Lee, the Confederacy's greatest general.

RECENT HISTORY:

In June 1957, for reasons yet to be determined, all the state's Negro inhabitants departed. Today, it is unique in being the only state in the Union that cannot count even one member of the Negro race among its citizens.

THE
AFRICAN

It was over now. Most of the men standing, slouching, or sitting on the porch of the Thomason Grocery Company had been at Tucker Caliban's farm on Thursday when it all started, though, with the possible exception of Mister Harper, none of them had known it was the start of anything. All during Friday and most of Saturday they had watched the Negroes of Sutton, with suitcases or empty-handed, waiting at the end of the porch for the hourly bus which would carry them up Eastern Ridge, through Harmon's Draw, to New Marsails and the Municipal Railroad Depot. From the radio and the newspapers they knew Sutton was not the only town, knew that all the Negroes in all the cities, towns, and crossroads in the state had been using any means of transportation available, including their own two legs to journey toward the state's borders, to cross over into Mississippi or Alabama or Tennessee, even if some (most did not) stopped right there and began looking for shelter and work. They knew most would not stop just over the borders, would go on until they came to a place where they had merely the smallest opportunity to live, or die decently, for the men had seen pictures of the depot jammed with black people, and being on the Highway between New Marsails and Willson City, had watched the line of cars crammed with Negroes and enough belongings to convince the men that the Negroes had not gone to all this trouble to move a mere hundred miles or so. And they all read the governor's statement: "There ain't nothing to worry about. We never needed them, never wanted them, and we'll get along fine without them; the South'll get along fine without them. Even though our population's been cut by a third, we'll fare all right. There's still lots of good men left."

They all wanted to believe this. They had not lived long enough in a world without black faces to know anything for certain, but hoped everything would be all right, tried to convince themselves it was really over, but sensed, that for them, it was just beginning.

Though they had been present at the very start, they had fallen behind the rest of the state, for they had not yet experienced the anger and bitter resentment which they read about in the papers, had not tried to stop the Negroes from leaving, as had other white men in other towns, feeling it was their right and duty to tear suitcases from any black hands which held them; or thrown any punches. They had been spared the disheartening discovery that such gestures were futile or had been barred from such demonstrations of righteous anger—Mister Harper had made them see that the Negroes could not be stopped; Harry Leland had gone so far as to express the idea that the Negroes had the right to leave—and so, now, late Saturday afternoon, as the sun swooped behind the flat-faced, unpainted buildings across the Highway, they turned back to Mister Harper and tried for the thousandth time in three days to discover how it ever began in the first place. They could not know it all, but what they did know might give them some part of an answer and they wondered if what Mister Harper said about "blood" could possibly be true.

Mister Harper usually appeared on the porch at eight in the morning, where for twenty years he had held court in a wheel chair as old and awkward as a throne. He was a retired army man, who had gone North to West Point, having been nominated to the Academy by the General himself, Dewey Willson. At West Point, Mister Harper had learned to wage the wars he would never have the opportunity to fight: he was too young for the War Between the States, did not arrive in Cuba until long after the Spanish-American War had ended, and was too old for World War I, which had taken his son from him. War had given him nothing, but had deprived him of everything, and so, thirty years before, he decided life was not worth meeting on foot, since it always knocked you down, and seated himself in a wheel chair to view the world from the porch, explaining its chaotic pattern to the men who clustered around him each day.

In all those thirty years, when the world could see it, he had climbed from the wheel chair only once—on Thursday, to go to Tucker Caliban's farm. Now he was again rooted as firmly as though he had never left it, his limp white hair, parted in the middle and long, falling almost like a woman's on either side of his face. His hands were folded over a small but protruding stomach.

Thomason, who, because he did so little business, was hardly ever in his store, stood just behind Mister Harper, his back pressed against the dirty plate glass of his show window. Bobby-Joe McCollum, the youngest member of the group, barely twenty, sat on the porch steps with his feet in the gutter, smoking a cigar. Loomis, a habitual member of the group, was in a chair, reared back on its two hind legs. He had been upstate to the university at Willson, though he had lasted only three weeks, and thought

Mister Harper's explanation of the happenings too fantastic, too simple. "Now, I just can't believe this here blood business."

"What else can it be?" Mister Harper turned to Loomis and squinted through his hair. He spoke differently from the rest of the men; his voice, high, breathy, dry, distinct, like a New Englander's. "Mind you, I'm not one of these superstitious folks; I don't take account of ghosts and such. But the way I see it, it's pure genetics: something special in the blood. And if anybody in this world got something special in his blood, his name is Tucker Caliban." He lowered his voice, spoke almost in a whisper. "I can see whatever was in his blood just a-laying there sleeping, waiting, and then one day waking up, making Tucker do what he did. Can't be no other reason. We never had no trouble with him, nor him with us. But all at once his blood started to itch in his veins, and he started this here . . . this here revolution. And I know all about revolution; that's one of the things we studied at the Point. Why d'you reckon I thought it was important enough to get up out of my chair?" He stared across the street. "It's got to be the African's blood! That's simple!"

Bobby-Joe's chin was cupped in his hands. He did not turn around to look at the old man, and so Mister Harper did not realize immediately the boy was making fun of him. "I hear tell about this African, and can even remember somebody telling the story to me a long time ago, but I JUST CAN'T seem to remember how it went." Mister Harper had told the story the day before, and many times before that. "Why don't you tell it, Mister Harper, and let us see how it got something to do with all this. How about that?"

By now Mister Harper realized what was going on, but it did not matter. He knew too some of the men thought he was too old and ought to be dead instead of coming to the porch each morning. But he liked to tell the story. Even so, they would have to coax him. "You all know that story as well as me."

THE AFRICAN

"Awh now, Mister Harper, we just want to hear you tell it again."
Bobby-Joe tried to make the man a child by the coddling tone in
his voice. Someone behind Mister Harper laughed.

"Hell! I don't care. I'll tell it even if you don't want to hear it
—just for spite!" He leaned back and took a deep breath. "Now,
ain't nobody claiming this here story is ALL true."

"That's true if nothing else is." Bobby-Joe drew on his cigar and
spat.

"All right, suppose you just let me tell this story."

"Yes, SIR." Bobby-Joe exaggerated his apology, but turning,
found no approval on the other men's shadowed faces; Mister Harper
had captured them already. "Yes, sir." This time Bobby-Joe meant
it.

Like I said, nobody's claiming this story is all truth. It must-a
started out that way, but somebody along the way or a whole parcel
of somebodies must-a figured they could improve on the truth. And
they did. It's a damn sight better story for being half lies. Can't a
story be good without some lies. You take the story of Samson.
Might not all be true as you read it in the Bible; folks must-a figured
if you got a man just a little bit stronger than most, it couldn't do
no real harm if you make him a whole lot stronger. So that's probably
what folks hereabouts did; take the African, who must-a been pretty
big and strong to start and make him even bigger and stronger.

I reckon they wanted to make certain we'd remember him. But
when you think on it, there's no reason why we'd ever forget the
African, even though this all happened a long time ago, because
just like Tucker Caliban, the African was working for the Willsons,
who was the most important folks around these parts. Only folks
liked those Willsons a hell of a lot more in them days than we do
now. They weren't so uppity as our Willsons.

But we're not talking about the Willsons of nowadays; we're

talking about the African, who was owned by the General's father, Dewitt Willson, even though Dewitt never got no work out of him. But he owned him all the same.

Now the first time New Marsails (it was still New Marseilles then, after the French city) ever saw the African was in the morning, just after the slave ship he was riding pulled into the harbor. In them days, a boat coming was always a big occasion and folks used to walk down to the dock to greet it; it wasn't a far piece since the town wasn't no bigger than Sutton is today.

The slaver came up, her sails all plump, and tied up, and let fall her gangplank. And the ship's owner, who was also the leading slave auctioneer in New Marsails—he talked so good and so fast he could sell a one-armed, one-legged, half-witted Negro for a premium price—he ambled up the gangplank. I'm told he was a spindly fellow, with no muscles whatever. He had hard-bargain-driving eyes and a nose all round and puffy and pocked like a rotten orange, and he always wore a blue old-time suit with lace at the collar, and a sort of derby of green felt. And following him, exactly three paces behind, was a Negro. Some folks said this was the auctioneer's son by a colored woman. I don't know that for certain, but I DO know this here Negro looked, walked, and talked just like his master. He had that same build, and the same crafty eyes, and dressed just like him too—green derby and all—so that the two of them looked like a print and a negative of the same photograph, since the Negro was brown and had kinky hair. This Negro was the auctioneer's bookkeeper and overseer and anything else you can think of. So then these two went up on deck, and while the Negro stood by, the auctioneer shook hands with the captain, who was standing on deck watching his men do their chores. You understand, they spoke different in them days, so I can't be certain exactly what they said, but I reckon it was something like: "How do. How was the trip?"

Already some folks standing on the dock could see the captain looked kind of sick. "Fine, excepting we had one real ornery son of a bitch. Had to chain him up, alone, away by himself."

"Let's have a look at him," said the auctioneer. The Negro behind him nodded, which he did every time the auctioneer spoke, so that he looked like he was a ventriloquist, and the auctioneer was his dummy, either that way or the other way around.

"Not yet. God damn! I'll bring him up after the rest of them niggers is OFF the boat. Then we can ALL hold him down. Damn!" He put his hand up to his brow, and that's when folks with good eyes could see the oily blue mark on his head like somebody spat axle grease on him and he hadn't had time yet to wipe it off. "God damn!" he said again.

Well, of course folks was getting real anxious, not just out of common interest like usual, but to see this son of a bitch that was causing all the trouble.

Dewitt Willson was there too. He hadn't come to see the boat, or even to buy slaves. He was there to pick up a grandfather clock. He was building himself a new house outside of Sutton and he'd ordered this clock from Europe and he wanted it to come as fast as possible, and the fastest way was for it to come by slaver. He'd heard how carrying things on a slaver was seven kinds of bad luck, but still, because he was so anxious to get the clock, he let them send it that way. The clock rode in the captain's cabin and was all padded up with cotton, and boxed in, and crated around, and wadded secure. And he'd come to get it, bringing in a wagon to carry it out to his house and surprise his wife with it.

Dewitt and everybody was waiting, but first the crew went down and cracked their whips and herded this long line of Negroes out of the hold. The women had breasts hanging most down to their waists, and some carried black babies. The men, their faces was all twisted up sullen as the inside of lemons. Most all the slaves was bone-naked and they stood on the deck, blinking; none of them had seen the sun in a long time. The auctioneer and his Negro walked up and down the row, as always, inspecting teeth, feeling muscles, looking over the goods, you might say. Then the auctioneer said, "Well, let's bring up this troublemaker, what say."

"No, sir!" yelled the captain.

"Why not?"

"I told you. I don't want him brung up until the rest of these niggers is off the boat."

"Yes, surely," said the auctioneer, but looked sort of blank. And so did his Negro.

The captain rubbed that shining grease-spot wound. "Don't you understand? He's their chief. If he says the word we'll have more trouble here than God has followers. I had enough already!" And he rubbed that spot again.

The crewmen pushed them Negroes down the gangplank and the folks on the dock stepped out of the way and watched them go by. Them Negroes even SMELLED angry, having been crammed together, each of them with no more room to himself than a baby in a crib. They was dirty, and mad, and ready for a fight. So the captain sent down some crewmen with rifles to keep them company. And the other crewmen, twenty or thirty there was, they just stood on deck fidgeting and shuffling. Folks on the dock knew right off what was the matter: them crewmen was afraid. You could see it in their eyes. All them grown men scared of whatever was down in the hold of that boat chained to the wall.

The captain looked sort of scared himself and fingered his wound and sighed and said to his mate: "I reckon you might as well go down there and get him." And to the twenty or thirty men standing around: "You go down there with him—all of you. Maybe you can manage."

Folks held their breath like youngsters at a circus waiting for a high-wire fellow to make it to his nest, because even if an old deaf-blind lady had-a been standing on that dock, she would-a known there was something down in the hold that was getting ready to make an appearance. Everybody got quiet and over the waves slapping against the hull they could hear all them crewmen tramping downstairs, the whole swarm of them in heavy bro-GANS, taking their time about informing that thing in the hold it was wanted on deck.

Then, out of the bottom of the ship, way off in some dark place, came this roar, louder'n a cornered bear or maybe two bears mating. It was so loud the sides of the boat bulged out. They all knew it was from one throat since there wasn't no blending, just one loud sound. And then, right in front of their eyes, in the side of the boat, way down near the water line, they saw a hole tear open, and splinters fly, splashing like when you toss a handful of pebbles into a pond. There was a lot of muffled fighting, pushing, and hollering going on, and after a while this fellow staggered on deck with blood dripping from his head. "God damn—if he ain't pulled his chain outen the wall of the boat," he says. And everybody stared at that hole again, and didn't take note that the crewman had just passed on from a cracked skull.

Well sir, you can believe that folks got into close knots for protection in case that thing in the bottom of the ship should somehow get loose and start a-raging through the peaceful town of New Marsails. Then it got sort of quiet again, even on the inside of the ship, and folks leaned forward, listening. They heard chains dragging and then they saw the African for the first time.

To begin with, they seen his head coming up out of the gangway, and then his shoulders, so broad he had to climb those stairs sideways; then his body began, and long after it should-a stopped it was still coming. Then he was full out, skin-naked except for a rag around his parts, standing at least two heads taller than any man on the deck. He was black and glistened like the captain's grease-spot wound. His head was as large as one of them kettles you see in a cannibal movie and looked as heavy. There was so many chains hung on him he looked like a fully trimmed Christmas tree. But it was his eyes they kept looking at; sunk deep in his head they was, making it look like a gigantic black skull.

There was something under his arm. At first they thought it was a tumor or growth and didn't pay it no mind, and it wasn't until it moved all by itself and they noticed it had eyes that they saw it was a baby. Yes sir, a baby tucked under his arm like a black lunch box, just peeping out at everybody.

So now they'd seen the African, and they stepped back a little as if the distance between him and them wasn't at all far enough, as if he could reach out over the railing of the ship, and down at them and pop off their heads with a flick of his fingers. But he was quiet now, not blinking in the sun like them others, just basking like it was his very own and he'd ordered it to come out and shine on him.

Dewitt Willson just stared. It was hard to tell what he was thinking but some folks said they heard him saying slowly to himself over and over again: "I'll own him. He'll work for me. I'll break him. I have to break him." They said he just stared and talked to himself.

And the auctioneer's Negro, he just stared too. But he wasn't mumbling or talking. Folks said he just looked like he was pricing something—looking at the African from head to toe and adding totals: so much for the head and the brain; so much for the build and the muscles; so much for the eyes—making notes on a piece of paper with a crayon.

The captain had yelled down to his men to get them Negroes over to the auction place, a mound of dirt in the center of New Marsails in what is now Auction Square. Some men cleared a way and some others came down off the boat and started pushing the line of chained Negroes. Then came all the people on the dock who was going over to the Square to see what the going price for a good slave was on that day, like folks read the stock market reports nowadays, and more important, to see how much the African would sell for. And after they'd gone away some, came the African and his escort, twenty men at least, each holding a chain so he looked like a Maypole with all the men around him in a circle staying a good healthy distance out of his reach.

When they got to the Square they pulled them other Negroes way off to one side and the African and his attendants went right up on the hill. Then the auctioneer, with his Negro behind him those same three steps, started his selling:

"Now folks, you see here before you about the most magnificent piece of property any man'd ever want to own. Note the height, the breadth, the weight; note the extraordinary muscular development, the regal bearing. This is a chief so he's got to have great leadership ability. He's gentle with children as you may be able to see there under his arm. True, he's capable of destruction, but I maintain this is merely a sign of his ability to get a job done. I don't think you need any proof of all I say; just to look at him is proof enough. Why, if I didn't own him already, and if I had a farm or a plantation, I'd sell half my land and all my slaves just to scrape up enough money to buy him to work the other half. But I DO own him, and I don't have any land. That's my problem. I can't use him; I don't need him; I got to get rid of him. And that's where you come in, friends. One of you has to take him off my hands. I'll pay you for that kindness. Yes, sir! Don't let anybody tell you I'm not grateful for the good turns my friends do for me. What I'll do is this: I'll toss right in this deal, at two for the price of one, that little baby he's got under his arm."

(Now some folks said they found out later the auctioneer HAD to make that deal, since it was the captain who'd tried in the first place to get that baby from the African, and that's how come he'd got his head smashed. So I reckon the auctioneer couldn't very well sell them two as separate items without having to kill one to get the other.)

"Now, you know that's a bargain," he was going on to say, "because that baby will grow up to be just like his daddy. So now just picture it: when this here man gets too old to work, you'll have his spitting image all set to take over for him.

"I reckon you must know I'm not very sharp when it comes to prices and costs, but I'd say right off this here worker shouldn't go for less than five hundred dollars. What say, Mister Willson, you figure he's worth that much?"

Dewitt Willson didn't answer, didn't say nothing, just reached into his pocket and pulled out one thousand cash, as calm as you'd pick lint off a suit, walked halfway up the hill and handed that money to the auctioneer.

The auctioneer rapped his green derby against his knee. "Sold!"

Nobody, not even folks what claims to-a seen it, is really certain about what happened next. It must-a been them crewmen, who was still holding all them chains, relaxed when they saw all that money, because the African spun around once and nobody was holding nothing except maybe a fist full of blood and skin where them chains had rushed through like a buzz saw. And now the African was holding ALL them chains, had gathered them up like a woman grabs up her skirts climbing into an auto, and right off he started for the auctioneer like he understood what that man was saying and doing, which could not-a been since he was African and likely spoke that gibberish them Africans use. But leastways, he `DID go after the auctioneer and some folks swears, though not all, that, using his chains, he sliced his head off—derby and all—and that the head sailed like a cannon ball through the air a quarter mile, bounced another quarter mile and still had up enough steam to cripple a horse some fellow was riding into New Marsails. Fellow came into town babbling about having to shoot his horse after its leg got splintered by a flying head wearing a green derby.

Some strange things happened just then. The auctioneer's Negro, who'd taken a step or two back when the African got loose and didn't seem to take notice of the headless auctioneer except to make certain he didn't have no blood splattered on him to ruin his clothes, he ran up to the African, who was just standing near the body which hadn't even had time to fall yet, and grabbed his arm and pointed and started yelling: "This way! This way!"

I reckon the African didn't really understand but he knew the Negro was trying to help him and started out in the direction the Negro was pointing, and the Negro followed him just like he'd followed the auctioneer, a distance of three steps back, and the African ran down off the hill though he must-a been carrying close to three hundred pounds of chains on him, swinging them, breaking seven or eight arms and a leg, carving himself and the Negro a path through the townspeople of New Marsails. Some men raised rifles and took aim, and maybe could-a hit them (not saying, mind you, they could-a stopped the African), but Dewitt Willson ran up on the hill like a crazy man, and got between the men and the African and Negro, screaming all the while: "Don't shoot my property! I'll sue! That's my property!" And by that time the African was out of range and heading south into the swamps at the end of town. So the men and Dewitt got horses and more rifles and after a while set out after him.

The African was traveling pretty fast (he must-a been carrying not only his baby and the chains but the Negro too because I don't see how that small Negro could-a kept up), and Dewitt and the men might-a never trailed him except that he went straight through the woods and swamps and left this trail of torn-up bushes, grass, and small trees where them chains had caught on things and he'd pulled them right out of the ground, heading straight for the sea. They just set out on this trail, wide enough for two horses to go abreast, as straight as a plumb line, and followed it through the swamp, right down to the sand and into the water. That's where it stopped.

The men figured the African must-a just tried to swim back home (some said he could-a made it—chains, baby and all) and that auctioneer's Negro must-a lit out on his own, and now they was sort of tired and wanted to go home and forget about it, but Dewitt was sure the African wasn't gone, not swimming, and was coming back, and got the men to look up and down the beach for some sign. They did, and half mile down the beach they found two sets of tracks going into the woods.

Right about now it got hard for Dewitt Willson to get men to help him chase his property. First of all, it was getting dark. Second of all, there wasn't no wide trail like before because the African must-a been holding them chains off the ground so they wouldn't catch on anything, like a little girl holds up her skirts around her waist when she goes wading. So the men just naturally cooled down when it came to tracking a wild man through the woods at night when, at best, it would be hard to see him and when you couldn't be sure where he was, and he could pay you a visit and slice off your head even before you knew he was calling. So they camped on the beach, and some men went for supplies and at daybreak they took out after him again.

But that one night was all the time the African and the auctioneer's Negro needed and it was going to be harder than ever to catch him now because when they came into a clearing about a mile into the woods, shining in the sun was a pile of broken stones, and links, and bracelets where the African had spent the night cleaning them off himself. So now he was loose, free of his chains, and was somewhere in the area. He was so big and so fast you didn't dare make a guess at WHERE he might be, since folks began to realize he could-a been anywhere within a distance of a hundred miles. But Dewitt, with fewer men now, kept going and tracked his property for two weeks, halfway to where Willson City is now, and back, which is a total of two hundred miles, and all along the Gulf Coast almost to Mississippi and the other way into Alabama, and finally, those men still with Dewitt noticed he was looking sort of funny. He didn't sleep at all, or eat, spent twenty-four hours a day on his horse and was talking to himself, saying: "I'll catch you . . . I'll catch you . . . I'll catch you." And then, nearly a month after the African got away, in which time Dewitt hadn't been home at all, while the men watched, he keeled off his horse and didn't wake up until they'd taken him home in a litter to his plantation and he'd slept in a featherbed for another week. His wife told folks he kept right on talking to himself and when he did wake up, he came up screaming: "But I am. I'm worth a thousand too! I am!"

Now the African changed his tactics.

One afternoon Dewitt and his wife was sitting on their front porch. Dewitt was trying to get back his strength by sipping something cool and taking in the sun. And up the front lawn, dressed in African clothes of bright colors, with a spear and a shield, comes the African, bearing down on the house like he was a train and it was a tunnel and he was going right through—which he did, on out the back door, across the back lawn to the slave quarters, where he freed every last one of Dewitt's Negroes and led them off into the dark of the woods before Dewitt could even set down his glass and get up out of his chair.

Well, if that wasn't enough, the next night almost the same thing happened to a fellow east of New Marsails. He came into town and told everybody about it: "I was sleeping peaceful when

A DIFFERENT DRUMMER

I heared this noise outside down by the slave cabins. God damn, when I rushed to the window if I didn't see all my niggers heading into the woods behind a man who was as big anyways as a black horse on its hind legs. And there was another one too," the fellow went on, "never more than a few steps behind the big one, waving his arms and telling MY niggers what to do and where to go."

Even though he was still ailing, Dewitt Willson came into town and stood up in front of a big meeting they was holding to try and solve the problem and said: "Now I swear to you, I'm not going home until I can take the African or what's left of him with me. And let everybody know this: white or black, anybody who can give me news that'll help me catch the African will be walking around the next day with a thousand of my dollars in his pocket." And that news spread like the smell of cooking cabbage, spread all up and down the region so that years after, if you'd gone into Tennessee and mentioned you was from down this way, somebody'd ask: "Say, who DID get Dewitt Willson's thousand?"

Dewitt Willson kept his word; he set out after the African again. He tracked and trailed him for another month all over the state. Sometimes they'd come pretty close to getting him too, but not quite close enough. They'd come on him and his band, which they managed to thin out and keep down to twelve or so what with killing and capturings, and have a battle, but the African'd always wriggle out some way. One time they thought they had him trapped with his back to the river and he just turned around, dove in and swam it underwater. And you know some fellows can't even throw a stone that far. They could never get their hands on that auctioneer's Negro neither. He was always around, holding the baby while the African fought, looking at what went on out of them money-filled eyes which gleamed under that green derby. Yes sir, he still had the derby, though nothing else, was dressed now like the African in one of them long, multi-colored sheets.

THE AFRICAN

Dewitt was changing again, doing the same things he'd done before he collapsed, not talking to anybody, not even to himself now, moody and silent all the time. And so it went on, the African raiding and freeing slaves, Dewitt Willson catching up with the band and taking most of the slaves back and killing more, keeping the African's men down to twelve or thirteen, and the African and the auctioneer's Negro never getting caught.

Then one night they was camped a little north of New Marsails. Everybody was asleep except Dewitt, who was sitting on his horse looking into the fire. He heard a voice behind him, what seemed like it could-a been the voice of the auctioneer's ghost, but wasn't. "You want the African? I'll take you to him."

Dewitt turned around and saw the auctioneer's Negro standing there, wearing his sheet and his derby; he'd got into camp without being heard or seen.

"Where is he?" Dewitt asked.

"I'll take you to him. I'll go up to him and slap him on the cheek if you want it that way," said the Negro.

So Dewitt went. He said later he wasn't sure he'd done the right thing following that Negro because it could-a been an ambush or a trap. But he said, too, he didn't think the African'd do something like that. Some of the men with him said Dewitt was crazy enough by that time to do anything to catch the African, would-a gone anywhere with anyone to get him.

So Dewitt roused his men, and they rode out after the Negro. They didn't have to go more than a mile before they came into the African's camp. There was no fire and the Negroes, maybe twelve, was lying on the bare ground with no cover, sleeping. Right in the middle of the clearing, his back against a huge rock, the black baby across his knees, sat the African. He had a cloth over his head and set up in front of him was a pile of stones, which he seemed to be a-mumbling at.

A DIFFERENT DRUMMER

Dewitt Willson couldn't figure out why no one'd warned the African, how come he'd been able to sneak up on him, and leaned down to the Negro and said: "Why aren't there no guards? He knew I was right close by. Why aren't there no guards?"

The Negro smiled up at him. "There WAS one guard. Me."

"Why'd you do this? Why'd you turn on him?"

The Negro smiled again. "I'm an American; I'm no savage. And besides, a man's got to follow where his pocket takes him, doesn't he?"

Dewitt Willson nodded. Some folks said he almost turned around and went back to his own camp and wanted to forget all about catching his property this way and then come back in the morning when the African would be gone and chase him until he caught him fair and square, because it seems like after all those weeks of chasing the African through the woods, after all that time of following his trail and thinking maybe he'd get him this time and finding he didn't any more have him than a dwarf has a chance of being a professional basketball player, after all the sweating and riding and bad food and hard sleeping, he'd come to respect this man, and I reckon he must-a been a little sad that when he finally caught up with his property it was because some fellow the African'd trusted would turncoat and lead the white men into camp. But the other men didn't feel that way. They wanted the African any way they could get him because he'd been making fools of them and they knew it and they wanted an end to that.

So the white men circled the camp and when they had it surrounded, Dewitt Willson called out for the Negroes to give up. The white men lit torches so the African could see he was ringed by fire, horses, and men with rifles. The Negroes jumped to their feet and right away saw it wasn't no use, since all they had was African weapons, and they threw them down on the ground. But the African bolted up on top of the rock straddling the baby and made a full circle taking stock of what he was up against because he was alone and he knew it, since by then all the Negroes had scattered into the bushes or were standing around like they'd never seen him before and didn't know him from a third-century Roman Catholic Pope.

There he stood on the rock, alone, glistening in the fire, almost naked, his eyes just hollows of black. Then he stepped down. Someone raised a rifle.

"Wait!" Dewitt shouted. "See if we can take him alive. Don't you understand? That's the point. Take him alive!" He was standing up in his stirrups waving his arms for attention in the firelight.

Some fellow took this to mean that he should be a hero, and thinking he could run down the African, raced his horse straight at him, but the African just grabbed the fellow off the horse's back like you might catch a ring on a carousel and popped his back over his knee like a dry wishbone and tossed him aside.

"If you shoot, aim for his limbs," Dewitt was yelling.

Someone from the other side of the circle fired, and they could see the bullet go right through the African's hand and dig into the ground near Dewitt's horse, but the African didn't seem to connect the report with any pain he might-a felt in his hand, didn't even wince or move. Someone else shot him just above the knee and blood ran down his leg like a ribbon.

Keeping his back to the rock, where the baby was sleeping, he made a full, slow circle, eying them all, eying the auctioneer's Negro too, who was standing next to Dewitt, but not stopping at him, or showing any anger or bitterness, stopping only when he came to Dewitt Willson and staring at him. They stared at each other, not like they was trying to stare each other down, more like they was discussing something without using words.

And finally it seemed like they came to an agreement because the African bowed slightly like a fighter bows at the beginning of a match, and Dewitt Willson raised his rifle, sighted the African's upturned face, and shot him cleanly just above the bridge of his wide nose.

It hit him all right, but the African just stood there, and then finally sunk to his knees, and then forward on his hands. He seemed to be melting away, and then suddenly, he looked up with shock on his face, like he'd just remembered something and had to do it before he passed on, and gave a loud wail, and started crawling toward the sleeping baby, his eyes filled with blood, and a good-sized rock in his fist. He raised the rock above the baby, but Dewitt Willson shattered the back of his head before he could smash it down. And so the African died.

None of the men moved. They sat, disappointed, on their horses because they, each of them, had wanted to go back and say they'd gotten the bullet into the African what had killed him.

Dewitt Willson climbed down off his horse, walked to the baby, which was still sleeping, not knowing his daddy was dead, not knowing, I reckon, his daddy'd ever been alive. Coming back to his horse, Dewitt tripped over that pile of stones the African'd been talking to. They was all very flat stones, and Dewitt Willson stared down at them for a long time, and after a while he bent over, picked up the smallest one, a white one, and put it in his pocket.

Mister Harper was getting hoarse. He paused for a moment, cleared his throat, went on. "Dewitt Willson went back to New Marsails, got his clock, which he hadn't called for yet, and rode on home, with the African's baby beside him on the wagon seat, the auctioneer's Negro and the clock ticking in the wagon bed, that same clock you saw out at Tucker's farm on Thursday." He stopped and turned to face those behind him. "Well, that's the story and you all know as well as me how that baby got named Caliban by the General, when the General was twelve years old."

"That's right. After the General read that there book by Shakespeare," Loomis added, sighing.

"Not a book, a play, *The Tempest*. Shakespeare didn't write no books; nobody wrote books then, just poems and plays. No books. You must not-a learned NOTHING your three weeks up at the university." Mister Harper stared Loomis down.

"All right then, a play," Loomis agreed, sheepishly.

It was near dinner time now. Several men left the porch. A warm wind blew down off Eastern Ridge. A car, filled with solemn-faced Negroes, sputtered through, going north.

"And Caliban, whose Christian name got to be First after he got a family and there was more than just one Caliban, was John Caliban's father, and John Caliban's grandson is Tucker Caliban and the African's blood is running in Tucker Caliban's veins." Mister Harper sat back, satisfied.

"That's what you say." Bobby-Joe tossed his cigar into the street.

"Boy, I'll forgive you for being so damned stupid. You'll find out one of these days that I'm no fool. You can believe me now or not—it makes no difference to me—but sooner or later you WILL agree and you'll have to apologize."

The men grumbled. "That's right."

"Now look here, Mister Harper," Bobby-Joe started very softly, not even turning to face the old man, rather looking up and down the street before him, "Tucker Caliban worked for the Willsons every day of his life. How come he picked Thursday to up and feel his African's blood." He turned now. "Tell me that?"

"Well, boy, a good man won't lie to you; he won't tell you something is true if he's not sure. And I'll tell you right out I can't answer your question. I just say Tucker Caliban felt the blood and had to move and even though it was different from what the African would-a done, it amounts to the same thing. But why on Thursday? I can't tell you." The old man nodded his head as he talked, looking over the roof tops at the sky.

They all heard the clomping of old woman's shoes, then saw Mister Harper's daughter. She was fifty-five, a spinster, with limp yellow hair. "You ready to come home and eat, Papa?"

"Yes, honey. Yes, I am."

"Will some of you men help him down?" She asked that same question each night.

"Well now, I don't reckon I'll be coming back tonight, so I'll see you all tomorrow after church." Mister Harper was in the street now, his daughter behind him, her hands on the high thronelike back, waiting.

"Yes, sir." They answered together.

"Good night then. Don't get into no trouble." The wheels creaked the old man away.

Once Mister Harper was out of earshot, Bobby-Joe turned to the other men. "You really believe that blood business? You think that explains all this?" He thought that once the old man was gone they would not be so kind to his opinions.

"If that's what Mister Harper says, it's got to be part of the answer anyways." Thomason pushed himself off the wall and started toward the door.

"Yes, that's so." Loomis rocked forward and placed his hands on his knees, preparing to get up.

"You REALLY think it's simple as that?"

"Well, put it this way." Thomason opened the door, went inside and pressed his nose against the screening. "Can you give a better reason?"

"No." Bobby-Joe looked at Thomason's stomach pressed flat against the screen door. "No, I can't right now. But I'm thinking on it."

HARRY
LELAND

Though it was well past ten that Thursday, Mister Harper, Bobby-Joe, and Mister Stewart had not yet appeared. Standing on the porch, a little apart from the others, peering from under the torn brim of his straw hat, Harry was waiting for his boy, Harold —the men called the boy Mister Leland—to turn the corner into the Square, and run (he always ran when he wasn't riding) down to Thomason's. That morning before they left for town Harry's wife had told him to visit Miss Rickett. "She's down with a broken hip, Harry, and she likes visitors. Don't come back here and say you-all didn't go by." He had only nodded—thinking: *Let the boy do it; I'll send the boy over. That woman gives me the willies. I can't see how Marge can't know about her and what she does. But I know she wants a screwing and I ain't about to give it to her. I'll just send the boy*—and so thinking, nodded again.

They had ridden the mile in from their farm, his boy in front of him on the saddle-less horse, between his extended arms, and when they reached the General's statue in the center of town, he pulled

Deac up, and told the boy to get down. "You don't have to stay too long, Harold. Just go and say, 'How do, Miss Rickett. My ma and pa heard you was feeling poorly and sent me by to see how you was doing.' "

Harold had just stared at him. Harry knew what he was thinking, and answering, did not lie. "I know I'm supposed to go by too, Harold. But I don't feel like it. You can go in and come right out. If I was to go, I'd have to stay a-visiting until sundown. So you do this favor for your pa. And if she asks for me, tell her I had some pressing business by Thomason's. Okay?" Still Harold did not move, continued to look up at him out of live gray eyes, like bits of a crushed, powdered, broken gray bottle. "I know, Harold. I don't like her neither. But I'm older and know more about her that I don't like." The boy nodded then—Harry liked that—with an expression saying he knew and understood and would go alone to save his father the hardship because his hardship was only a boy's and his father's was that of a man, larger and worse. Then he turned and started west up Lee Street.

Harry had sat the horse and watched him, in his blue overalls and horizontally striped blue and white T shirt, which, with the long sandy hair—like his own—that obscured his ears and shaded his gray eyes gave him the appearance of a miniature prison escapee. Harry had watched him until he turned the corner, then he rode on to Thomason's.

But now, standing on the porch, listening to the aimless grumbles of the men talking (Mister Harper was not there to give their conversation form and scope), he began to feel guilty: *It's like I sent my own son into a she-lion's den. The boy got more guts than me. God knows, I should be able to keep a forty-year-old bitch with a broken hip at arm's length. But I sold my own boy out. When he gets back, I'll buy him something.* He leaned against a post, his post; it did not have his name on it, but no one else used it; he took no part in the talk, continued looking up the street toward the General, waiting for the boy to turn the corner.

Through his denim work shirt and jacket, he felt a fleshy hand on his shoulder. "Where'd you send Mister Leland, Harry?" It was Thomason, his best friend among the men, an apron tied high around his chest like a dirty white strapless evening gown.

"Sent him up to Miss Rickett's. She's—"

"You don't have to say it. Don't you think he's too young for that?" He was grinning broadly. "Seems like he wouldn't be big enough yet to fill that. Some of US can't hardly fill THAT."

Behind them, the men laughed.

"At least, I ain't fallen so low as to ever need to want to fill that. So I; for one, don't know nothing about its dimensions." He pushed his elbow back, hitting Thomason in the ribs, then laughed. "Leastways, that's why I sent him. I want to keep her away from me."

"But ain't you afraid for him? You trying to bring him up decent, ain't you?" Thomason's alarm was exaggerated.

"She won't bother him none. Maybe give him something sweet."

"That's what I'm talking about! And take him in her arms and say he should come back in six years and when he's as big and good-looking as his pa she'll show him something REAL special!"

The men laughed again.

"Awh, shut up!" Harry, not really angry, turned away and looked up the street again. And then he saw the boy turn the corner, running.

"Here he comes." Thomason clapped Harry's shoulder. "A-running. I reckon she didn't get him this time. But then that boy runs everywhere. Still, he got too much spunk left." He turned away and backed to his space against the wall.

The boy had now come opposite the store; he stopped, looked up and down the street, then toward the Ridge where something seemed to arrest his attention. He took one more look and ran furiously across the strteet and hopped onto the porch. "Papa, a truck's coming." At the same time he reached out and pushed something into his father's hand: three long, tapering, mud-colored cigars.

"Where'd you get these?"

"Miss Rickett give them to me and said they was for you and asked you to come by and see her sometime." He paused, looked down toward the edge of town, as if expecting something to appear. "A truck's coming."

As the men behind him burst into laughter, Harry took the cigars and slid them into his shirt pocket. He turned to them. "She ever send you fellows any presents?" He pretended great pride.

"Papa, I seen a truck coming. It was—" And then the truck had appeared behind him, large, black, square, its back heaped high with white crystals that shifted and glistened in the late morning sun, air squeezing its wheels to a standstill and small bits of its cargo falling to the pavement with the sound of hard breakfast cereal in a bowl.

Some of the men ambled to the edge of the porch and visored the sun with their hands. Harry placed his hand on top of the boy's head just as the driver, in denim pants, slid across the leather seat and leaned out of the already open window. "Where's the Caliban place?"

"Up the road about a mile and a half." Harry took a step down, reached out and rested his hands on the window sill. "Can't miss it. Looks like three flat white boxes end to end. What you got in back? Rock salt?"

"Don't see where it's any of your business unless the name is Caliban." The men laughed. The driver hesitated for a second, not realizing he had come close to calling Harry a Negro. "But you're right. Just up the road? Three white boxes?"

"You got it. Salt, you say?"

31

"That's right. Salt. He wants salt; I'm bringing him salt. Just up the road, you say? Flat?"

"What he want all that salt for? You know?"

"No, I don't. He called for it. Ten tons. If he's got the money, I got the salt. Just up the road?"

"That's it."

"Good." The driver rolled up the window, which being broken would close only part way, slid back across the seat and started the motor. Then he was gone, barreling up the Highway, swirling dust at the road-edge on either side of him.

"That's a damn funny thing for that nigger to be buying. Ten tons of salt." Thomason turned to Harry. "Come on, I got something to show you." He smiled and motioned the man into the store. The boy followed them.

Inside, the storekeeper reached under the counter and produced a bottle of whisky and two thick-bottomed glasses. Harry leaned over an urn of pickles. Next to him, Harold stood on tiptoes, looking with wrinkled brows and through shaggy hair in the direction of a jar of chocolate drops on a low shelf. "Say, Thomason, give me five cents' worth of them, will you?" *Didn't say nothing to him about it so nobody could hold me to it, but I made the promise to myself. That's enough.*

Thomason took up the ladle, weighed them out—there were only about ten—and put them in a bag. Harry motioned Thomason to give them to the boy, who took them in shocked delight, too surprised to say anything. He began to eat them, closing and re-opening the bag after each drop, as if fresh air would ruin them. Harry turned back to the storekeeper: "Wonder what he wants all that salt for?"

Thomason poured two drinks and shrugged. "Damned if I know. Must be good for his farm, else he wouldn't-a ordered it."

Harold looked up from his candy. "Papa, that Tucker, the good nigger, you talking about?" Harry felt the boy tugging at the loops of his pants.

Thomason leaned over the counter and spoke down to the boy. "Who told you he's a good nigger, boy? He's evil a nigger as you'd want to know."

Harry felt the boy's face pressing his leg. He looked down and found him peering up and out at him shyly. They both knew what had happened: he had been told not to use NIGGER. And too, Harry and his wife did not want him to pick up stray opinions, good or bad, about anything, wanted to know exactly where he learned things. Harry could hear his wife already: "You let that boy stand there with all your filthy-mouthed friends; no wonder he comes in here with crazy ideas."

"Who told you Tucker's a good Negro, Harold?"

"Nobody." He spoke into Harry's leg. "I just——" He stopped. Harry turned back to Thomason.

"What about another drink?" He slapped the counter so it sounded as if he were driving nails with a hammer.

"Why sure, coming up." He grasped the neck of the bottle. "But we got to watch for my wife. She always seems to show up——"

Harry raised his hand and pressed back the words. "Harold, go watch for Missus Thomason and say 'Hello' when she comes." He smiled at Thomason. "Real loud."

The boy went and sat on the floor, pressing his nose against the bottom of the kick-bulged screening. The men clicked full glasses and delivered toasts, raised the liquor to their lips and tossed it off.

"Papa?"

Thomason swept the glasses and the bottle off the counter and placed them quickly but clumsily underneath. Both men stood straight and wiped their mouths.

"Papa, Mister Harper's coming."

Thomason laughed nervously. Harry came to the door and put

his hand on the boy's head. "Next time say it's Mister Harper right off. You about killed Thomason there." The storekeeper blushed.

They went back onto the porch. Harry leaned against his post; the boy stood next to him. Mister Harper, late this morning, was being wheeled down the center of the Highway by his daughter. When he reached the porch the men lifted the chair into their midst and exchanged greetings with him. Almost at once his daughter started up the street back home. The old man leaned back. "Well, what's happening today, Harry?"

"Nothing much. A truck—" He started but Mister Harper had turned to Harold.

"How's Mister Leland, there?"

Harry felt the boy slide in behind him, jamming between his hip and the post: *Funny how he don't like Mister Harper, who never done him no harm. I reckon he don't understand how a man can be so old and still be human.* "He's okay, Mister Harper."

They lounged on the porch and talked. Harry embraced the post with one arm, his boy sitting in front of him, a stick in his hand, carving in the cracks at the edge of the Highway and every so often leaning back so his head bumped gently against Harry's knee. Behind them, the men would ask Mister Harper questions of world events and when he answered, whether they really understood or not, they would nod and grumble. Then, as it neared lunch time, they started to vacate the porch, knowing the old man wanted to be alone while he ate. Soon, his daughter came briskly down the center of the Highway carrying a gray metal lunch box under her arm.

Harry and the boy went into the store and Harry bought their meal. They went around to the back of the store and sat in the sun. When they finished the cheese and crackers and milk in waxed containers, Harry lit one of the cigars Miss Rickett had sent him. He watched Harold as he pretended to smoke a faded yellow straw, and reached over, struck a match, burned the end of it so there was an ash. The boy moved closer to him and rested his head on his shoulder. "Papa, why'd Tucker buy all that salt? You know?"

"No, son." He drew on the cigar. "Tucker's strange, ain't he? I heard tell of him doing stranger things than that even." Suddenly remembering, he turned sharply. "And say now, what did your mama and me tell you about using NIGGER?"

The boy cast his head downward, searched the ground between his legs for the answer. "You said . . . you said not to use it any."

"You remember why?" Harry did not want to sound too stern: *It's hard for him. Everybody uses it hereabouts. It's even hard for me not to use it.*

"You said it was a bad name and that you don't call nobody a bad name unless you want to hurt them." The boy looked up then, anxious to have given the right answer.

"That's right. Now you remember that, you hear?"

"Yes, sir."

"Listen, Harold." He turned to the boy, searching for words strange even to him, not knowing exactly why he felt the way he did, but sensing somehow it was right to feel this way and to tell his son these feelings. "Someday, when you get to be my age, things may not be the same as they is now, and you got to be ready for that, you see? If you're like some of my friends, you won't be able to get on with all kinds of folks. You understand?"

The boy did not answer. He was looking up into his face, his eyes veiled by his sandy hair.

Harry went on. "You see, I don't think no word starts out being bad. It's just a word, and then folks give it a meaning. And it may be you don't mean it the same as everybody else means it. Like if someone at school should call you a sissy, that don't mean it's right off bad to be a sissy; it's just like saying your eyes is gray. That don't mean it's bad to have gray eyes. But if you call a colored person a nigger he thinks you saying he's bad, and maybe you don't even mean it that way, you see?"

"Yes, sir."

"All right, Harold. I wasn't mad at you, you know that, don't you? Here." He pushed the wet end of the cigar close to the boy's mouth. "Now don't take in on it—you'll get sick. And for God's sake, don't tell your ma."

He watched the boy holding the cigar between his teeth, making a grimace against its bitterness, but still proud to be almost smoking. Then he took it away. "I reckon we can go on back. Mister Harper'll be over his lunch by now." He started to get up.

They were the first to reappear on the porch. Gradually the others returned, stood in small clusters, talking, staring off at birds flying above the low roof tops. Harry leaned on his post, scanning the horizon beyond the town. Harold sat on the porch edge, no longer carving. So they remained, into the early afternoon, listening to the stillness, watching the few passing cars, tourists, with oddly colored license plates, having seen all there was to see in the old French city on the coast, speeding through without realizing they had ignored the General's birthplace, going on to the capital.

Then they saw the wagon, approaching the town from the north, behind a red horse with a spine, not sagging, but crooked as if it had been rammed out of shape by a sidelong blast from a sledgehammer, and then they could see the man driving, whipping the animal frantically, as though being chased by ghosts or a thousand angry Negroes, the man as red as the horse from the drinking he had begun to do regularly almost as soon as he had discovered there were beverages other than his mother's sweet milk. They all heard the popping of hoofs on the pavement as Steward skidded, pulling his horse to such a stop that the reins drew blood from the animal's mouth, and the iron-rimmed wheels of the troughlike wagon left filings for ten feet. He hopped down from the seat, stumbling in the gutter. "Just seen the God-damnedest thing. How do, Mister Harper, Harry. I just seen the damnedest thing."

"What did you see—a herd of elephants?" Harry exhaled; the smoke hung heavily over Stewart's head. The men laughed, but stopped abruptly when they realized Mister Harper was sitting straight in his chair, his mouth closed and narrow as a crease in a piece of paper.

Stewart caught his breath, ignoring the comment and laughter, spoke only to Mister Harper. "Driving by there, coming from out home, I seen him, Tucker Caliban that is—now this is the gospel truth—tossing salt, rock salt, on his field. When I called to him, he wouldn't answer me. Just kept tossing. Kept filling this satchel hung over his shoulder from a big pile of salt in his front yard."

Harry drew in sharply; no one noticed. *The truck. That's what he's bought it for; that's what he's doing with it. And there's some of it right under Stewart's feet.* A few crystals lay at Stewart's feet, unnoticed and forgotten by the rest, though they too had seen the truck and its bed heaped high.

"What's that you say—salt?" Mister Harper had leaned forward almost immediately and cupped a hand behind his ear, pushing away a tumble of white hair. "How long ago'd you see this?"

"Long as it took me to drive in here." Stewart did not think the men believed him and began to sweat, pulled off his dog-eared black hat and mopped his naked head with a crinkled yellow handkerchief. "I swear it." He crossed his heart with a tobacco-stained index finger.

"Must be so, Mister Harper." Harry turned to the old man. "We all seen the truck, heaped up full." The other men nodded.

"I wonder what he's gone and done that for?" Stewart put one foot up on the porch. Harry felt the boy inch closer to him. "Must be nuts." Some of the men murmured agreement, but Mister Harper paid no attention.

"Lift me on that wagon." He pulled himself out of the chair, which rolled back from him, its dry wheels squealing, as if surprised to be no longer supporting his weight. He spread his arms out like a scrawny bird, waiting for someone to help him into Stewart's wagon. "Stewart, you get in back. I'm commandeering your wagon. Harry, YOU drive. I want to die in bed, not all twisted around a pole."

Most of the men had never seen Mister Harper on his feet, and immediately, as if an unknown and distant voice on Thomason's store radio had announced the coming of a tornado, the streets were filled with running men. Stewart struggled his bulk onto the tail gate. Other men, Negroes too, fetched horses without understanding what they were doing, why they were doing it, or where they were going.

The boy, next to Harry on the wagon seat, climbed to his knees and cupped his hands around his father's ear so Mister Harper, now being hoisted into the wagon next to them, would not hear. "Papa, I thought he couldn't walk. You said he couldn't walk."

"No, Harold. I didn't say that. I said that he didn't think there was anything important enough for him to walk to. Maybe he's found something."

Mister Harper was on the wagon seat now, breathing heavily, and Harold moved as close to his father as possible. Harry whispered to the red animal, looking down at its back like a twisted red circus balloon and headed it out of town, past the rows of stores and houses, past the people who had come out of the stores and houses to gape as at a Confederate Day Parade. Many who saw—without word, without explanation—hooked up wagons, saddled horses, started motors and followed the wagon, gazing mesmerized at Mister Harper.

Near the edge of town and to the right the wagon passed the low wind-chapped buildings where Negroes lived. They, too, watched Mister Harper and put aside what they had been doing, stopped talking, and leaving a proper space, formed a line of their own to follow the old man.

A short distance out they passed Wallace Bedlow sitting as broad and black as a coal car on the back of an orange horse the size of a large dog. As always, he wore the white dinner jacket he had won at a pile-driving convention. He pulled up short, turned, and joined the Negro line at its head.

The two groups went up the Highway toward Tucker Caliban's farm and finally Harry saw in the distance the white farm house, three joined sections side by side, bought and painted the summer before, and behind that the barn, sturdy and faded, and in front the square corral, no bigger than a good-sized parlor, and a gaunt and leafless maple, dead and rotted many years, and the small figure of a tiny man at work in a field that with every wave of his arm took on the white color of an autumn frost.

They sat at the side of the Highway in the wagons, the cars, atop horses and waited for Mister Harper to do something. Elbows jutting from his thin body, he asked Harry and Thomason to help him down and walk him to the fence. He said nothing, did not call to Tucker as he would have to any of the men with him or to any other Negro, but instead leaned against the fence watching the boy-sized Negro at work, almost as if he respected the work being done and would not interrupt until it was completed.

Tucker had finished almost a quarter of the field since Stewart had seen him and whipped the crippled horse into town, and now was close to half done. Across the field Harry could see him, one small speck of white shirt; he wore black pants and was himself black and barely discernible against the darkness of the trees enclosing the farm. Harry watched as Tucker ran out of salt and came slowly toward the house and mound, stepping high over the furrows. Then he was close by, his head lowered, and Harry could see the small features seeming lost on the large head, the steel-rimmed spectacles on his flat nose. If he had gone insane, was running wild as Stewart had suggested at the porch, he did not show it. To Harry, he seemed quiet and thoughtful as if he was doing nothing out of the ordinary. *Just like he's planting seed. Just like it's spring planting time and he started early and don't have to worry none about missing the first good days. Just like all of us every spring, getting up early and eating and then going out into the field and tossing in seed. Only he ain't planting nothing; he's surely killing the land and he don't even look like he hates it. It ain't at all like he got up one morning and said to hisself, "I ain't busting my backbone another day. I'm getting that land before it gets me." Not running out like a mad dog and putting down the salt like it* WAS *salt, but putting it down like it was cotton or corn, like come fall, it'd be a paying crop. He's so tiny to be doing such a terrible thing, no bigger than Harold even, doing that like a boy building a model plane or working with a little hoe beside his daddy, pretending he is his daddy and it's his field and his own little son is working beside him.*

Tucker was close enough now for Mister Harper to reach out and pound his shoulder. But the old man only whispered, barely heard by even Harry, who stood close by. "Tucker? What you doing, boy?" The men waited for an answer. It had not surprised them that Tucker had not spoken to Stewart before, but they were certain if a man had a tongue in his head, he would answer Mister Harper. Tucker, however, showed no signs of recognition, just filled his satchel. "Tucker, Tucker Caliban." Mister Harper spoke again to his back. "You hear? What you doing?"

Stewart was already on the second rung of the fence, his face red and twisted. "I'll teach that nigger some respect." Mister Harper reached out and grabbed his arm; the men were surprised that both could move so quickly.

"Leave him alone." Mister Harper turned away from the fence. "You can't stop him, Stewart. You can't even hurt him."

"What d'you mean?" Stewart stumbled after the old man.

"He's already started something. You can't do NOTHING to him now. Even if you were to put him in the hospital, when he got healed up, he'd be out here with that satchel planting that salt." He let Harry help him to the wagon. "Get me back up there. I might as well watch this sitting down. It'll take a long time."

The Negroes had arrived shortly after Mister Harper returned to the wagon and had clustered down the road. The white men had watched them carefully, looking for something that might help them to understand what they were seeing. But they had found only a re-flection of their own dismay, tempered perhaps with tolerance. *They don't know nothing neither. You can see that. It's like he's an Egyptian, and they don't know no more about this than they know, than we all know, about riding a camel.*

Out across the partially whitened field, Tucker had continued to fling the hail-like crystals, had made trip after trip, filling the satchel and emptying its contents, handful after abundant handful on the field. The sun had curved down toward the trees; when Tucker was finished it was no more than three fingers above the horizon. He came back across the field and tossed the satchel on the still unex-hausted mound, and in the silence of the late afternoon, wiping sweat from his face with his sleeve, surveyed his day's work and then went into the house.

"Would you look at that?" Stewart turned from the fence. "What a waste of good salt. I bet you could make a lot of ice cream with that much salt." He was joking.

"Keep quiet, Stewart." Mister Harper leaned forward. "Maybe you'll learn something."

The door opened and Tucker came into the yard carrying, in one hand, an ax, in the other, a rifle. He leaned both against the corral fence and disappeared around the house. When he came back he was leading his horse, an old gray animal with a slight limp, and a cow the color of freshly cut lumber. He opened the gate of the corral and for an instant stared at the animals, petting first one and then the other. Harry saw him stand straighter and heave, then pull them into the corral, close the gate, climb and sit on the fence with the rifle across his knees.

He shot the horse in the head just behind the ear and sticky blood ran down its neck and left foreleg. It stood for a full ten seconds, its lids stretched over bulging eyes, took a blind step and collapsed. The cow, smelling death and blood, steamed across the corral at top speed, her udders swinging violently. After she was hit, she kept moving until she banged into the fence, bounced back, turned to Tucker with the quizzical expression of a woman who has just been slapped for no apparent reason, screamed and crumpled. Tucker climbed down and looked them over.

Tears had begun to roll down Harold's cheeks when Tucker first shot the horse, but he had cried so softly, so much within himself that Harry would not have known if he had not glanced down at him. Putting his arm around his small shoulder, he squeezed it, feeling the tiny bones, but otherwise let him alone, did not hurry to clean his face or clear his nose until later when he was certain the boy had stopped crying.

Mister Harper sat smoking his pipe. Loomis looked at the carcasses lying in the corral corners and shook his head. "That's a shame. A real shame. Them were two fine animals. I might-a bought them if I'd known."

Thomason laughed. "Oh, shut up. You got to borrow from me any time you want a drink. Where you expect to get the money to buy a cow and horse?" The other men took the opportunity to laugh, watching Mister Harper from the corners of confused eyes. He did not laugh and they turned back to the yard.

Tucker had come out of the corral and picked up the ax, which, in the late afternoon sun, glinted like a single match flare in darkness.

Then he advanced on the twisted tree. It had once been the southwest boundary of the Willson Plantation, on which his great-grandfather and grandfather had been slaves and then workers. And it was told how the General had ridden out to this spot each day to watch the sun go down. Now it belonged to Tucker, as did this land. He put his hand on the trunk, running it over the ridges and smooth places, closed his eyes and moved his lips. Then stepping back one good pace, he cut it down. It was old, dry, tired inside and when it fell, it creaked like the wheels on Mister Harper's chair. With no trace of anger or madness, only intensity, he splintered the tree, laid the ax in the dull gray chips and gathered some of the remaining salt into the satchel, and tenderly, as he might have planted seedlings, banked the salt high around the dead roots. When he was done he went toward the house.

"Say, Tucker!" Wallace Bedlow was calling to him from down the fence. "You planing on growing a salt tree?" The Negroes laughed uproariously, slapping their thighs. Tucker said nothing, and the men from the store porch were more bewildered than ever. They had climbed out of the wagons and cars and now lined the fence like birds. Stewart's skin was greasy and he reached for his yellow handkerchief and tried to clean his face. "This is crazy. If one nigger can't make out another nigger, no one can. Maybe we should call someone to come and take him away. He's gone crazy."

Harry called down from the wagon. "It's his land. He can do anything he wants to it." He glanced at the boy, who sat wide-eyed.

The streaks of dirty tears lining Harold's face made him look as old as Mister Harper. "Is Mister Stewart telling the truth, Papa? Tucker gone crazy? Is that what happened?"

Harry could not answer. *If I'd-a met someone tomorrow and they'd* TOLD *me about what I just seen I would say that Tucker Caliban's crazy for sure. But I can't say that sitting here watching it happen because I know this, if I don't know nothing else. Craziness ain't driving him. I don't know what IS pushing at him, but it ain't craziness.*

The afternoon had crept away and now above the corral, where the dead animals were beginning to collect flies from half the county, and away from the three-part farm house, and beyond the field, white and vacant, and the trees, tall strips of black velvet trimmed with green, the sun went down like a burning new penny.

Tucker had gone into the house, and now the door opened and Harry could see his thin back, a broad sweat stain showing his dark brown skin gray through his white shirt. He was pulling something heavy. A shove made him stumble back a step. Bethrah, his wife, must be behind, in the doorway.

Wallace Bedlow climbed over the fence and went toward the house, removing his white coat, beneath which he wore nothing but a torn undershirt. "You tell Bethrah to stop shoving that thing in her condition. I'll help you, whatever the hell you doing."

"I don't need any help, Mister Bedlow." Bethrah's voice came from darkness. "You go on now. Thank you anyway."

Tucker just stared up at the man who was at least ten hands taller.

"Missus Caliban?" Bedlow spoke over Tucker's head. "You don't want to be working hard like that, not NOW." He had his coat draped over his shoulder; its green plaid lining was ripped.

"We realize you're trying to be helpful, but we have to do this ourselves. Thank you anyway, but go on now." Her voice was very sweet, and firm.

Tucker just stared.

Bedlow came back to the fence. Tucker turned to his work and soon Harry could see by the leftover light of day he was struggling with Dewitt Willson's grandfather clock, the same clock which had come on the African's ship, boxed and packed in cotton, and had traveled, after the African's betrayal and death, with the African's baby and the auctioneer's Negro to the Willson Plantation. It had been given to that baby, First Caliban, when he reached his seventy-fifth year, or what they thought anyway was his seventy-fifth year, a present from the General for First's years of good and faithful service, first as a slave and later as an employee; and passed down to Tucker.

The clock was outside now, standing in the yard, and beside it, in the final bloated stages of pregnancy, stood Bethrah, almost as tall, looking down at her tiny husband who had gone across the yard and returned with the ax. He raised it and arched it down on the glass protecting the clock's fragile hands, popping the glass, shattering it at his feet. He swung until the finely worked steel and imported wood were nothing but scrap metal and kindling.

Bethrah had gone into the house and was coming out with a baby. She carried only the sleeping child and a large red carpetbag. "Tucker, we're ready."

He nodded. He was staring at the pieces of wood strewn in the dust of his yard. Then he looked toward the corral and beyond to the field, gray now in the late dusk light. The baby began to cry and Bethrah rocked it, swaying back and forth as if to a silent lullaby, until it was asleep again.

Tucker looked at the house. For the first time he seemed hesitant and perhaps a little frightened.

"I know." Bethrah nodded. "Go ahead now."

He went inside, leaving the door open. When he came out, he wore a black chauffeur's coat and a black tie. He closed the door gently behind him.

Orange flame climbed the white curtains in the center section of the house, moved on slowly to the other windows like someone inspecting the house to buy it, burst through the roof with the sound of paper tearing, and lit the faces of the men, the sides of the wagons, and the faces of the Negroes.

Harry watched the blaze and the orange coating it gave the trees across the field. Sparks curled up and then died, dissolving against dark blue sky. Harry lifted the boy from the wagon and led him to the fence, where they stood watching. After an hour the flames faded, showing here and there tenacious fits and starts on still unconsumed scraps of wood, cloth, and shingle. Finally only glowing coals remained, and the rubble of the destroyed house looked like a huge city seen at night from a great distance.

Tucker and Bethrah came toward the fence, and Harry thought, but only for an instant, they would say something, a final word of explanation; instead they walked around the wagon and went up the road in the direction of Willson City.

The men turned from the fence, each realizing how warm and wet the fire had made the front of his body, each mumbling to the man next to him something like "Well, ain't that a bitch!" or "That tears all, don't it?" or "Never in all my born days have I . . ." They climbed into the wagons, unhitched horses, started the popping, bubbling motors.

Harry lingered at the fence and when he had seen everything he thought there was to see, reached down his hand for the boy to grab it. The boy was not there. He looked around him, then up the road and saw Harold, his neck craned backwards, talking quietly with Tucker in the silent shadows. Bethrah waited beyond them. He saw Tucker turn, join Bethrah, and disappear, enveloped in the thick night. Harold started toward him, walking backwards as if the blackness would not swallow the two figures as long as he watched. When he reached him, Harry said nothing, just put his hand on the boy's shoulder.

By now the men were settled in Stewart's wagon, ready to return to town. Harry handed the boy up to one of them, climbed up himself, and the crippled horse pulled them toward Sutton, leading, as before, two separated groups. Harold sat close to him. It was cold and he was shivering. Harry looked down at him and, holding the reins in first one hand and then the other, took off his jacket.

"Here." He pushed the coat into the boy's arms. "Put that on."

MISTER
LELAND

Tucker Caliban had never said very much to him, but Mister Leland considered him his friend. As far as he was concerned, Tucker had proved that friendship, its depth and permanence, forever, one morning the summer before.

Early that morning, even before Mister Harper had appeared at the porch, he and his father had come to town, his father to talk with a doctor about a cough he could not throw off, and Mister Leland had been sitting alone on the curb in front of Mister Thomason's store carving in a crack at the edge of the Highway. After he gouged down about an inch into the hard mud, and there was no more dirt in that crack, he had stood and peered into the store window, not concerned with the cans of food, or the guns, or fishing equipment, or even toys, concerned only with the vial of hairy brown peanuts, wishing someone would come along *like them fairy godfathers you hear about who knows what I'm thinking and just up and buy me some.*

MISTER LELAND

He had heard footsteps behind him—had seen, as he pulled back from the glass, the large black head on the short thin body reflected darkly before him, the figure not so tall as his father's, hardly taller than himself.

Tucker Caliban entered the store and purchased a bag of feed, started out, then stopped and pointed to the window, speaking to Mister Thomason, who weighed out a full pound of peanuts and poured them into a brown paper sack. Then he came out onto the porch and stood in front of Mister Leland. "You Harry Leland's boy?" He looked down at him as if he might hit him, not raising his hand, simply looking fierce.

Mister Leland ducked. "Yes, sir." *He's a nigger—a Negro, but Papa says to say* SIR *to anyone what's older than me, even nig—Negroes.*

"You wants peanuts, Mister Leland?" Tucker shoved the bag into his arms. "Here's peanuts. Tell your pa I knows what he trying to do with you." He turned and climbed into his wagon. He never looked at Mister Leland after that, never smiled or said good-by, just hit his horse with a piece of knotted rope tied to a short brown stick and drove away up the street, leaving Mister Leland to wonder what his father WAS trying to do with him. *Tucker said it like there was something wrong with it, mad-like, but then if it was bad and he didn't like it, why'd he buy me the peanuts? I reckon that's just his way, like Papa and Mister Thomason is always arguing, with their faces all mad, but Papa says Mister Thomason is his best friend ever, except for Mama, but Mama and Papa is always fighting too, so it must not really matter at all how folks look or what they says, just what they does.* He decided, however, he would ask his father what was being done to him, and when he did ask, his father had looked at him, very deeply, very seriously. "Your mama and me is trying to make you a passable human being."

That did not really explain it to him, but he felt sure that if his father wanted him to be that, even if he did not quite understand what and why, it was all right with him. And if it earned him peanuts, that made it even more all right. He did not ponder it further.

This, then, had been all that passed between him and Tucker Caliban, all he had to bolster the belief in their friendship, except those times when they might meet in town and Tucker would nod or even say, "How do, Mister Leland."

But it was enough so that as he watched Tucker's farm house burn and crumble, as he heard around him his father's friends speak of Tucker in mocking tones, calling him evil and crazy, he had begun to cry again, and pushed through the forest of legs, running up the road after the Negro, feeling betrayed because Tucker had done such things and seemed to deserve being called evil and crazy, wanting also to be given some explanation so he might defend his friend to the others, to be able to say, when they said he was evil and crazy: "He is not. He did it because . . ."

He caught up to the two Negroes and called to them, but they did not turn, stop, or give any sign of hearing him. He grabbed at Tucker's coattail, using it as a rein to halt him.

"Go on back, Mister Leland. Do like I say."

"Why you going?" He cleared his nose and tilted his head. "You ain't really evil—is you, Tucker?"

Tucker stopped and put his hand on the boy's head. The boy stiffened. "That what they saying, Mister Leland?"

"Yes, sir."

"Does you think I is?"

Mister Leland stared into Tucker's eyes. They were large and too bright. "I . . . But why'd you do all them evil, crazy things?"

"You young, ain't you, Mister Leland."

"Yes, sir."

"And you ain't lost nothing, has you."

The boy did not understand and said nothing.

"Go on back."

He found himself backing up, not really wanting to, not having decided to, rather as if the finality and quiet command of Tucker's voice was pushing him as would a heavy autumn wind. Then his father's hand was on his shoulder, light, not guiding him, but being guided by him, as if his father was a blind man and he was leading him. Then he had been lifted into the wagon and began to shiver and his father had given him the jacket and he was warmed, not so much by the oily denim as by the smells of his father's body, of tobacco and sweat and soil. He had fallen asleep on the way to Mister Thomason's, his head resting against his father's muscle. They had let the men out and his father handed the reins to Mister Stewart, who asked if they needed a ride home. "No, thanks, Stewart, we come in on Deac this morning." They went around to the back of Mister Thomason's store, through the cold shadows, and found the horse where his father had left him, tied to a twisted, tiny bush and his father lifted him up, then swung up himself and next he knew they were turning off the Highway into their road, out three quarters of the way to Tucker's, but not so far and he was waking up. "Papa?"

"Yes, Harold." He could feel his father's breath past his ear.

"Tucker said he'd-a lost something." He remembered that Tucker had really asked him whether he had lost anything yet. "He said I was young and ain't lost nothing yet." His father said nothing. "What'd he mean by that?"

He could feel his father thinking.

"Papa, I lost things, ain't I? Like marbles and the time I lost that quarter you give me. Ain't that losing something?"

Still he could feel his father behind him, his arms reaching around him, almost a hug except that if his father did not have to guide Deac, he might not have hugged him either; he could feel the man thinking. Finally: "I don't think he meant it that way, son. I think he's talking about something else. Maybe like . . ."

He waited but his father did not go on. He could not tell what he had been about to say, or what Tucker meant, but he had the feeling (he did not put it into thoughts; the absence of worries, of thoughts, somehow gave him the feeling) that it was not important.

They came to their house, turned off the road, went into the barn, and his father took off Deac's bridle and led the horse into his battered stall. Then they went into the house.

His mother did not say hello to them. "Harry, here you go again bringing that child in here at ten o'clock. Harry?" She was waving her arms. She was still dressed, her hair still up, long and black as . . . *like Papa says, the inside of a blueberry pie . . . that black.*

"Honest, Marge, couldn't help it this time." His father spoke timidly. "We—"

"That's what you always say. Honestly, all your drunken cronies call him MISTER but leastways YOU should know he ain't but eight." She was a Sunday-school teacher. "Did you go see poor old Miss Rickett?" She had put her hands on her hips and turned away from his father, was speaking to Mister Leland now.

"Yes, Mama. We went and sat and she give Papa some cigars." He lied, he knew it, and turned to look at his father, and saw the fleeting smile of relief and gratitude cross the man's lips, then realized it was not like a lie at all, not really, *more like the soldiers in Korea, where Papa fought, looking out for each other because they was all soldiers and had to keep each other alive else the enemy would-a done them harm. And the enemy, Papa says, could be a Red or a captain or even a sergeant though Papa was a sergeant hisself, but was also under sergeants who was just as much enemies as the men they shot at and who shot at them.*

She turned on his father again. "Did you feed him?"

"Not much. You see . . ." He and his father stood together just inside the door, his mother confronting them across the room behind the kitchen table.

"Harold, sit down and eat." She turned abruptly to the stove, took a plate from the top of a pot of boiling water, where she had left it to keep it warm, brought it to the table and although he thought she might bang it down, set it down quite gently. Mister Leland sat behind it. There were drops of warm water on the underside. He was really too sleepy to be hungry, but knew if he did not eat heartily his father would be answering for more.

His father took one step into the room. "Marge?"

She ignored him. "Eat, Harold." She did not have to say this; he was already doing so.

When he finished (his father having come forward like a boy late for school and snuck into a seat across from him, following his mother with his whole head as she bustled around the kitchen), she took him off to bed, where his brother, Walter, already slept as silent, as immovable as the General's statue, waited while he undressed, helped him with his prayers, and went out, her kiss still warm and sweet on his forehead. He tried to listen for his parents in the kitchen, but could hear nothing.

He woke up later and it was night. He never considered the darkness at the end of each day truly night, only darkness. Night was when he woke up and the room, the house, and all outside were silent and he had to go to the bathroom. He got up and went down the hall past his parents' open door and they were hugging one another in the bed into which, he was told, he had been born, into which he knew his brother to have been born. And if he had been troubled (he had not been), he no longer was and did his business and went back to sleep. . . .

"Harold-boy, get up." It was his father and it was Friday morning. "Come on, boy. We got to hurry."

In an instant he was fully awake. "What happened?"

"Nothing yet. Something might. Don't want to miss it, do you?" His father was already dressed, even to his hat.

"No, sir." He was already climbing from bed, was standing, making certain he had left his brother covered.

"I'll go see what I can do for breakfast." His father strode from the room, and soon he could hear him in the kitchen clanking pans. He put on his overalls and a clean shirt—it was the same kind as the day before; he had seven and his mother had printed the day of the week inside the collar—and went to the bathroom, spying, through the open door, his mother alone and tiny in bed, as fast asleep as ever Walter had been, her black braid looping around her throat like a friendly snake. He brushed his teeth, wet his hair, combed it straight back, and arrived in the kitchen just as his father was sitting down with a mug of coffee. Already at his own place was a glass of orange juice and a bowl of oatmeal. He sat down and began to drink the juice; it was cold and tasted bitter because of the toothpaste. "Why we going so early?"

"Want to be there when it starts." His father was blowing at his coffee.

"What's starting, Papa?"

"Don't know." His father's eyes were glassy, a bit red. "Whatever's started already. You remember what Mister Harper said? I don't think it's over yet, and you want to be there to see it, don't you?"

"Yes, sir."

"All right then." His father's face woke up momentarily with a smile. "Hurry up."

He ate as fast as he could—once, at the start, he scalded his tongue because he scooped a big spoonful from the center of the bowl, but now ate small rapid spoonfuls from around the edges— and his father sat across from him, drinking his mug of coffee.

MISTER LELAND

When his mother drank coffee, she used a cup, but his father's mug was twice as big. The coffee steamed up into the thin, dark, kind face, making sweat at the end of his nose.

When they were through, after silently putting the dishes in the sink and running water over them, they went out the back door and got Deac. His father lifted him up, climbed up himself, and they began the ride into town. It was still early enough for the fields, the bushes, and tall grass to be angel-haired with mist: *going up just like Papa's coffee steam.*

They arrived at Mister Thomason's and discovered they were not the only ones who had decided to come to the porch early. There were Bobby-Joe, Mister Loomis, and of course Mister Thomason, inside now dusting cans. It was still too early for Mister Harper to have arrived or Mister Stewart: *Papa says Mister Stewart starts asking Missus Stewart if he can come into town soon as he wakes up, and worries her so bad, she finally lets him, but not until four or five when she's made him do all the chores.*

They took Deac around back, tied him to the same bush, and returned to their places on the porch, Mister Leland sitting on the steps beside Bobby-Joe, and just in front of his father who leaned against his post. No one greeted them—they all knew each other too well for that—they simply began to talk, not about Tucker Caliban, but about the weather, trying to decide if it would be a nice day. They talked about such things until Wallace Bedlow came, not riding his orange horse as on the day before—*I hope he ain't shot it*—rather lumbering toward them from the north of town on foot, wearing his white coat and a good pair of pants of thin material that rustled in the breeze of his stride. He carried an old cardboard suitcase, and upon arriving at the porch, only nodded, saying nothing, and set down the suitcase beside the BUS STOP sign, at the end of the porch away from the men.

The men eyed him furtively, Bobby-Joe with a touch of contempt, but Mister Leland's father was the first to speak, assuming, in Mister Harper's absence, with the tacit consent of the others, the position of spokesman. "How do, Wallace."

Wallace Bedlow turned and smiled, as though his presence had just been discovered, as though he had not known they were watching him. "How do, Mister Harry."

The boy's father took a step away from the post toward the Negro. "Where you going? Into New Marsails?"

"Yes, sir." The smile had fled his face suddenly with a deathlike completeness. Mister Leland was thinking that Wallace Bedlow had used SIR: *Like Papa is older than him, which ain't so because when Wallace Bedlow takes off his hat, you can see crinkly gray hairs. Still he calls Papa* SIR *the same's I'd call him or my papa* SIR.

"Staying long, Wallace?" His father spoke as if these questions were not important, as if no one besides himself listened, examined every word.

"Yes, sir."

"How long?" There was an amount of accusation in the question.

"Don't reckon I'll be back, sir." Wallace Bedlow answered with more defiance than seemed necessary.

"What?"

"I don't reckon I'll be back, sir." He eyed all the men. "I'm waiting for the bus and going into New Marsails and I don't reckon I'll be back . . . at all."

"You moving into the Northside?" The Northside was where New Marsails' Negroes lived. Mister Leland had seen that when they took the bus to go to the movies. The bus had to go through the Northside to get downtown.

"No, sir." Wallace Bedlow's face seemed to die still more.

"Where you going?" His father almost whispered. Mister Leland heard someone sigh.

MISTER LELAND

"I reckon I'm going North to stay with my younger brother Carlyle in New York." Wallace Bedlow stared back at them, as his father said, "Oh." He looked like he was daring them to stop him. The men did nothing, casually turned away to their small conversations; Wallace Bedlow too turned away, standing very quietly waiting for the bus to come. When it came, he got on it. By that time, seven Negroes had joined him; they too carried suitcases, wore their best clothes, some even with neckties. Waiting, they said nothing to each other, rather stood patiently, self-engrossed, as if the white men did not exist, and when the bus came careening, its wheels hissing, down from the Ridge and stopped at the porch, they boarded silently, dropped their money in the plastic box (all seemed to have exact fare), moved to the back, and the bus took them away.

Shortly after the bus departed, Mister David Willson came around the corner from his house in the rich section of town, the Swells. He was a nice-looking man, with sad brown eyes, a bit shorter than Mister Leland's father. He was not a farmer, was descended from the General, though he seemed to possess none of his greatness, and was considered rather some kind of usurper of the family name. He owned much of the land on which Mister Leland's father's friends share-cropped; he was not their friend. He came on foot, thinking deeply, his hands knit behind his back, and without speaking to or even looking at the men on the porch, went inside, bought a newspaper, and retraced his steps up the street past the General.

Bobby-Joe spat into the street. "God-damn uppity bastard!"

Each hour for the next four, the bus came from New Marsails. At least ten Negroes were waiting silently, patiently, each hour, as if enclosed in invisible coffins, no longer having the power of communication or even possessing anything to communicate to the world around them, or each other. They all carried suitcases or boxes or shopping bags or bundles tied with string; all wore their best clothes.

Mister Harper was there by then. He had come after the second bus. He did not speak. More white men gathered on the porch, those who happened by or had come to the realization slower than the first batch that something was happening, changing. Some of these were even so dull as to ask Mister Harper why the Negroes were leaving (which they should have known) and where they were going (which did not matter and could not be answered unless they were to ask each Negro individually), but Mister Harper did not honor their questions with so much as a nod, just sat smoking his pipe, shifting in his wheel chair from time to time, watching the buses come and depart, watching the Negroes with suitcases waiting down the porch silently, getting on with exact fare ready, sometimes whole families from grandmother to grandchild, and the buses making the turn behind the General's back, climbing the hill to Harmon's Draw with much shifting of gears and black smoke, and then disappearing.

When the noon bus came, the bus driver, instead of letting the Negroes on immediately, made them wait, climbed out with his money changer like a tiny xylophone, and a bag of coins, went around to the window near the wheel, reached high inside and closed the door. Then he went into Mister Thomason's and bought a cream-filled cupcake and a container of milk and came out on the porch again.

Mister Leland had seen him twice this morning; the driver reminded him, with his hat, of a flyer he had seen once in an Air Force movie about Korea. When he finished eating, he lit a cigarette, glanced down at the Negroes, shook his head, took a deep drag and contemplated the cooling ash. Mister Leland was sitting on the edge of the porch, had abandoned carving in the cracks in favor of an inspection of the bus wheels, which were at least as big as he was, but turned up to see that the man's face was deeply troubled.

Mister Harper wheeled up behind them. "Say, now, where do all these people seem to be going?"

"Just been wondering that myself." The bus driver dropped his cigarette and twisted his toe on it. It became a small spot of paper, ash and tobacco, but Mister Leland could still see the printing in fine blue letters. "Today, I carried more niggers, men, women, and children, into New Marsails than I ever carried any day before, even more than on that day that ball club what had the first nigger in the major leagues played in New Marsails, but not one—that's right, not even ONE—out of New Marsails. I leave them all at the depot and they all go inside. I see all kinds of niggers going in the depot, and the thing is, I ain't seen one nigger come out. Now I ask YOU, where they going? And don't make no mistake about it, it ain't just from Sutton; it's from all along the Highway. They come running out of the woods and wave me down and get on and move to the back. Back there looks like it's jammed up with black sardines—with suitcases."

"Mmmm." Mister Harper nodded. He said nothing more, wheeled back to his place against the wall, staring into the Highway, not even attempting to control the conversations around him.

He said nothing until his daughter appeared with his lunch box and then only, "Thank you, honey."

Mister Leland turned to watch him open it, to see what he would be eating, but his father tapped him on the shoulder and nodded for him to get up, and they went around back, sat in the sun, watched a group of birds swirling like wind-torn smoke far off above the Ridge, and ate sandwiches his father had made before waking him that morning. When they were through with the sandwiches, his father reached into his jacket pocket and pulled out two apples, shined one on his chest and handed it to Mister Leland.

"Where all them ni-groes going, Papa?" He inspected the apple, trying to pick the exact spot to take the first bite.

"Don't know, Harold." His father bit into his, chewed, swallowed. "I reckon they all heading for some place where they think they can get on better."

"Ain't none of them coming back?"

"I don't reckon so, Harold. I reckon they making what we called in the Army a STRATEGIC WITHDRAWAL. That's when you got thirty men and the other side got thirty thousand and you turn and run saying to yourself, 'Shucks, ain't no use in being brave and getting ourselves killed. We'll back up a ways and maybe fight some tomorrow.' I reckon them Negroes is backing up all the way."

"Don't that make them scaredy cats, Papa?"

"Don't think so. Seems like this time it should take more guts to go, boy."

Mister Leland had nothing more to ask, but to himself wondered about it, munching on the warm, almost bitter apple. How could you have more guts to run than to stay? Perhaps it was like the time Eden MacDonald at school had said his father could beat the tar out of Mister Leland's and Mister Leland had answered, "No, my papa can beat the tar out of your'n because my papa ain't scared of nothing or nobody." And Eden had said, "I bet if he met hisself a bear and he didn't have no gun, he'd run faster than a nigger." And Mister Leland had said, "That ain't so." And Eden had said, "Well, then he'd get killed." When Mister Leland came home and asked his father if he would run from a bear when he didn't have a gun, his father had said, "I reckon I would, Harold. That'd be the smart thing, don't you think?" And when Mister Leland thought about it, it seemed like his father was right, even though he did not like to think of his father running away from a bear or anything else. But at least it was better than having his father all messed up and bloody and dead. And perhaps it was the same with the Negroes. He was about to ask his father if it was really like that when the man got up, stretched, and went to the barrel against the wall to toss away the waxed paper from the sandwiches. So he got up and followed him around to the porch, deciding to ask him about it later.

They began the afternoon in the same places, doing the same things as in the morning: waiting for more Negroes with suitcases to appear on the porch and for the bus to come down from the Ridge on sticky-sounding wheels. But the car came first.

It was black, polished like a pair of Sunday shoes, moving faster than any bus, faster even than the truck Mister Leland had seen yesterday with its wheels straddling the broken white line, its back heaped with salt. The car was traveling so fast Mister Leland could not adjust his eyes to its speed; it seemed always blurred. There was silver all over it, like a chariot in a movie, and its back looked to him like that of a rocket ship. There was a light-skinned Negro driving (his skin looked green behind the glass) and someone sat in back. He could not be seen too well until the car stopped in front of the porch and he rolled down the window and stuck his head out. Then Mister Leland saw he was a Negro, just as black as the car, and almost as shiny, with long hair almost obscuring his ears and bundled at the back of his neck like an ancient warrior, black sprinkled gray like ashes. He was dressed in black, and wore a pair of blue sunglasses with gold rims. Attached to a gold chain that looped down and into a buttonhole in his vest, was a golden cross with Jesus Christ nailed to it, so big you could see the nails in His hands. He looked at no one, spoke only to Mister Leland. "God bless and protect you, young man."

He talks like Mister Harper, who Papa says learned to talk up North. So he must come from up North too. No wonder them nig-Negroes is going North; Negroes in the North must live like kings. He was a bit flabber-

61

gasted but managed to squeeze out: "How do . . . sir." Sitting on the edge of the porch, he could see the inside roof of the car. *It's all out-a soft cloth. It's all over everywhere.*

"How do." His father spoke from high above him, his knees just behind Mister Leland's head. But the Negro did not avert his gaze, continued to stare at the boy.

"Are you Mister Leland?"

"Yes, sir."

As if this in itself was worthy of reward, the Negro reached out of the car pushing his index and middle fingers toward the boy. Pinched between them was a five dollar bill. Mister Leland took it timidly, wondering why the money had been bestowed, a slow fear beginning deep within him because now the Negro's face had taken on an almost savage expression, as if just by being Mister Leland was not only worthy of reward but at the same time evil.

"I've been led to believe, Mister Leland, that you were well acquainted with a Negro, Tucker Caliban. Is that true?"

"Yes, sir." Mister Leland still held the five dollars gingerly in his hand, as if it had been given him only to hold, as he would hold a sample being passed around his classroom by the teacher. He stood, backing up so he was almost leaning against his father, gained security from the hand his father placed on his shoulder. Around them, he noticed the other men, lining the car's curbside, peering through the windows, though not touching the car, as if it was moulten hot. Only Bobby-Joe seemed more than just curious; he squinted as if in pain or wanting to inflict pain.

Still the Negro ignored all but him. "In that case, Mister Leland, would you be so kind as to tell me all you saw yesterday?"

Mister Leland was not certain he should do this, so tilted his head almost straight back, and, upside down, saw his father nodding Yes. He looked at the Negro again. "Well, first of all there was this coal—"

The Negro did not let him finish, but finally acknowledged his father's presence. "You're the boy's father, I presume."

His father nodded.

"In that case, I wonder if I might request that you permit him to show me where this farm is?"

"You mean I can ride in that car?" Mister Leland had ridden in a bus several times, but never in a car.

His father said nothing, stood staring at the Negro.

Mister Leland looked upwards at his father again. "Papa, can I?"

His father looked thoughtful, more thoughtful than just trying to decide whether the boy could go, trying to think why the Negro wanted him to go, what was in his mind.

The Negro watched his father for a short while, then reached into his inside breast pocket, produced a wallet, a large one, took out ten dollars and handed it to his father. "Here," and he chuckled as if something was very funny, "let me buy him from you for a short time." He leaned out with his arm extended, but unlike Mister Leland, his father did not reach out for it, made no sign of acceptance, stared deep into the blue glass protecting the Negro's eyes.

"Not sufficient?" The Negro added another ten. Mister Leland was thinking that he could pull ten dollar bills out of his wallet all day. He could see the wallet choked with money. This was only a fleeting thought; his main concern was riding in the car. "Papa, can I?"

Still his father did nothing, finally turned his head the slightest bit toward Mister Harper, who had wheeled to the edge of the porch. Mister Harper nodded just once. His father turned back to the Negro. "When'll you bring him back?" At the same time, he reached out and took the money. Someone behind them let out an involuntary whistle.

"In approximately one hour. We're simply going to Caliban's farm."

The boy felt his father ruffle his hair. "Harold, you want to go?"

Certain of wanting to ride in the car, he was not at all certain he liked the Negro, who was not like Tucker Caliban, really friendly although you did not think so at first. Still, he MUST ride in the car. "Yes, Papa."

His father let fall his hand to the back of his neck, and gave him a gentle push. "Come over here." They went a short distance from the men, the car, and the Negro; Mister Leland led, his father directed, then stopped him, turned him around, his hands now on the boy's shoulders.

"Harold, remember what I said to you this morning? About something starting?"

"Yes, sir." Staring deeply into his father's eyes, he could see them serious and large, shaded under the brim of his hat, but bright and gentle too.

"Well, it's started, son, and this Negro knows it. So you remember EVERYTHING he says." He paused. "Everything, exactly the way he says it even if you can't understand the words. Don't worry about that; I can't understand half of what he says neither, but Mister Harper can."

"Yes, Papa."

"You ain't scared, are you?"

He was not sure, but he wanted to ride in the car. "No, sir."

"All right then. Now be good, on your best manners, and remember everything he says." He stopped and looked toward the car, then turned back. "For me."

"Yes, Papa." Mister Leland felt like a spy. They went back to the car. The Negro opened the door so he could see the inside of it as soft as a bed. The Negro slid over on the seat and he climbed in and saw his father grasp the handle and close the door. He sat in the corner, and then suddenly felt himself pushed, by an invisible force, deeper into the seat, although he heard no roaring motor.

There were rugs on the floor; the windows made everything outside green, ghastly. Music was coming from somewhere behind him. When he turned around to wave good-by to his father and the men, the town had already disappeared.

"Now, Mister Leland, tell me what happened, won't you?"

He opened his mouth and a slight fear propelled the story out furiously. "First we seen the coal truck coming down off the Ridge, all black and going as fast as anything. It was carrying salt, and the driver said he wanted to take it to the Caliban place; and asked us where that was, and my papa told him and he went away. And then later, Mister Stewart come in and he said Tucker was putting the salt on his field, and so we all went out there, all of us on the porch and some Negroes too, and watched him all afternoon. He made the field so it looked all white like he put fertilizer on it, but it weren't that, it was salt. And then he went in the house and come out with his rifle and his ax and sat on the fence of his corral and first he shot the horse and the blood squirted out like as if you stuck a pin in a balloon filled with blood, and the cow was a-running and screaming and he shot her too, and she turned around and you could see the hole in her head like she was dead but didn't know it at all, and then she died for real. And then he picked up the ax and chopped down the tree in his yard where the General used to ride out in old times because he liked that tree best of all, and then went in the house and set it on fire and come out and walked away." He stopped abruptly. He would not tell the Negro what Tucker had said to him. The Negro did not know Tucker. That would be like telling a special secret that Tucker had told to him.

"Was there anything else?" The Negro was looking at him through the sunglasses.

"No, sir. Not about Tucker Caliban." He lied, then modified it. "There was more happened this morning when my papa and me come into town."

"And what was that?"

"Well, first a ni—gro named Wallace Bedlow come with a suit-case and good clothes what ain't used for working and flimsy pants that blow in the breeze and he said he wasn't ever coming back to Sutton, and waited for the bus and got on it and went away. And there was more Negroes too, and they all had suitcases and good clothes and got on the buses and went away."

He heard the Negro exhale sharply, almost angrily. "How many would you say, Mister Leland?"

"Maybe fifty that I seen, but them was only Negroes what didn't have cars; there's some that got cars and went that way."

"Just as I suspected." The Negro was talking to himself.

When they arrived at Tucker Caliban's farm or what was left of it, it seemed the same as it had been the night before, but in some ways different. It looked as though it could not have been only yesterday that Tucker destroyed and left it, but a long time before, for already the ashes had settled into a kind of paste, and the place looked as run down as if long abandoned, like farms back in the hills his father had showed him one time they went fishing early in the morning. The field was not as white—the dew had melted some of the salt—and had driven it further into the ground so that now the field was more gray, ashen, than white and glistening. The sky above the corral was black with flies, and already the meat of the animals had begun to smell sweet like the oppressive odor of a candy shop.

The Negro's chauffeur parked the car in front of where the front door had stood and Mister Leland hopped out, followed by the Negro, who the boy noticed was a bit paunchy around the waist, though his arms and shoulders seemed quite thin. As he bent over to step out, his cross dangled and glittered.

They walked slowly around the farm until, in the middle of the yard, the Negro found the remains of the clock, a pile of iron, brass, little wheels, and springs, bits of finely polished wood. "What's this, Mister Leland?"

He had forgotten about the clock and told the Negro what it had been.

"What happened to it?"

"It was after he chopped the tree down, he brung the clock into the yard. My papa told me about it on the way home. He says it was a clock what the General hisself—you know who the General is? That's General Dewey Willson of the Army. He—"

The Negro had begun to laugh.

"Sir?" The boy walked closer.

"I was just laughing at what you said. There were two armies, young man."

"Sir?"

"It's not at all important. Don't worry yourself about it. Go on."

Puzzled for an instant, he looked at the Negro, but decided it WAS, after all, not very important, although he did feel it was rude of the Negro to laugh at him. "Well, the General give it to Tucker's great-great . . . great-great-great . . . great-great-grandfather and it was Tucker's and he chopped it to pieces. He—"

"Isn't that gloriously primitive!" It was not a question. Mister Leland did not know what it meant, but remembered it anyway for his father.

"Well, that seems to be about all, doesn't it, Mister Leland." The Negro started toward the car. "Unless, you've remembered something else." He looked down, it seemed, suspiciously.

Mister Leland wondered if the Negro knew he had not told everything about Tucker. After all, the Negro had known his name and whoever had told him that perhaps told him Mister Leland had talked to Tucker. The Negro might get angry and tell his father he had lied. "Well, there was one thing . . . but Tucker told it to me and I don't know if I should tell you because . . ."

"Suit yourself, young man. I would never persuade you to betray a confidence."

"Sir?"

"Oh yes, of course." Then miraculously, the Negro began to talk almost like Wallace Bedlow or Tucker himself would have talked. "I won't make you tell no tales out-a school, Mister Leland. What your friends tells you in secret is supposen to stay secret." He paused and added, "Don't you reckon that's so, Mister Leland?"

The boy was surprised; someone else's voice was coming out of the man's body. "Yes, sir. Well, maybe . . . well, you give me the money to tell you ALL about yesterday and that wouldn't be honest if I was to . . . well, Tucker said . . . I run after him when he left and he said . . . that I was young and ain't lost nothing yet and I didn't understand what he meant when he said that and he made me go back." He tilted his head and looked the Negro in the eye and found him smiling more warmly than he had smiled since first Mister Leland had seen him. He hesitated, then asked, "You know what he meant by that?"

"I think he meant that he had been robbed of something but had never known it because he never even knew he owned what had been taken from him. Do you understand that?" The boy realized his face must have been revealing his thoughts. "No, I don't think you do. No, well, it's of no importance to you now, Mister Leland; when you grow a bit older, you'll understand perfectly enough." They had reached the car. "I'll get in first, all right?"

"Yes, sir." He was still thinking about what the Negro had said, and continued to think about it, as the car nosed toward town on quiet wheels, as the Negro sat beside him deep in thought staring ahead over the chauffeur's shoulder and far down the road . . . *If Tucker lost something but didn't know he had it, he couldn't know he lost it. That's silly. You got to know you got something to know you lost it, unless, when you lost it, you go to look for it and find it ain't where you left it, but then if you left it somewhere you must-a knowed that you had it, so that ain't the same thing. Maybe it's like if somebody give you something at night when you're sleeping, but before you find it in the morning, somebody like Walter comes in and sneaks it out, and plays with it in the woods and leaves it there so you won't never find it, and then next day the person what left it for you comes in and says, "Harold, did you find what I left for you?" And you says, "No." And he says, "Well, I left it right in plain sight on the dresser so how come you didn't find it this morning?" And you says, "I don't know." And then you think on it and says, "Walter, he must-a took it before I woke up. I'll go beat the tar out-a him." And Walter says that he left it in the woods and don't know where and so you lost it and never even had it in the first place, but know you lost it all right. Maybe it's like that. . . .*

By that time they had pulled into town and stopped across the street from Mister Thomason's.

The Negro rolled down the window, and Mister Leland peered across the street and saw his father resting on his post, then straighten up, saw Bobby-Joe spit into the street, and Mister Harper leaning forward.

"Thank you and God keep you, sir." The Negro called to his father, then turned to him. "Thank you too, Mister Leland. You're a fine young man, and if ever you should come North, do pay me a visit." He reached into a tiny pocket in his vest and produced a card. Mister Leland took it, running his fingers across the raised surface of the letters, not looking at it. The Negro reached over and they shook hands—his hand was soft and flabby like a fat woman's—then opened the door and Mister Leland hopped out. By the time he reached the porch, the car was halfway up to Harmon's Draw.

He handed the card to his father, who in turn handed it, without reading it, to Mister Harper, who read it aloud to all the men. "THE REVEREND B. T. BRADSHAW. THE RESURRECTED CHURCH OF THE BLACK JESUS CHRIST OF AMERICA, INC., NEW YORK CITY."

Mister Thomason brought out a chair and motioned for his father to sit down, and when he had done so, his father pulled Mister Leland onto his lap. Mister Harper wheeled up to him and leaned deeply toward him where he could smell the old man's old breath, and questioned him. He told all he knew, all he could remember; he had remembered everything. Mister Harper made no comments until he had told about the clock and the Negro saying: "Isn't that gloriously primitive!" and then only nodded his head and almost sighed: "Yes, yes, he's right there." But that was all. And the other men simply listened.

It was not quite four in the afternoon, but when he had finished, his father looked down at him gravely. "Well, let's get on home."

His father did not speak to him again until they were just turning into their own road, and Mister Leland could hear the horse's hoofs as they left the asphalt and began to chomp in the dirt. "Harold, don't tell your ma about going with the Negro." He paused for a second. "She might not like it."

"Yes, Papa."

He did not turn, but did lean back so he was resting his head against his father's chest and could hear the man's large heart beating, and his voice, hollow and far away, rumbling. "It ain't that it's bad, you understand. It ain't like yesterday when you had to tell a lie to keep me out of trouble. This is to save her worry because she don't like you going off with strangers and since it's done and nothing happened to you, ain't no need to worry her about it. You understand?"

He nodded, feeling the back of his head rubbing the cloth of his father's shirt.

"Look." He took one hand off the reins and Mister Leland could feel it behind him going through his father's pockets and then coming out again, heard then tissue paper sizzling and then his father's hand was coming out from behind him, reaching over his shoulder and he saw the package. "Open it; I want you to see it." Mister Leland took it, undid the paper, and saw a scarf of yellow silk—somehow he knew it was silk because it was finer, smoother, more delicate than any cloth he had ever seen—with a tiny sewn border like a tube. He held it up and felt it even lighter than the slight wind blowing; it flew bravely, elegantly in that wind. "Yellow's her favorite color and she likes nice things. I bought it with some of that twenty dollars. Say, you want me to hold that five you got?" And then he added, "You don't have to give it to me if you ain't a mind to. It's yours." But Mister Leland had already gone into his overall pocket, pulled out the money, and handed it to his father. "I'll save it for you so you'll have plenty when the circus comes to New Marsails." The boy nodded.

His father told his mother he had made twenty dollars fixing a rich tourist's flat tire, then gave her the scarf. She cried into it, and kissed it and wore it at supper. She looked prettier than Mister Leland had ever seen her.

Saturday they did not go into town. Mister Leland thought they might, that there might be more to see, but when he asked whether they were going, his father answered, "No; chances are all we'd see would be more Negroes with suitcases going away, and besides, we left your ma here alone for two days, and I figure it'd be a good idea if we stuck around and did everything she asks us, else she might get a little testy and mean. And she'd be right when you think on it, seeing as she been doing all the things we should-a been doing and that weren't very kind of us. I reckon we'll stay home today."

So Mister Leland played with Walter most of the day. He tried

to recount everything he had seen in the past days, but Walter could
only understand the animals being shot and blood squirting out of
them like water out of balloons. He wished he had seen that. Mister
Leland assured him it had been something to see all right. Of course,
Walter wanted his brother to take him over to see the animals—
he must have been secretly hoping their blood was still squirting
out—and Tucker's burned-down house. Mister Leland said he was
too little to go. And Walter said he was not too little at all, but
proved that he was by starting to jump up and down and fume and
cry and carry on. Finally, because he really wanted to go himself,
Mister Leland took him. They went back through the woods, along
the smooth, narrow dirt paths, and came out in the back of the
gray field, and could see, far across, the jagged bits of house timber
jutting up like burned cotton stalks, and the dark, fly-filled sky
above the corral. They were halfway across the field when a white
man pedaled up the Highway from the direction of town on a bicycle.
It was an old American bike, had once been cream and the red color
of bricks, but use and weather had transformed those colors into a
dark gray rust. Its fenders were gone; its headlight broken. The
man pulled off the road, lay down the bicycle, and stood staring
around him. Then he saw the two boys. "You're Harry Leland's
boys, aren't you?"

He too talked as if he had learned up North, but more like Mister
Harper than the Negro. The boys said nothing. They had stopped
in the middle of the field and Mister Leland had taken his brother's
hand.

The man called to them again. "I'm Dewey Willson."

That's a lie; Dewey Willson is the General and he's dead. He gripped
Walter's hand so he winced and protested. "Now you be quiet,
Walter. This man may be crazy" . . . *not crazy like Tucker, but really
crazy because he thinks he's a dead man.* He pulled his brother along

behind him, and presently they could see the man better. He was shorter than their father, but had the same sandy hair, though cut shorter. He was wearing a light blue suit with a great many buttons—three or four—and a drab tie with diagonal stripes.

"Do you know anything about the fire, little boy?" He waited for an answer but Mister Leland gave him none. "I'm a friend of Tucker Caliban's. Just back from up North. Do you know what happened?"

"You a friend of Tucker's?" Mister Leland spoke in spite of himself, but did not believe this last statement any more than he believed this man was the General. Still, the man did not sound like he was lying.

"Yes. Look." The man reached into his pocket, and Mister Leland's heart jumped—*more money!*—but the man had pulled out only a piece of paper. "It's a letter from him. He was a very good friend of mine." The man grew sad after he said this.

"He was?" They were standing quite close to him now; he looked down at them with the piece of paper extended in his right hand. The flies seemed to drone a great deal louder. "You know why he done it?"

"What did he do?"

And then he could not keep it back any longer because he wanted very much to find out what this man knew. "Why, he burned down his house and killed his animals and all."

The man only stared at him; he did not believe. "My father was right! Is that what he did?"

"That's what he done—really." Still the man looked as if he did not believe it. Mister Leland added, "He done all that two days ago."

"Two days ago?"

Mister Leland decided the man did not hear very well, not that he did not believe. He asked him to repeat everything. "Uh-huh, I seen it myself. He just burned down his house and shot his animals and—"

"Blood squirted out of them like water out of a pricked balloon," Walter chimed in.

"Hush, Walter." Mister Leland squeezed his hand and felt the little boy jump in pain. "Really he did those things." He turned to the man.

"I believe you." The man nodded.

"It's the truth." Walter chimed in again.

"Hush, Walter."

"Tell me about it, will you please?" The man looked very sad.

Mister Leland unraveled the tale of salt and killing and burning and the clock (he did not forget it this time) and the sparks going up and disappearing in the sky. But even when he had finished, the man looked no less sad, no less disbelieving. "You a friend of his —really?"

The man nodded his hand and looked so very strange that Mister Leland thought it would be best to get away from him as quickly as possible. "We got to go now. Good-by." He immediately started for the Highway—that would be the safest way to go home because the man might follow them into the woods—and did not hear the man answer: "Yes, good-by."

When they got to the Highway, he turned to Walter, let his hand go, and yelled very loudly, "Let's race!"

"I don't feel like it."

He leaned toward his ear. "That'll be our reason to run. He can still catch us and he looks dangerous."

"All right, let's race." Walter looked back over his shoulder.

They ran wildly to the top of the hill; when they got out of the man's sight, they stopped, heaving deeply. Walter caught up. "He was crazy."

"How do you know?" Mister Leland did not like his brother to jump to conclusions.

"Didn't he look crazy?"

"Yes." He was forced to tell the truth.

"Well, there then, he must be crazy."

Mister Leland was about to say that this was not always true; that Tucker had done crazy things, even looked crazy, but was certainly not crazy because he seemed to have a reason for doing those things, even though they were both too young to understand the reason, but he decided to let it drop because he did not think Walter would know what he was talking about.

They were a quarter way to the bottom of the hill, walking toward where their road turned off the Highway. They could see the next hill and the Highway coming out of the trees. Then they saw the black car appear, coming just as fast as it had yesterday from the Ridge, just as fast as the coal truck the day before that. The same light-skinned Negro was driving, and the dust swirled at the sides of the road and closed in behind it like Walter's hands closing too late when Mister Leland tossed him a ball. Mister Leland started to wave, and Walter, thinking it was some kind of game, raised his arms and waved frantically. They both waved until the car passed them, but no one in the car waved back. Mister Leland, in the instant of its passing, even saw the Negro in the back, his blue sunglasses perched on his nose, staring straight ahead of him. Then the car had disappeared over the hill. They walked on.

"What'd we do that for, Harold?" Walter had begun to skip around him in large, uneven circles. "Did you know them?"

Mister Leland had not told Walter about the Negro and his ride in the car because he knew Walter would have told his mother, and would have caused trouble for his father. "Yes. I saw them in town yesterday."

"What'd they do? You didn't tell me about that."

"It ain't at all important, Walter. You forget it."

"Well, who WAS that?"

"Just nobody." He turned and looked his brother in the eye, trying to make his face honest as possible. "Nobody, is all."

ONE
LONG AGO
AUTUMN
BIRTHDAY

When Dewey Willson III had blinked full awake on the clear, mistless, autumn morning of his tenth birthday, it was standing in the corner of his room: an American bicycle with bright gaudy colors, shining chrome, and white-wall tires.

He climbed slowly and uncertainly from bed, thinking that if he moved too quickly it would surely disappear. The floor was cold and sent a shiver through him. And then he had reached it, had not shocked it out of existence, and now stood stroking the black pigskin seat. He longed to ride it, but realized painfully he did not know how; Tucker had tried to teach him several times, but finally had given up because Dewey could not balance or steer or pedal.

Watching it constantly, he dressed as fast as he could and then ran downstairs in search of Tucker. This time he WOULD learn if only he could convince Tucker to attempt once again to teach him.

A DIFFERENT DRUMMER

Tucker was in the back yard with John, his grandfather, removing the dried film of recently applied wax from the side of the car. John, white-haired, the many wrinkles in his face making him almost featureless, was nearly seventy-five. Tucker was doing most of the work, though he was only thirteen and could barely reach the top of the car doors. Dewey stood off and watched them, afraid Tucker would tell him he was a stupid little boy who would never learn to ride a bicycle, but finally he got up the courage to ask.

"Can't now, Dewey. I got to help Grandpap." Tucker turned around, holding a piece of white toweling in his right hand, a can of orange polish in his left. Already he looked at people in a way that made it seem he was about to lash out and strike at something, although he might be thinking of something completely different; already his eyes were framed by steel-rimmed spectacles.

"I'll learn this time. I promise." He fidgeted under Tucker's gaze and averted his eyes to the rubber toes of his sneakers.

"Maybe you will, maybe not, but later. I got to help Grandpap." Tucker turned back to the old man, who was puffing as he made desperate swipes at the top of the car. "Later on."

Dewey spent most of his birthday on the back steps, the bicycle on its stand beside him, watching Tucker at work. He wondered whether Tucker was envious of his having received a new bicycle. He wished he did not have to bother Tucker at all, wished he could get on the bicycle and discover he was part of a miracle and could ride it away, never looking back, never fearing he would fall or crash.

Tucker did not finish his work until late in the day, when the wind was coming off the Gulf, full of the metallic smell of salt. The sun seemed dark and rode just above the horizon in a chariot of clouds. They would not have much time.

They stood near the back steps, Dewey staring up at Tucker, who was looking around the yard, scowling. "Can't learn to ride here; ain't enough room. You'll knock down every bush in sight and get us in trouble. Come on." He kicked up the stand, grasped the handle bars, and began to wheel the bicycle toward the gravel driveway.

"Where we going?" Dewey scurried after him. He was a little angry that Tucker rather than himself was wheeling his bicycle.

"Come on now. We ain't got no time to talk."

They went a half mile north of Sutton to a place just off the Highway where someone had started to build a restaurant but had never finished, had completed only a parking lot, a huge open black space sprouting with several concrete pillars.

By now it was almost dark; the sun had dropped without notice behind the tall trees on their side of the road. Tucker wheeled the bicycle up to one corner of the lot and stopped. "You remember what I told you before?"

"I think so." He was not sure. Tucker could see it.

"All right, now listen." He recited the lesson in a high-pitched monotone. "You can't balance too good when you're going slow, better when you going fast. But when you going fast you got to remember to steer. It's real easy if you just keep your head. Can you do it?"

"I think so."

"All right. Get on and I'll hold it for you and run alongside, pushing. I'll tell you when I'm letting go. All right?"

"I think so."

Tucker helped him up on the new seat. Dewey put his feet on the pedals. Tucker looked at them. "I told you and told you—don't NEVER ride no bike in no sneakers. Your feet'll slip and you'll hurt yourself."

"I'm sorry."

"Ain't much you can do about it now." Tucker sighed. "Well, let's try it."

Dewey squirmed on the seat, and Tucker began to push him along. "Now keep your balance. Get the feel of them two wheels. Don't be scared. And DON'T oversteer."

The handle bars jerked like the horns of a wild bull. Dewey turned to Tucker.

"I'm letting go now." He did and almost immediately Dewey wobbled from the straight course and Tucker had to catch him just before he crashed into one of the concrete posts. They tried again, and again: Tucker running beside him, breathing hard, coughing now and then; Dewey sitting, not knowing what to do, but trying hard to do something. He wanted to cry, but did not want Tucker to see; that would have made him more ashamed of himself than he was already.

Dusk hung now on the hills; the wind was rising. They had tried countless times.

"We best go on home, Dewey-boy."

"Please, Tucker, just once more. Please."

"Now, Dewey, you knows it won't make your pa happy, us holding up his dinner."

"Tucker, I GOT to learn." He could feel hot tears just behind his eyes and perhaps already spilling out, scalding his face, because Tucker looked down at him and nodded, then helped him up and held the seat tightly so the bicycle would not tip over, and started to push. Dewey tried to get the feel of it, and when he thought he had it, turned to tell Tucker to let go.

Tucker was no longer there. Without warning he had stopped running, and Dewey was alone, rolling, riding, gliding, sailing, flying all by himself and could feel the bicycle balanced on the thin white wheels, and pride welling up inside him. And then fear appeared out of nowhere, and dark panic glazed his eyes and stopped up his ears, making it almost impossible to hear Tucker shouting: "Keep straight! Steer now! Keep straight!"

But his confidence had already ebbed from him in small oily drops; he was losing his battle with the fighting handle bars. The black pavement came up to meet him and skinned his knees, but now off the bicycle, safe once more on earth, he could not feel the stinging and was as proud of himself as he had ever been.

"You did it! You did it! You did it!" Tucker ran to him, swooped him up, clapped his shoulder; they danced in huge circles around the bicycle. Tucker shook his hand, and hugged him, even kissed him, and they whooped and hollered until they were tired and hoarse.

They started home then, along the black straight road, their faces lit and shining in the headlight glare of the few passing cars.

"Tucker, would you teach me how to start alone?"

"As soon as you can stop another way besides falling off."

"Tucker, would you——?" A car went by, glinting light off Tucker's glasses, turning his face almost white, and Dewey saw the expression of resignation there, and knew Tucker's mind was already at home, knew he should keep quiet.

When he thought of that day later, Dewey realized Tucker must have known what would happen even when he said they could stay. He was supposed to be the responsible one; it was up to him to keep track of time, but he had not kept track of it or so it seemed to Dewey's father, who had spoken to John about it, who had instructed his daughter-in-law to make the punishment one to be remembered. And so as Dewey ate dinner that night, he could hear the smacking of the hot strap across Tucker's buttocks.

Later that evening, Dewey told his father he had learned to ride. He thought his father would be happy, since the bicycle had been his present, but his father had only nodded and had not even looked up from his newspaper. For the longest while, until he went to college, Dewey felt guilty that he had begged Tucker to stay, and wanted to say something to him, but never did. And Tucker never mentioned it.

THE
WILLSONS

It was Saturday afternoon. The telephone poles, embedded at the edge of the river in the built-up concrete-fieldstone bank, snapped by his window so fast that, after a while, Dewey, eighteen now and returning home from his first year up North at college, stopped trying to think the mounting total, gave up his counting to watch the train race ahead of the river's current. But soon, as he had done many times in the month since he received it, he began to think of Tucker's letter. He was still not certain he understood what Tucker meant. Not that the letter communicated many deep or complex thoughts—it was the simplest of letters—rather it brought up a subject and a time he could hardly remember, and he knew in order to understand what Tucker meant he had to remember, examine that time, that day; and not only this, but also the feelings he had experienced that day. He wished those feelings were written down someplace where he could pull them out to read and know them perfectly. And so again he reviewed the particular day Tucker mentioned, and still he could not understand; Tucker's message, written in a code he could not remember or had never known, evaded him. He started again, took the letter from the now shredded envelope, unfolded the yellow copy paper, and read the typed words, dictated to Bethrah (he was sure), and signed in the hand not of a twenty-two-year-old man, but of a fourteen-year-old boy, the age Tucker had dropped from school:

Dear Dewey:

    I hope you're well. I'm fine myself. So is Bethrah. So is the baby.

    The reason I wrote is because I wanted to ask you if you remember when I taught you to ride a bike? That was a very important day for you. I remember you wanted to learn a lot. I am glad I could teach you. But you would have learned anyway, because you wanted to learn so much.

    When you were home for Christmas you wanted me to write to you. Well, I wanted to ask you about the bike.

Sincerely yours,
Tucker Caliban

It was as futile this time as it had been all the other times and Dewey was still puzzled and disappointed. But he would be home soon and would ask Tucker himself to explain the letter, though it meant he would have to admit his intellect did not possess the lightning snatch he prided himself it possessed.

The train entered the tunnels leading to the New Marsails Municipal Depot. The darkness was lit in round patches by dim bulbs in steel shades. Men worked by lantern with picks and shovels, and one, the foreman, held a blood-colored lamp and waved it as the train went by. Dewey got to his feet, stretched, searched for the tangled arms of his suit coat and the cigarettes he was certain he had left in his breast pocket. And then it was once again late afternoon, and the roar of the tunnel was replaced by the murmuring in the car.

Afterwards, when Dewey thought of how the station had looked that afternoon, he could not remember whether he had taken notice of the great number of Negroes on the platform, in the colored waiting room; could not remember the many thoughtful dark faces of the men or that they wore newly pressed suits and clean shirts or that most of them carried chipped leather suitcases or frayed cloth carpetbags or shopping bags crammed with clothing, sheets, blankets, and pictures; could not remember the women in their summer dresses carrying sweaters and coats, their own and their children's, or the picnic baskets in the crooks of their arms, or the walking shoes cleaned until the scars and scratches were hidden; could not remember the scampering, skipping children, running ahead of their parents or the littler ones hanging onto their mothers' dresses; could not remember the babies sleeping in the grownups' arms or on the benches; could not remember the old people hobbling proudly on canes, or sitting quietly waiting for the trains to be called; could not remember that the Negroes spoke in whispers, avoided the glances of white people, and tried not to be remembered.

He remembered there had been Negroes, there had always been Negroes at the depot, the porters in their gray suits and red hats, but he had not taken notice of the many others there that day or that most of them were boarding outgoing trains. All he could really remember was looking through the dirt-streaked window, finding his family amid the crowds as the train's air brakes threw him forward, and his happiness at seeing Dymphna, his sister—whom he was old enough now to appreciate and like—for the first time since Christmas; his disappointment at not seeing Tucker and Bethrah anywhere on the platform; and finally, his surprise, no, it was a far more wrenching sensation than that, his utter shock at seeing his parents, HIS mother and father, smiling at one another and HOLDING HANDS (!) as gleefully as teen-agers. When he had left home after a dreary Christmas holiday, his mother had been muttering constantly about getting a divorce.

The train had stopped now. He reached up, tipped his two bags off the rack above his seat, and, after waiting for a few passengers to trudge by, fell in behind two girls, who, like himself, were returning home from school. They wore heavy crew-necked sweaters, though it was quite warm, and many beaded necklaces.

"So then he asked me if I had a block or some such thing and started to talk to me real soft, but I didn't fall for it a bit. He told me it was natural for men and women to do it."

"That's just exactly what he told me."

"Well, anyway, all of a sudden, honey, I realized I wanted to kiss him more than anything. And after that, I just fell apart."

"Me too."

At the door, a smiling conductor in a frayed blue suit guided passengers down the slippery steps. He reached for Dewey's arm, but the boy shook free politely and hopped the last high step to the platform.

Dymphna was bouncing up and down. With each jump she turned a quarter circle, and finally she was facing him. She saw and recognized him, waved her arms, and, still in flight, tried to tell his parents. Then she disappeared below a bank of people, and when next he saw her, she was no more than thirty steps from him, running, her arms spread wide, her coat flapping behind her. Grabbing him tightly around the waist, even before he could drop his bags, she hugged him. "Dewey! Hiiiii!"

"Hello. How are you?" He was too stunned by her attack to say anything else.

She did not let him go, rather she hugged him tighter. "Fine.

Is that all you have to say to me?" She leaned back from him. "How do you like me?"

"You cut your hair off." Over her head he saw his parents advancing, still holding hands, and he wanted to know what to expect. He bent close to her, whispering. "They're REALLY holding hands. What the hell's happening around here—miracles?"

She hugged him tightly again. "Yes! Yes! Yes! I don't know how it happened. But it looks like we have a chance to avoid a 'broken home.' It's wonderful."

His parents arrived. Dymphna turned him loose and his mother came forward and hugged him. She sounded as if she were sobbing and he could not understand what she said into his chest, but when she stepped back to inspect him, her eyes were dry and she was smiling. She had aged; he had never remembered gray hair wisping over her ears, but saw it now.

His father stood behind her, hands behind his back. "How are you, Dewey?" He reached out his hand and bent forward, almost timidly, taking no steps, as if there was between them a trench two arm lengths across and bottomless.

"All right, Dad."

The man nodded, withdrew his hand and put it, with the other, behind him. "You look well, son."

"He's lost some weight," his mother clucked.

They all looked at each other in silence and Dewey realized now just how much they had changed: his mother, still pretty, but no longer young, was almost matronly. Her once sharp features had softened, her brown eyes had dulled. But more than anything she looked tired. His father seemed to have shrunk and wasted away more than aged, but he looked happier than Dewey had ever remembered him, less oppressed, less as if something were pushing down on him. Dymphna had become quite an attractive young lady, was dressed fashionably, a copy of her mother as she must have looked twenty years before.

He had expected something drastically different; he would not have been even surprised if only one of his parents had come to meet him, bringing the news that divorce proceedings had already begun. Or if both had come, he would have expected them to keep their distance from one another, to talk only to him, not to each other, with Dymphna standing between them like a partition of flesh and blood so they would not, even accidentally, touch. But all this; they were—too happy.

No one had spoken. They stood now on a near-empty platform. Toward the back of the train a brakeman blew his whistle and the line of cars began to back up. An outgoing train was announced; it would be heading North. After a few seconds, Negroes began to stream through the main doors, marching toward the next track.

"You ladies go ahead." His father stepped forward and picked up one of Dewey's bags. "We'll join you at the car."

Dymphna stood by watching; she knew Dewey and their father had never been very close, at times had argued bitterly, and she had been wondering how, when Dewey came back, her father would get along with him. She made no move until her mother pinched her arm.

"Come on, Dymphnie. This'll give us time to put on new lipstick."

Dewey watched them through the door, noticing Dymphna turn back once or twice. He smiled. "God, she's such a busybody." He shook his head and spoke out loud.

"She is that." His father stepped to his side.

Dewey turned, resenting the intrusion. "What did you want to say to me?" He had been trying to hurt the man, and was surprised to find he had.

His father looked at the ground in front of him. "Dewey," he started, sighing, "I realize your mother and I haven't made things too easy for you."

"You mean YOU haven't."

"That may be so, son." Dewey had scored again; something was wrong, or changed; his father seemed almost human. He had started to say in answer that he KNEW it was so, but decided to hear his father out.

"Yes, it probably is so, son. But we've . . . I've been trying to get things going again." He looked up shyly. "Maybe when we, you and I, get to know each other better, I can tell you what it was all about." He looked away. "Let's walk, all right?" He looked up as if he expected a fight on this request too.

"Yes, all right."

"Well, at any rate, it looks like your mother and I might be able to . . ." He did not finish. "And I was hoping that perhaps you and I could get to know each other a bit."

Dewey found himself wanting very much to say: of course they could, that this is what he had been hoping all his life. But he stopped himself; there was too much separating them to wave away all at once. "I don't know."

"Maybe we could try. We have all summer. Maybe we could try."

"Maybe we could."

They entered the huge marbled waiting room; reflections replaced shadows beneath their feet. They went on to the parking lot, a large concrete open space with rows of dull metal parking meters ordered like the crosses of a military cemetery. There were only a few cars. From the front seat of one of them, his mother smiled and waved at them. Dymphna, who was sitting in the back, waved too. They looked very much alike.

When they reached the car, his father swung open the trunk and

Dewey shoved in his luggage, then climbed in back with Dymphna. His father started the motor, stomped the gas pedal, and steered into the street.

There were a great many more Negroes than usual downtown, all, it seemed, carrying suitcases, wearing dark clothes.

"Dear? Did you hear me?" His mother had been talking to him. "I asked if you liked school?"

"Yes, Mama. It was fine."

They were in the Northside. The streets were filled with Negroes, some sitting on white steps in front of tall, narrow, dirty brick buildings. Children played tag amid the garbage of vacant lots. Every so often, at the call of various black women with their breasts pressed flat against stone window sills, a child would break from the group and run into the house. Their good-bys seemed always quite final.

They passed a group of men standing on the corner in front of a bar with an unlighted neon sign. Their heads were bowed together as if one of them was telling a dirty joke. Dewey waited for an explosion of laughter, but none came. Instead, the men pulled apart and ambled their separate ways, solemn and alone. The entire Northside seemed strangely silent for a Saturday afternoon.

They crossed the river, and through the black steel network, seeming from the car no bigger than fly screening, the water swelled around the pillars, and the bridge, rather than water, seemed to be moving.

"Say, Dymphnie, how are Tucker and Bethrah? And the baby?" He noticed the silence. "Did you hear me? Dymphnie? How are——"

"I heard you, Dewey." She stopped short. "We don't know."

"Pardon?"

His mother swiveled around to face him. "They aren't working for us any more, dear."

"Really?" That saddened him, but he decided it could not be helped. "Who are they working for?"

"No one."

There was another silence.

"Where are they?"

"They were out at the farm." Dymphna put her hand on his arm. He turned to face her. "They stopped working for us in April—"

"And we knew you'd be studying hard and didn't want to worry you so we didn't write," his mother finished.

He sat back and knit his hands behind his head. "Oh, then they're at the farm and not working for anybody. That's good; I wanted to talk to Tucker about something. He wrote me a letter. Did he tell you?"

There was still another silence.

"What's everybody so mysterious and solemn about?"

"Dewey," Dymphna started as if she were going to tell him he had done something terribly wrong and did not quite know how to say it.

"There was a fire out there Thursday." His mother looked at him seriously.

He jumped forward. "They're not . . . Are they? Are they?"

"No, dear, they got out." She shook her head frantically, as if the words were not enough.

"But nobody knows where they are," Dymphna whispered ominously. "It's really mysterious as the DICKENS."

"Oh, for God's sake. Don't joke; it's not funny . . ." He paused, seized on that as a possibility. "Or is it? Are you folks joking with me? What a bunch—"

"No, Dewey, they're not joking." His father, speaking calmly, kept his eyes on the road. "There was a fire and Tucker and Bethrah AND the baby got out safely. And Dymphna is correct. Nobody knows where they are."

Dewey was leaning forward now, gripping the back of the seat. "How did it start?" And then a horrible picture flashed through his mind: men in sheets, flaming crosses, catcalls. "It wasn't . . . it wasn't the . . ."

His father knew what he was thinking. "No, they didn't have anything to do with it."

"The paper said he set it himself. Honestly!" Dymphna bounced on the seat like a small girl.

"Set it himself!" He threw his hands up. "Now you ARE joking."

"No, dear, that's what the paper said. But they weren't certain. And no one's seen Tucker or Bethrah since. I can't really believe he set it himself, though."

"I can," his father asserted quite without emotion. "I'm quite certain he did."

"How do you know?" Dewey was leaning over his father's shoulder.

"It's quite involved, son, and I'd like to go into it when we have more time."

The old resentment flooded up: "God damn it, that's what you ALWAYS say. You NEVER have enough time for ANYTHING."

His mother looked worried, once again seeing a familiar nightmare. "Dewey, I don't think your father would say that if—"

"Oh, Mama, grow up. That's the kind of thing he's been saying all my life."

"But this time it's different, dear."

"How different?" He had spoken before he realized he was almost arguing with his mother, who was actually speaking in behalf of his father. In the past, the arguments had been between him and his father, with Dewey defending his silent mother. "Well, maybe it is, but I'm finding out for myself."

This interested Dymphna. "How?"

"I'm going out there and see, talk to somebody. THAT'S how."
He had taken her simple question as a challenge.

"Would you like to take the car?" His father made a peace of-
fering.

"No!" He decided that was too harsh. "No, I'll ride my bike,
thanks. I've . . . I've been sitting for two days straight." He stopped,
then added, "Thanks, anyway."

His father nodded.

No one had any more to say.

The road widened. They passed two Negroes, heavily laden, walking toward New Marsails in the dust they themselves were kicking
up. As the car passed them, Dewey thought he recognized them
from Sutton, but the car had sped by too fast and he could not be
certain.

DYMPHNA WILLSON

I saw some odd things coming home from school yesterday. That was Friday. I go to school in New Marsails; MISS BINFORD'S SCHOOL. It's very exclusive.

Anyway, when I got on the bus at the depot—they'd let us out early and it was about noon—I noticed there were an awful lot of colored people there. I mean hundreds. But I really didn't think too much of that. But when the bus came into Sutton, there was a crowd of colored people there too. They were standing on Mister Thomason's porch with suitcases. As soon as I got off they all got on.

The only reason I'm mentioning this is because I've been thinking about the one colored person I really know, Bethrah Caliban, a lot the past couple of days, especially since the fire. I've been thinking about when she first came to work for us, and how she happened to marry Tucker, and plenty of other things.

I can remember it all pretty well because I was going through a period in my life when everything was symbolic of SOMETHING, when each second, I thought, I was deciding something big and dramatic. Girls are like that when they're fifteen, which I was that summer. That was two years ago, almost exactly.

Bethrah came to work for us because Missus Caliban, Tucker's mother, was doing all the work. John wasn't much good for anything; I guess he must've been at least eighty. And you couldn't get Tucker to do any house cleaning. It wasn't that he'd refuse; you just wouldn't dare ask him. He'd come in and lift heavy things, but he wouldn't do anything else. He was in the garage most times. So Mother decided Missus Caliban needed some help and called an agency.

They sent the first woman on a Wednesday, but nobody liked her and she was gone by Thursday night.

Friday morning, when the doorbell rang, I was sitting in the parlor waiting for some friends to come and pick me up. So I yelled back to the kitchen that it was for me and went on to the door.

"Hello, I'm Bethrah Scott. I came to apply for the maid's job." And she smiled.

I was stunned. She didn't look at all like a maid. Maids are fat and very dark and have thick Negro accents. I mumbled something like: "I'm Dymphna . . . Willson. I . . . ." and looked at her again.

She was tall—that was the first thing I thought about—almost six feet (in heels, she said later, six feet, one and a half) and slim; I guess willowy is a better word. Her hair was dark red, like old rust, straight and shiny, wavy and cut off short. She was wearing a light gray summer suit with a plain white blouse and the cutest pair of black shoes you ever saw. Her eyes were big and hazel. She was just beautiful, that's all, and I loved her the first moment I ever saw her. Not only didn't she look like a maid, she hardly looked like she was colored, except maybe her nose. She looked very young and when she smiled, her eyes smiled too so that her whole face seemed happy.

I just stared up at her and smiled, asked her to come in, and told her I'd get my mother. I saw her inside and closed the door. I wanted to say something profound, but didn't know what so I ran down the hall to the kitchen where Mother was having a late morning cup of coffee and talking to Missus Caliban about what they needed at the store that week. I told Mother a girl had come who wanted to be a maid. I started to say that she didn't look like a maid, but didn't finish the sentence.

Mother noticed how confused I looked. "What's wrong, dear?"

"Nothing. But she . . . Oh, you'll see. Come on." So I turned back into the hall, where Bethrah was standing patiently. When Mother came, I noticed she was a bit startled too, but she handled it much better than I did.

"I'm Missus Willson. Let's go back into the kitchen and have a cup of coffee and talk." She reached out her hand; Bethrah removed a pair of white gloves and they shook hands.

"I'm Bethrah Scott, Missus Willson. Very nice to meet you." And she smiled again. It was such a wonderful smile.

"Bertha?"

"No, ma'am. Beth-rah." And she spelled it.

"Bethrah. All right. I have it. Well, come along, dear. Let's have some coffee."

I went right after them and stared at her. I'm sort of a schemer, and I was thinking some very selfish thoughts. First of all, I wanted to ask her where she bought her shoes, because they didn't look like any I'd ever seen in New Marsails. I would've known because I go and shop just about every week. The other thing I was thinking was even more selfish: there aren't too many girls around here, at least that I can talk to; they're all farm girls. And most of my girl friends are in New Marsails. But here was this nice-looking girl who couldn't have been more than three years older than me, and it seemed like it would be very nice to know her. And a good thing about having HER for a friend was that she was colored and there wouldn't be any competition between us as far as boys were concerned, because that kind of thing always makes girls enemies even if they're very close.

Anyway, Mother sat at the kitchen table. Missus Caliban stood behind her, and I could see she liked Bethrah very much too. Bethrah was sitting across from Mother and I sat down on a stool by the door so I could see her face and the shoes too, all at once.

"Well, Beth . . . rah," Mother said, "why don't you tell me something about yourself. Do you have any experience?" She was trying to be businesslike, which she isn't. That question would have frightened me. You know how it is when someone says: Why don't you tell me about yourself. You don't know where to start and you get all nervous and your hands sweat. But Bethrah didn't seem nervous at all. She could cope with anything.

"No, Missus Willson, I haven't. But I know how to do the job. My mother was a maid and I watched and helped her a great deal."

I guess if just anyone came and said they had no experience Mother would have told her right away she couldn't have the job. But Mother told me later she wanted to hire Bethrah the minute she saw her, and now she had to find a good reason WHY to hire her.

"Tell me this, dear, why does a girl like yourself want to work as a maid? I'd guess you've had an education."

"Yes, Missus Willson, I have. That's why I need the job. I went to college for two years and need the money to finish. I'll be honest and tell you I can only work for two years. Then, I think I'll have enough to go on back to school."

That was exactly what Mother wanted. "Well, then, I'd say you have the job." She was very happy with her ingenuity. "We'd like to help get you through college. We pay well, and two years is a long time. By then we can find another maid, don't you think?"

Bethrah smiled. I looked at Missus Caliban and she was really glowing and proud to see a colored girl going to college and willing to work as a maid to do it.

"You can save some money too." Mother was really very pleased. "You can stay here with us, and still get a good salary."

"That would be nice, thank you," Bethrah said.

So we hired her right then. We sat around in the kitchen (I didn't go out) and felt happy and liked each other very much.

Bethrah moved in and started to work, and I just talked to her all the time. In fact, I don't know what I would've done without her, and now I'm not speaking about shoes and silly things. She really taught me a lot about life. Like the time I went to a party in New Marsails with Dewey and I met this boy there, whose name was Paul. We danced all night together, and so I told Dewey I wanted Paul to take me home.

Well, of course we parked on the Ridge, which was all right because I wanted to park with him. I was sitting there in the car looking at the stars. They looked like lightning bugs pipping around. I was blinking in a way to make them look like they were hanging on silver threads. It was very romantic.

Paul slid over and yawned and then let his arm fall around my shoulder. Boys are so funny; they always stretch or yawn to get an arm around your shoulder. I leaned against him. "Isn't it a beautiful night though?" I said. I thought he was shy and I wanted to get him in the mood.

So he took me under the chin with his hand and turned my face up and kissed me, and I kissed him back. We did that for a little while.

Then all of a sudden I felt like I was surrounded by hands. There was a hand on my breast. That was all right, I suppose. Can't very much happen with a hand on your breast, at least not to me—I'm not very sexy there. All it does is relax me.

Then I felt a hand on my knee. At first I forgave him because I thought maybe it had slipped. After all, I didn't know him very well and I was giving him the benefit of the doubt. But then the hand wasn't on my knee any more. It was way up under my dress. I didn't want to destroy the mood, so I sort of pulled away from him and whispered in his ear, "Don't do that." After all, it's not really bad if a boy wants to put his hands on you. It means you're attractive anyway. So I just whispered, "Don't do that."

But he didn't hear me or maybe he'd heard me but didn't want to destroy the mood by moving away like he'd been shot. Anyway, his hand was still there, so just for good measure, I said again, "Don't do that." But this time I made it a little more definite.

"Shhhh, be quiet," he said. "Don't destroy the mood."

Don't destroy the mood! Golly! All of a sudden I felt my garter undone. Now I knew he'd heard me, so I had to do something else. I decided to get mad. I pulled away from him altogether and said, "That isn't very nice!"

I wasn't really angry, but you have to pretend sometimes to keep boys in line. I glared at him and he just sat there smiling, almost like he thought I wasn't serious about him stopping. So to make certain I repeated myself. "That isn't very nice!" I tried to make it sound really fierce.

"What isn't?" He just sat there smiling at me.

"You know. What you were doing. That isn't very nice." I was getting really scared, so I added, "Listen, if you want to get in trouble, you can. Tomorrow, I'll get my father to have you arrested. And he can do it too!" Later, I thought that was a sneaky way to get out of there, but at the time I couldn't think of anything else.

He grabbed the wheel very tightly. "Boy! BOY! You girls! YOU want to come out here and then you scream PAPA as soon as something happens. Boy!"

"You just take me home this minute," I said. So he started the car, took me home and let me out. And to show you what kind of GENTLEMAN he was, he wouldn't even walk me to the door.

I ran inside and closed the door and locked it. I was relieved, but then I just started to shake all over, and then I started to cry. I must have been scared as anything because I just stood there leaning against the door, shaking and crying.

That was when I heard footsteps in the kitchen and thought it was Mother and started to run up the stairs, because you know mothers don't at all understand things like that.

I ran into my room and closed the door and stood there breathing really hard. I couldn't stop crying or keep quiet. So I went to the bed and put my head in the pillow to muffle the noise. The door opened and closed and I turned around and started to think up a lie to tell Mother, but it was Bethrah standing there in a bathrobe. She looked at me and got really alarmed when she saw my face, and came over, sat next to me, put her arm around my shoulder, and asked me what happened.

At first I was going to lie to her. After all, you don't like to tell anyone you got trapped in a car because everybody knows you really got there because you wanted to. But then I just couldn't think of a good enough lie, so I told her the truth. "You don't think that's bad, do you, Bethrah?" It sounded really strange asking her opinion when she was colored.

"No. Why should I?" She hugged me. It was like she was my big sister and I felt a little better. "No. That's happened to me, too."

"Really?" I looked at her and she nodded.

"When I was a freshman, honey, I went out with this basketball player. I always had to go out with basketball players because I'm so tall." (You see how she was, how she could talk that way about being tall. Most tall girls are ashamed of it and slouch. But Bethrah

used to stand very straight. I once asked her whether she was ashamed of being tall and why she stood so straight and she said: "How else can I let a boy know I have breasts if I don't stand up straight.")
"I went out with this basketball player and we parked in his car, and I thought he must be a magician, his hands moved so fast. You know what I did?"

"Tell me. Nothing I did worked. He just laughed at me."

"Well, this'll work all right! I just balled up my fist and hit him right in the——" She clicked her tongue. Then she laughed sort of embarrassed.

"You did? Really?"

"Yes, I did!" She was leaning toward me now, whispering. "And he yelled! I thought he was going to die right there, and I'd have to drive home. I couldn't drive a car then and would've killed myself too." She laughed again. And I started to laugh and felt a great deal better.

"But could I do that? I mean, suppose he told?"

"He wouldn't tell that. How could he? He'd be too embarrassed. And if he did, it would probably make you the most popular girl ever. You'd be a challenge to boys." She stood up.

"Why don't you take a bath. It'll make you feel better." She started to the door.

"You won't tell Mother, will you?" I was worried about that.

"Tell your mother what?" She smiled again. "You take that bath. I'm glad you had such a GOOD TIME at the party."

At first I didn't understand her; I wasn't very subtle then. Finally I got what she meant. "Thank you, Bethrah."

"One girl to another. Good night, Miss Dymphna." That sounded strange after we'd been so close.

"Bethrah, don't you call me that. You call me Dee or Dymphnie like everyone else."

"All right, but just when we're alone. Your mother might not like it."

I said okay and she went out. I guess she was right, although Mother is very good about this race business and got along very well with Missus Caliban, just like I did with Bethrah, although I don't think Missus Caliban ever called Mother by her first name.

So you can see how nice Bethrah was and how smart. She knew how to handle anything. That was before she fell in love with Tucker.

This is how I found out about that. I went into the kitchen one day to get some orange juice and she was looking out of the back window into the garden. I went over beside her and looked too. One of the cars was in front of the garage with two legs sticking out from under it and she was staring at the legs. I couldn't believe it. She was going back to school and all that. Tucker may have been able to fix anything—he was very handy—but I couldn't imagine them together. She was smart, not just clever but really intelligent. She and Dewey used to talk about things I couldn't even understand. And besides, Tucker was even shorter than I am. But there she was staring at his legs.

She turned and saw I didn't believe she could be interested in him. She looked very serious. "What does he think of me?" she asked. "Does he ever say anything about me?"

"Gee, I don't know. What's wrong?" You see, I couldn't believe it. "Is he mean to you?"

"No. He isn't ANYTHING to me. I don't think he's ever looked at me."

"Well, he doesn't say very much to anybody." I tried to make her feel better.

"Dee, will you do me a favor? If it ever comes up, if you ever get a chance to talk to him, see if you can find out what he . . . thinks . . . about me." She felt embarrassed and looked down at her hands. "That sounds silly, doesn't it? But I'd really like to know."

"Okay, Bethrah. But Tucker's so . . ." I stopped. You can't just tell a girl the boy she likes is nondescript.

After that, I used to watch the way she looked at him when he came into the kitchen. Sometimes he'd talk to her in that really high voice he had, but he'd never look at her. He always pretended to be doing something else like bending down under the sink looking for leaks.

She'd stand by the stove and just look at him like he was simply beautiful, so upset by him she'd stutter. "Tucker, would you take out the garbage, please?" She'd sound like she was apologizing for something.

He'd look at her then, but like he was angry at her. Then he'd pick up the garbage pail or whatever it was and go outside.

When he was gone, she'd sigh like she was relieved to get him out of the room, like the strain of having him around was too much for her. I guess that's what it was, and I could understand that. She'd look at me and even though I was only fifteen, I'd understand. Then she'd turn back to the stove.

I don't know how much later it was, but Tucker took me into New Marsails to get a tooth pulled. When he came to get me, I hopped in beside him instead of getting in the back.

I wanted him to say something first, so I groaned. Actually the tooth didn't hurt. It was so rotten it just about fell out by itself. But I groaned anyway. He didn't say anything at all.

Tucker used to drive like you think a race driver does, bent over the steering wheel, staring at the road, his eyes squinty, his shoulders hunched. He looked silly, because he was so tiny. He looked like a too-serious little boy.

I groaned again. But still he didn't say anything. Maybe he didn't hear me over the motor. So finally I just said, "Isn't Bethrah nice, Tucker?"

He didn't move. You would imagine that if a man was thinking about marrying a girl, when someone mentioned her name, he would at least twitch. He didn't.

I wanted to know for myself now. I suppose it wasn't actually any of my business; Bethrah just wanted to know if he ever thought about her. "I mean, do you like her at all?"

He sounded like it hurt him to say it. "Yes, Miss Dymphna."

That was all I could get out of him, and that wasn't very much. It wasn't that I expected him to go overboard and tell me everything, but I couldn't even tell whether he REALLY liked her, or whether he was just trying to keep me quiet.

But he did like her after all because they got married in September. And it seemed like no time at all before she was plodding around the house pregnant. Even after they were married, he didn't say much to her. It might be he didn't want to be mushy with everybody watching. But I think it's nice to have someone tell you he loves you in front of everybody. He didn't though; he didn't say anything.

So then I went back to MISS BINFORD'S and I guess that was about the time my parents started to get along really badly. Not that they argued in front of us. In fact, I doubt if they argued at all. It was much beyond that. It was that gradually, going back as far as I can remember, they kept saying less and less to each other until the time came—this is the time I'm talking about—that they didn't say anything at all to each other . . . except maybe at night when I guess married people feel most alone, when they realize how little they have in common, and how much they've lost.

I don't think trouble came to them out of nowhere. I think it was there all along, but they didn't have time to think about it because they were raising Dewey and me. But now that we were mostly grown up, they didn't have so much to do to hide the trouble behind and it started to show, to come out.

I'd hear them sometimes at night. I'd be going by to the bathroom and hear them, and I'd stop at the door and listen. I guess that's nosy, but when your parents are having trouble, you can't go by and put on your cold cream like nothing at all was the matter.

First I'd hear Mother say: "But why, David?" She'd sound very teary and maybe was already crying.

"I don't know. There's nothing you could understand." He never raised his voice.

"But I used to understand. Didn't I, David?"

There'd be a silence, and you could hear them shifting around. It wasn't the sound of them making love. They were just trying to get to sleep. Then all at once Mother would say: "David? I love you."

And he wouldn't say anything.

I guess that was the first time I felt really close to Mother. I get along with her about as well as a daughter can, but they say girls always get along better with their fathers, and boys with their mothers. And that's true in this family because Daddy never really got along with my brother. I used to watch him look at Dewey sometimes. He'd look at him for a long time, and shake his head and turn away. It wasn't like he was disgusted with him—like Dewey thinks—more like he wanted to say something to him and didn't know how. It must sound like TV, but that's the way he would look. I think lots of times he wanted to say something to Dewey, but said it to me instead. I get along with Daddy about as well as anybody in the world, and that's not really saying much.

After my parents stopped talking to each other, Dewey and my father couldn't talk without arguing. It was like Dewey was arguing in place of Mother. Daddy would say something, anything, and

Dewey always hopped in on it. I stayed out of it. I used to try to break it up by doing something silly or cracking a joke, but it never worked, so I just started to leave the room.

When all this was going on, Bethrah was the only person who saved me from being miserable all the time. She'd talk to me and cheer me up. But she had things to worry about too—after all, she was expecting a baby soon—and couldn't afford to get all messed with my problems.

She had the baby in August and it was beautiful, a very light coffee brown with light brown eyes. I loved to take care of it. I'd do all kinds of nutty things like hold it, and close my eyes and pretend I was nursing it. I'm certainly going to nurse my children when I have them. Bethrah used to answer all the questions I had about breast feeding, and she'd tell me some very funny things. Like there was the time she went into New Marsails to a hen party and came home that night and asked me, "What time did my baby eat?"

"He started to cry at seven and I gave him a bottle," I told her.

"I thought so." And she smiled to herself and giggled. "At about seven, I started to drip, and ache, oh goodness, I just ached like I'd been punched and I had to get up and go drain. I knew my little boy was hungry."

Just imagine, she was twenty or thirty miles from her baby and she knew he was hungry. It must be wonderful to feel that close to someone.

I learned about what was happening to Tucker and Bethrah because of breast feeding. That may sound really crazy, but it's true. Bethrah used to say that a mother who breast-fed her baby had to stay very relaxed or she'd dry up and the baby would have to go on a bottle. She had promised herself that when she had a baby, she'd stay relaxed and make it work.

Anyway, in September after Dewey left for college and Tucker had bought the farm, she just dried up. That was all; she was doing very well, but she dried up like a desert. I can even remember the particular night she told me. I remember because I started to grow up. That's silly, I know. I guess you can't say you just suddenly overnight grow up. What I mean is that I started to think about some things in a grown-up way.

What happened was I went down to the kitchen to get some orange juice (I love the stuff) before I started my homework, and was just sitting there, sipping it in the dark near the window where I could see the stars. It was like looking at a picture because there was a square of stars framed in the wall.

Then the door swung open and Bethrah came in. It was so quiet, and nice I didn't say anything, and I don't think she knew I was there because I don't guess she'd have started crying. But all at once, I could hear her sobbing across from me in a dark corner near the stove, then saying: "I don't understand you, Tucker. I try. I try. I try, but I don't." That was all, over and over.

I didn't know what to do. I didn't want to let her know I was there if she had come into the kitchen to be alone. But if I kept quiet and she found out, she might've thought I was a snoop. But then: "Miss Dymphna?"

"Bethrah? What's . . ."

"Oh, Dee—" There were footsteps and then she grabbed me, and started to cry on my shoulder. I was really surprised; I'd always seen her when she was strong and knew exactly what to do when something went wrong, but this was completely different from anything that had ever happened. I put my arms around her and patted her back. And after a while she stopped crying, and stood up, all shaking. I could just make out her face; she was looking at me. "I'm drying up." She started to cry all over again, and I hugged her again for a long time until she stopped, looked up, and started to tell me what was wrong.

She was sobbing and shaking so it was all very confused, but this is what she was saying, more or less. Tucker didn't tell her anything. He did a lot of confusing, strange things and never talked them over with her, and never told her why he did them. He'd bought the farm from Daddy and Bethrah said she knew he wasn't just going to become a farmer. He was planning something else, and she didn't know what. She even doubted if HE knew what he was planning. He didn't think about things; he just did them. And all this had confused and worried and upset her so that now she was drying up.

By the time she finished telling me that, she was much calmer. She got up and went for an ash tray, tried to light a cigarette, but I could see the flame shaking, and she couldn't get it lit. She cursed it and put the cigarette back into the package. "I don't really need this kind of treatment, Dymphna." Then she got really mad. "You think this is the first time? It isn't. But it's sure the last time."

Then she told me about one time when they first got married and she took him to meet some of her old college friends. As she told it, I remembered that night because I'd heard them drive in afterwards on the gravel in the yard and when the motor stopped, I'd heard her say: "How could you act that way? How could you embarrass me like that?"

I don't think he answered; at least I didn't hear him say anything. There was just the two sets of footsteps on the gravel like crushing ice.

And then Bethrah said: "All I wanted was a dollar. You could've given me a dollar."

"I didn't want to," he said finally.

"I guess THAT'S clear! But even so, if you didn't agree with him about the Society you could have given him the dollar because I asked you to."

"That ain't no reason," he said. That had even made ME mad. I should think a husband would do something for his wife if she really wanted him to.

So Bethrah told me about that in the kitchen. "Did I make a mistake that night! You can't imagine! I never should have taken him. Do you know what he did? I almost lost every friend I have . . . or had." She got up and started to pace.

It seems some friends of hers had invited them to a party. "Tucker didn't want to go. And I ACTUALLY convinced him. I got him to give in so he could do THAT to me. Dymphna, I know he doesn't have any education. But, honestly, I'm proud of him. I wanted them to meet him."

As she told what happened, I could see the whole thing; she didn't have to tell me how it happened, only what it was about. I'd lived with Tucker long enough to know just what he'd say, just how he said it, and looked saying it. And that surprised me at the time because I never realized I knew so much about him. I never thought I paid much attention to him like Dewey does.

But I knew; I could see them all sitting there, talking about things I guess college people talk about: the world situation and old teachers. And Bethrah said that colored college students ALWAYS get around to the race question. Then one member of the group said he was an officer in the local chapter of the National Society for Colored Affairs and he might as well use the opportunity to drum up membership.

Bethrah told him she had let her membership lapse and she'd give him a dollar and to please send her a card. Then she looked at Tucker, who'd been very quiet, who hadn't said a word since being introduced to them all. I could really see him when she told me that, sitting in a chair straight up, his hands folded in his lap and the party lights playing on his glasses so you couldn't see his eyes, as little and ugly as he could be. Bethrah said, "Tucker, give him a dollar for me, will you please?"

Tucker just sat there, his face angry-looking and said, "No."

I could see everybody, all her old friends look at him really slow and surprised, but not wanting to show it, and then darting a look at Bethrah and then away, thinking: the poor thing; she married a real cheap skate.

I blushed for her when she told me, like it had been me and I knew how embarrassed she must have felt.

Then she said to him, "Please, dear, give him a dollar. The Society needs the help and I believe in what they're doing. I'll pay you back when we get home." She was thinking that it was all right that he'd worried about money. Her friends could understand that; they all had to skrimp to make ends meet and pay for their schooling.

But that wasn't it! That wasn't what he was talking about because he reached into his pocket and pulled out all the money he had—she said it was close to twenty dollars—and reached over and handed it to her, while all her friends were looking on, embarrassed for themselves and for her. Then he said: "I don't want you to pay me back. Here's all I got. But don't give none to him for no piece of cardboard."

That's what really upset her; she leaned very close to me and her eyes were angry. "He could be cheap. Dee, he could be as tightfisted as a boxer. But all of my friends and me too, we believe in the Society. We believe they're doing something important and doing it well. But for him to sum up all their work that way . . . a piece of cardboard. I don't expect you to understand how I feel about this." She looked me in the eye.

But I did understand. I don't think much about race, and certainly didn't then, but I know next year I'll go up North to college like Dewey and there'll be colored people there and I'm sort of looking forward to it because Dewey says it's really an education in itself. But that wasn't even what she was talking about. She was surprised and hurt to find he didn't believe AT ALL in something she believed in very strongly.

Then, she said, the person who'd asked for the dollar said to Tucker that it was more than a piece of cardboard, that the Society was working for Tucker's rights and the rights of all colored people.

This is when he started to sound stupid, sitting there just looking at the Society-person, and maybe even smiling a little, and then not smiling any more and saying: "They ain't working for my rights. Ain't nobody working for my rights; I wouldn't let them."

The Society-person said that whether or not Tucker let them, they were doing it anyway, that the decisions they won in the courts would help his children go to school and get a good education.

"So what?" That was Tucker's answer. "So what?" he said in that high, chirpy voice like an old man's.

Bethrah was looking around the room apologizing with her eyes, and some people turned away, not angry, just ashamed, and her very close friends looked at her with pity, and that was the most painful thing of all.

The Society-person went on: "Don't you want your children to have a good education?"

"I don't care about that," Tucker said.

"Well, whether you like it or not, the Society is fighting your battles in the courts and you should support them."

Tucker just sat there. "Ain't none of my battles being fought in no courts. I'm fighting all my battles myself."

"You can't fight all this alone. What battles?"

"My very own battles . . . all mine, and either I beat them or they beat me. And ain't no piece of cardboard making no difference in how it turns out." Then he got up and walked out of the room. Bethrah said she got up too and apologized to everyone, and felt like crying, but didn't because she was so mad she wouldn't let Tucker have the satisfaction of seeing her cry.

She wanted a cigarette now, and this time succeeded. "I think he must be crazy. Education is the most important thing there is, Dymphna. Especially for Negroes. And if he thinks he's keeping my child as ignorant as he is, then he's in for a fight. My friends must've thought he was a terrible Uncle Tom. And what they must've thought of me for marrying him?" Then she was sad. "Why doesn't he explain anything to me? That's all I want. Is that too much?"

"No, Bethrah," I said. I don't think I should have said that because it was all she needed: someone to agree with her.

She looked at me seriously. "I've had it, honey."

I don't know if she cried after that. I don't think she did. It wasn't fifteen minutes before she'd packed some things for herself and the baby and was walking down the hill to catch the bus to her mother's house in New Marsails. She wouldn't have had time to cry.

She was back in a week. We all missed her a lot, even Tucker. He didn't say so, especially not to me, but I could tell. He didn't seem as crisp as before; he trudged around like a zombie, in a daze, and I said to myself: It serves him right; I hope she never comes back.

But I only said that for her sake and to see him punished. For me, it was bad having her gone.

Then I walked into the kitchen and there she was, cooking. I couldn't understand why she'd come back, and must've looked confused because she looked at me real level and grave for a long while. "I KNOW, Dee. He was right. And when I found out I was wrong and why, I called him and told him to come get me and he did."

I was still looking at her like I didn't understand, which I didn't. But all she said was: "It's so new and good I want to be selfish about it for a while. I'll tell you one of these days. It's better anyway if you figure it out yourself. Try." And she smiled. But her smile was a little different, like she knew a wonderful secret and she was more than just happy, but contented too.

She got pregnant again. I guess it must've been in December because she was just starting to gain weight in April when she came into the kitchen and said, "Missus Willson, Tucker and I have to leave. We're sorry, but we have to."

Mother almost cried, right at that moment. "But, Bethrah . . ."

"I'm sorry, Missus Willson, but Tucker wants to go. He wants to move to the farm."

Mother's lashes were already wet. "But, Bethrah, you're pregnant and it's much better for you to be in town . . . isn't it?"

I just stood there with my mouth open.

"We have to go. Tucker wants it. And I have to go with him."

I just turned around, went to my room, and cried for hours. I guess I didn't have a right, but I really felt betrayed because I'd have to be in that house all by myself with my parents. I even thought about moving out, but I could only go into New Marsails to my grandmother's, Mother's mother, and she was really primitive. She doesn't have a modern idea in her head. She'd want me in at nine on Saturdays. So I didn't move out. I guess I wouldn't have anyway.

The night before Bethrah left, I sat in my room being really grumpy. It was late and I was feeling very, very sorry for myself. I couldn't even sleep. I heard a knock on my door and sort of bitterly told whoever it was to come in. It was Bethrah. I guess I knew that before I saw her.

"Can I talk to you for a minute?" She seemed very apologetic. "I want to tell you something."

"Sure." I wasn't very friendly.

She sat on my bed at the other end, and stared at the floor between her legs. "I know how you feel about my leaving. I'm sorry. I have to go, though, I know that." She looked at me; very slowly I turned away, because I might have been starting to cry. I don't know.

"Remember the time before I left Tucker that we talked in the kitchen?" I didn't say anything; she knew I remembered.

"You see, the trouble with me was that I was a college girl. I wasn't at college, but I thought like a little coed. There was something I couldn't figure out about Tucker and it upset me because I took it like I'd take a flunk on a test.

"I don't really know, but maybe those of us who go to school, Dewey, myself, not so much your mother, I guess your father, maybe we lost something Tucker has. It may be we lost a faith in ourselves. When we have to do something, we don't just do it, we THINK about doing it; we think about all the people who say certain things shouldn't be done. And when we're through thinking about it, we end up not doing it at all. But Tucker, he just knows what he has to do. He doesn't think about it; he just knows. And he wants to go now and I'm going too. I'm not going to tell him he's leaving a secure job and people who honestly care about him. I'm just going with him. And not just because I love him, but because I love myself. I think maybe, if I do whatever he tells me to do, and don't think about it, well, for a while, I'll be following him and something inside him, but I think maybe some day I'll be following something inside me that I don't even know about yet. He'll teach me to listen to it.

"I wanted you to know why I was going because maybe it'll help you get along better here. If you understand what's making me go, maybe it'll help you find something inside yourself that will make you survive whatever your parents decide to do. And your helping yourself, your finding some comfort inside yourself, will be much better than any comfort I can ever give you.

"Well, that's what I wanted to say." She got up and started for the door. I still hadn't looked at her.

I jumped up just as she put her hand on the door knob and called her in sort of a cracking voice, and ran to her and hugged her, and cried. So did she. And then we stood apart and looked at each other.

"Come see me a lot, all right?" She smiled at me. I promised her I would.

Now she's gone for good and I don't even know where. I'm just hoping she writes me.

That's all I know about everything; I guess it isn't much. As for my parents, they seemed to get on better today than I've ever seen them, holding hands and all. Maybe something happened yesterday, but I can't imagine what. Anyway, I try not to worry about it. I don't think I'm hard or anything, but it's really their problem and I haven't got anything to say about it. Either they figure it out and stay together or they don't and split up. That's the whole point; at least I think that's what Bethrah was saying although it's difficult to accept. I mean it seems horrible that the most you can do for people you love is leave them alone.

DEWEY
WILLSON III

We were standing on the Ridge looking down into the sheer cut called *Harmon's Draw. The General was a few steps away from us, barely old enough to be my father, in gray pants with yellow piping, his shirt sleeves rolled up past his elbows. His hair was white and long.*

We watched the Yankees advance under a canopy of dust, coming down the paved Highway, passing the statue of the General, down the main street through Sutton, past Mister Thomason's store and then up the hill toward us. Sweating horses pulled cannon; the men marched in order and even at this distance, I could see the faces of each man shaded under his blue visor. The General stood quietly watching them. "Hold your fire until you're sure you can't miss," he kept saying.

The Yankees saw us and charged, rushing up the hill, yelling. As we shot them they broke into little pieces—they were made of blue ice—and the pieces melted, changing from blue to red blood, flowing down the hill in many rivers.

At the bottom of the hill the blood collected into the gulleys in the soil,

forming pools, scabbed over, grew hard, and before my eyes, the shapes of men began to grow up, fully uniformed, fully armed, broke loose their roots, and began to charge once more up the hill toward us.

All around me as I fired at the charging Yankees, our men died, melting too, but only once, into gray pools in which bits of hair and thread floated, pools smelling of garbage, and death, and sickness. Soon there were so few of us it seemed we could hold them off no longer and the General turned to me, tore his head roughly from his shoulders, so I could hear the veins and bones cracking and groaning, the sound of pulling up a handful of grass, and tossed the head to me. His trunk stood facing me. I cradled the bleeding head in my arms like a baby, and all the while it yelled up at me, "Run, boy! Save it! Run for a touchdown, boy!" And as always, always, I would stand tasting a sickness from the pit of my stomach, the blood soaking into the cloth of my shirt until the cloth stuck to me, and I would know I wouldn't be able to move, would realize already even before I attempted the first step that I was paralyzed from the waist down.

That was the first thing I thought about when those kids left; that God-damn nightmare. I don't think I've thought about it or even dreamed it for about two years. I used to have it all the time when I was younger and was afraid of my father. I knew why I dreamed it; guilt feelings brought it on. I'd get a B on a test and —boom—the dream; I'd forget to do something he asked me and—boom—the dream. But when I got to be a senior in high school, I began to really hate him—that's about the time he completely stopped talking to Mama, distant and withdrawn, and really a bastard—and stopped being afraid of him.

Anyway, that's what I was thinking about, only it didn't take as long as it did to tell it. I imagine I thought about that because just standing there in the middle of all that mess, and finding out from the kids how it happened gave me that same sick feeling. I was scared because I didn't really know or understand what was happening, and when I get scared I get sick. I have a doctor friend at school who tells me I'm a gut-reactor. Some people get headaches; others, like myself, get sick to their stomach.

The dream wasn't the only thing I was thinking about. I tried to think a little bit more constructively after a while, tried to find some cause, some reason for Tucker doing what he did, like something that had happened to him in the past, that he could brood about, that would get him mad, and the only thing I could think about was last summer, when John died.

But to say just this doesn't seem like enough. There's more to a man than the day, and the way he died; there's his whole life, no matter how dull or unimportant, before that. I'm too young to know much about John's life firsthand. I knew him only when he was an old man. But when I was a little kid, I'd somehow get my hands on a stack of photograph albums, kept religiously by the Willson women who have carefully collected stray Sunday afternoon pictures, report cards, and scrawled drawings from as far back as anyone would care to remember. In these albums there are pictures of the Calibans too. This is how I knew John, although when I began to look at the albums it wasn't for John's sake, rather the old funny clothes, and the square black cars he once tended and drove, and before them, the horse-drawn buggies. The first picture of John is when he is a boy, about fourteen, in front of a brand-new buggy. He is wearing a white starched shirt, which bulges rigidly because his chest is thrust way out. If you don't know better, you'd think he owns the buggy, but he doesn't. It belongs to the General. John drove, sitting high on the seat, never having to crack the whip, steering the matched team gently, the reins loose in his hands. He'd just begun to drive the buggy for the General, because John's father, First Caliban, was already too old, nearly sightless and sat in front of his cabin at the Willson Plantation smoking a pipe and resting. And John, still in his teens, though a man when he drove or tended horses or fixed buggies, is driving now. Glittering on that chest is a diamond stickpin the General had just given him for his birthday; he wore it when he died.

Then you'll see him with more, newer buggies, and then cars, and finally you'll come to a picture of him in front of a square-nosed Packard with a great shining grill. He stands with a little boy, who already wears glasses, whose head is too large for his spindly body. Behind the glasses there are great, hard brown eyes, with more in them than should be there. That's Tucker. And soon Tucker is in front of the cars alone, for John is already too old to drive or crawl beneath and now tells the boy what to do—what to tighten, loosen, or adjust—all John can do is tend the flowers in the garden of the house in the Swells, still as proud when they bloom as he would be if they were his own.

And now I really knew him.

On Saturdays John would put on his best suit, a wide tie with the diamond stickpin the General had given him so long ago, and a pearl-gray hat, and get into the bus at Mister Thomason's store and ride into the Municipal Depot in New Marsails, making the trip to the Northside where he'd sit in the dark friendly saloons and talk to the old Negro men, who, like himself, were too old to do anything else.

Then, one Saturday in June last summer, I answered the phone and heard the voice on the other end. "Got a nigger here in the depot, old man, dropped dead. What you want me to do with the body?"

"Wait a minute," I said. "We'll be right there."

Tucker, Missus Caliban, Bethrah, and I climbed into the black car. Tucker drove; Bethrah sat beside him, the line of her shoulders well above the back of the seat, a maternity dress sloping straight from her shoulders to her knees like a children's playground slide. Missus Caliban and I sat in back. She was small and black, was not yet, at fifty-three, graying or growing old, and reminded me of a smooth black China doll Dymphna once had. I felt strange riding with so many Negroes, even though they were my friends.

No one spoke; no one cried. We still waited to see John dead, wished for some mistake, hoped the police had called the wrong house, wanted to arrive at the depot and find a total stranger lying before us.

When we arrived in New Marsails we went to the depot police office. The bus driver was sitting in a small fan-cooled room, a can of beer in his fist, waiting. He was big, balding, and flies seemed always to swarm around his head.

"We're here to claim the body of John Caliban."

"Surely." He pulled himself to his feet, placed his beer can carefully into the circle it had sweat on the table. "Come on then." He went out of the room and we followed him.

"Knew old John well." He was speaking to me. "Boarded out at Thomason's just like every Saturday. I never paid much attention to him after that; only when we got to the depot and everybody's a-hopping off, I looked up in the mirror before I closed the door, and there he was, sleeping, or so I thought. His head was leaning on the post. So I got up and went on back and shook his shoulder, but I noticed he was sort of cold. I knew then. I says to myself: I ain't never waking up this old nig—" He stopped and looked at Missus Caliban, who hadn't even heard him. "This old man, even if I stand here and shake him for the next thousand years. He dead." We had come almost to the bus. Empty of passengers, it looked ghostly.

"I never touched him after that; no one moved him. I went and found the PO-lice and they went through his clothes and come up with your number, was all. Here, let me go around and open the door." He went to the other side of the bus and reached into the window. The door sighed open.

DEWEY WILLSON III

We found him as he had been left, as he had died, his eyes shut over his life. As we climbed the narrow rubber-carpeted steps, we could see the pearl-colored hat in his lap, and the round patch of bristling white hair leaning heavily on the chrome-plated cross bar that separated the back of the bus from the front. Hanging from the bar was a white sign inscribed with thick black letters, which, had his eyes been open, had he been alive and just resting, would have been the only thing he could see.

It was John, but even then no one cried. We were too busy signing release papers, and getting an undertaker down from the Northside, a Negro who had known John. When he came Missus Caliban said to him: "I wants you to do it. That way he'll look like he looked when he was alive and won't be stuffed all full of cotton." After that we drove back to Sutton.

That night I went into the kitchen and sat watching Missus Caliban prepare dinner. I had finally realized John was gone and would never return, had realized this because I had not heard him humming below my window in the garden as he had done almost every day of my life. I remembered then, the long-ago times when I was small, smaller even than Tucker (he had stopped growing at the age of fourteen and I had passed him within the year), and John would take us in his lap, one on each thin knee, and would sing to us and laugh. Now I could only remember him singing and laughing.

And sitting in the kitchen, I began to cry, ashamed of myself because I was almost grown-up, or so I thought and Missus Caliban turned from the stove and tried gently to make me stop, tried to comfort me, but could not stop me, and finally sat across from me, and took my hands in hers, and we cried softly together.

The funeral was in the Northside two days later. The church was a new one, occupied before it was really completed so that the inside walls were no more than cinder blocks painted gray. A small plaque near the entrance of the church stated that the cross had been donated by a woman in remembrance of her sister. It was pale sky-blue with bronze edges.

Very few people came. I realized for the first time the Calibans weren't very popular among their own people, that their devotion to us and our love for them had separated them from other Negroes, so that there weren't a great many people who would want to call them friend. My mother and I went; my father and sister did not. I doubt whether Dymphna would have wanted to go to anyone's funeral; my father would just have been out of place. Bethrah, Tucker, and Missus Caliban were in the front pews, nearest the coffin.

The service was quiet and simple. Finally the time came for a friend to stand and say a few words. He was a tall Negro man with a great bald dome and pocked skin hanging loosely from strong bones. He rose, turned, and began to speak.

"Dear Friends: We've come here today to give our last tribute to our close friend, John Caliban.

"The facts of a man's life ain't very important, but it seems like they should get said anyways. So, what did John do? Well, he never went into business; he worked all his life for one family, and I knows by the way he talked about them, he liked them, and he never felt like it was a job he was doing for them, almost like he would do it anyways, even if they didn't pay him. I know he'd want me to say that for him, because he was taken so fast he didn't have time to say it to them hisself." Some people turned to look at us and I felt embarrassed, hot and cold.

"And that's it; we can't stand up here and talk about all the great things he done, because he never done nothing great. But he was always doing GOOD things. We'll all remember John because when he come into our lives he was always smiling and happy and made us feel good just to look at him. He was a simple fellow and never done nothing big; he was just around making you feel happy.

"Maybe one thing you COULD say, and I think he'd want me to say this for him too, was that he was the best man with a horse anybody ever seen. But that don't really stack him up; I reckon the simplest thing to say is the best thing. John Caliban was the kind of man would always sacrifice hisself to help others. He was a good man and a good worker in all kinds of ways, a gentle soul."

The Negro paused and someone in the front of the church stood, I thought, to second these sentiments with an AMEN. Then I heard a high male voice say in disbelief: "Sacrifice? Is THAT all? Is that really all? Sacrifice be damned!" It was not for an instant that I realized from what part of the church the figure rose, not until I marked the thin black-coated figure, the short-cropped hair on the large head, the steel-rimmed glasses, not until I saw the arm raised and brought down in a motion of disgust, as if to wipe away the words, that I realized it was Tucker.

The church was silent as he pushed his way to the aisle. And now Bethrah too was on her feet. "Tucker?"

He reached the aisle and was heading out of the church, his mouth clamped shut, his eyes blank and hard. Bethrah had excused her way out and followed him, leaning backward against the weight of her unborn child, a look of bewilderment on her face. And then they were gone, and a general buzz filled the church for a second or two, then died away.

The Negro finished, stumbling over his words, his composure and self-assurance broken, and we filed from the church and piled into the cars and prepared to go to the cemetery. Through the windshield of the car that took my mother and me, I could see Tucker and Bethrah ahead of us. They did not speak all the way out.

A DIFFERENT DRUMMER

We took John to the cemetery, and saw him buried, and each of us tossed a rose wired to a green stick onto the coffin as it was lowered into the ground. The undertaker said a few kind words, which did not quite ring true, and we left, came home to Sutton.

I hadn't said anything to Tucker about how I felt and went to find him later that evening. He was sitting on an old crate in the garage, where he and his grandfather had spent so much time together. I went in and told him I was sorry John was dead. He didn't look up. His eyes were as dry as small, hot stones. "So am I," he said finally.

I turned to go, then heard him grunt. "Not another time. This is the end of it."

"What, Tucker?"

"Nothing, Dewey. Just thinking aloud, is all."

Two months later he bought the farm, a piece of land at the southwestern corner of what had been Dewitt Willson's plantation, on which Tucker's people had worked as slaves and then employees, until my grandfather Demetrius broke up the plantation into small share-cropping plots, bought the house in the Swells and moved the Willsons and the Calibans into Sutton. I couldn't, still can't, understand how he ever got my father to sell it.

That was clicking through my mind too after the kids left. But that didn't seem like a big enough reason for Tucker to have done all this. An old man dies, whom I too loved a great deal, and the last thing he sees is the COLORED sign on a segregated bus, but that is little more than ironic. I decided it had to be something else, but before I could think about that, I heard the sound of an engine coming over the hill, and then the car itself, new, expensive, a limousine, with a light-skinned Negro driving, sitting at attention and uniformed like a West Point plebe; it slowed and pulled off the road, and I could see the elegantly dressed Negro sitting in

124

back, behind the green glass. The chauffeur stopped, rushed around to the near side, opened the door, and the Negro, a gold cross hanging from his vest by a gold chain, stepped out. He was wearing blue sunglasses.

"God bless you, Mister Willson? I thought perhaps you might come to this place." He wore a dark-gray three-button suit. His shoes were black and highly polished. He smiled. "I bid you welcome, Mister Willson." He sounded almost British and there was a quality to his voice that I recognized.

He reached into his breast pocket and produced a cigarette holder and a pack of Turkish cigarettes. "Do you smoke, Mister Willson? If not, do you mind if I indulge in one of the less harmful vices?"

"No. Go ahead," I stammered.

The chauffeur lit his cigarette and the Negro took a deep drag. "Why don't you get back into the car, Clement." He was talking to the chauffeur. "I'm sure Mister Willson will be kind enough to be my guide."

I couldn't say anything. He laughed. "Come-come, Mister Willson, pull yourself together."

"Who are you?" I struggled out. "Just who are you?" My voice was high and squeaky. "How do you know me?"

He answered without hesitation. "I am quite in the habit of becoming acquainted with the records of those young people I feel show promise. An old habit. As for my identity, why not call me Uncle Tom." He laughed. "At least it is an old and respected name in some circles. But I see that displeases you. Then I think Bradshaw ought to do. The Reverend Bennett T. Bradshaw. But come, Mister Willson, you know, or shall I say knew, Tucker Caliban quite well, I understand. I would be very grateful for any insight you might have into his somewhat unorthodox personality."

"What do you know about it?" This was really eerie.

"I would not be so bold as to venture any answer with absolute

125

certainty. You see, I am not truly an expert on the southern mentality, black or white. Admittedly, we have the same racial tensions in the North, but not on the open, primitive, refreshingly barbaric level one finds here. This is why I ask you. You can be an interpreter of sorts, having had some small part of your education in the North, but being also a native of the area. Perhaps my question is too general. Don't you feel you're on the site of some significant event?" He gestured widely. "Isn't there something here that taps in you an epic vein, reminiscent of the Bible or the *Iliad*?"

I nodded. I didn't like the feeling of disadvantage he was giving me; he knew so much about me.

"Since I seem unable to secure an articulate answer from you, perhaps we should tour the farm. Perhaps it will stimulate one of the utterances for which your college is famous." We walked around the farm, stopping at the rubble of what had been Dewitt Willson's clock, and again at the heap of ashes where the house had stood. After this, we came back to his car. "What do you think now, Mister Willson?"

"I don't know. What do YOU think?" I was feeling pretty stupid.

"Mister Willson, you disappoint me," he scolded. "You were in the depot this afternoon. What did you see?"

I couldn't remember anything about the depot, except my parents holding hands; I remained silent.

He frowned; perhaps really disappointed with me. To tell the truth, I was disappointed with myself. "Negroes, Mister Willson, Negroes. Colored folks. Darkies. Coons. Boots. Spooks. NIGGERS. Negroes. More Negroes in the New Marsails Municipal Depot, I daresay, than had ever been there before, and more than will ever be there again."

I couldn't remember. "Well, so what?"

He pointed straight down. "This is where it began, Mister Willson. Your friend Tucker Caliban started it all. You must give him credit. As for me, I stand corrected; I'd never have imagined such a movement could be started from within, could be started at the grass roots, through spontaneous combustion, you might say."

I was unbelievably dense. "What movement?"

"All the Negroes, Mister Willson, are leaving, going away."

I didn't say anything, but I must have looked as if I didn't believe him.

"All right, come with me. Let's go in and watch it." He opened the car door for me.

I wasn't sure I wanted to go anywhere with him, but on the other hand, I knew I was going. "What about my bike?" I said stupidly.

"We can put that in the trunk."

The trunk of the car was large enough to hold my bicycle and perhaps another one besides. With the chauffeur's help, I secured it with rope so it wouldn't bounce and rip the upholstery. Then I climbed in beside Reverend Bradshaw and we set out for New Marsails.

"Why don't you tell me all you know about Tucker's nose-thumbing at the world." He settled back and turned to me.

"Like what?" I had gone over what I knew by myself, but perhaps he could help me to bring something to light.

"Like anything. Strange doings around the household, you might say. A set of the jaw, a determined stride. Anything."

"He wrote me a letter. I don't understand it at all." I pulled the letter from my pocket and read it to him, then told him what I remembered of my tenth birthday. And perhaps because I knew I had an ear and a mind that would hear and give it thought, I didn't stop with my recollections but continued, speculating. "You know, when he says, 'But you would have learned anyway, because you wanted to learn so much,' well, I don't know if I would've, I don't know if I could've learned without him, but maybe he was trying to say I could do anything if I really set my mind to it. But that doesn't really mean very much, does it! That's what everybody tells you. I guess that's too simple."

He seemed excited. "No, I don't think so. You forget who you're dealing with, Mister Willson. We're not talking about a sophisticate drawing inspiration from Plato; we're talking about an ignorant southern Negro. We're not talking about the new, complex ideas: the unique thunderbolts of thought that come to men of genius. We're talking about the old ideas, the simple ones, the fundamental ideas that perhaps we've overlooked, or never even tried. But Tucker Caliban cannot overlook them; he has just discovered them. I like your analysis, Mister Willson. What else can you think of? I can see him already, raging against untold and countless wrongs and humiliations; this anger welling up in his soul, the blood of vengeance just behind his eyes."

"No, that's wrong. You're wrong. There's no anger in Tucker. He accepted everything almost as if he knew it was going to happen and there was no way he could stop it."

"Perhaps so. Well, continue."

I was thinking about last summer again, but trying to sort out the important parts. I didn't say anything for a few moments. We were passing through Sutton now, past Mister Thomason's porch, which perhaps because it was around dinner time was empty, or perhaps it was because of this movement Reverend Bradshaw was talking about. "Well, something finally made those loafers move."

"And why not? Tucker Caliban has made us chase up and down the countryside trying to find out what makes him tick." He shook his head. "This is truly remarkable, a miracle."

We climbed up and over the Ridge, and in the orange dusk light, far off down the hill and across the river, we could see the city, from this distance seeming just as it had always been, blissful, carefree.

I had last summer sorted out now, and told him, finishing with my surprise that my father had ever sold Tucker the land and farm in the first place.

Reverend Bradshaw smiled to himself. "Men do strange things sometimes, Mister Willson, especially of our—your father's and my—generation. Don't forget, we came along in a time when people were truly idealistic, when discontentment with the existing order of society caused us to break the pattern of our lives, break patterns our ancestors, our parents, had formed for us."

I started to laugh. "My father? My father. If you knew him, you'd know better."

"I do know him," he stated flatly. I turned to him astonished.

"You know him?"

He smiled at me this time. "No need to be alarmed, Mister Willson. I know him as I know them all. All of the boys, now men, all of us who grew up with the Depression, cut our teeth on the Spanish Civil War, and flirted with Dame Communism. Some of us even married her. Others married, then divorced her and could never really fall in love again." His eyes went dull, far away, as if he could not only remember but see and feel those days.

"Not my father!" I broke in on his memories.

He turned to me. "Men, I still maintain, do strange things when weaned in strange times."

"Not my father." I repeated softer this time, then laughed because I sounded like an echo.

Reverend Bradshaw didn't laugh. "You shall discover many a strange thing about your father as you grow older." He smiled again, but it was more a leer.

We had moved closer to New Marsails, past the empty, darkening fields where already corn and cotton shot small green plants in rows, and now crossed the black bridge into the Northside. The streets were littered with the bits and scraps of a vacated, discarded life: worn-out clothing, mattresses, broken toys, picture frames, chipped furniture, all the things the Negroes could not carry in their satchels or on their backs. There were not many people, a few stragglers carrying bundles of brown paper tied with cord or white laundry string. On a cane, an old man hobbled by, probably toward the depot. He wore a Mexican sombrero, sported a knotted white beard. A woman, alone, sped along the gutter in a wheel chair, a small suitcase in her lap. She was a pale gray color, though she should have been very dark, and looked like she hadn't been out in the sunlight in many years.

We drove on toward the depot, but when we came within three blocks we found we couldn't go any farther because the way was cut off by state troopers in cowboy hats and steel-blue puttees, and New Marsails policemen in light blue. Beyond the roadblock, crushing toward the depot, were the Negroes, all kinds, light, dark, short, fat, thousands of them. A few sang hymns and spirituals, but most stood quietly, inching forward, thoughtful, triumphant, knowing they couldn't be stopped. They shuffled steadily forward, gazing ahead and slightly upward at the depot building, seeing only the very crest of the white stone dome.

Bradshaw bent to a microphone at his left side. "Clement, we're getting out. Wait for us here."

"Yes, sir." Clement's voice coming through the wires was metallic. "I'll back up and park, sir."

"Come, Mister Willson, and with God's blessing we'll have some questions answered."

I nodded. We got out of the limousine, skirted the roadblock, and found ourselves almost immediately engulfed by the crowd. We moved forward next to a family of seven—two adults and five children, ranging in ages of ten to a baby in the woman's arms. The father already had his fare out, a number of bills clutched in his fist. He was very tall, as thin and strong and black as a weathered fence post. His hair was straight. His wife was as tall as I was, and a murky brown. The children tagged after them, wide-eyed and sleepy, walking like little zombies. "Elwood, I'm tired. I'm tired." A small girl, just beyond toddling years, turned to her brother. He was a little older.

"Mama say we'll be there soon. Quiet."

"But I'm tired."

Reverend Bradshaw reached out and put his hand on the father's arm. "God bless you, brother. I'm the Reverend Bennett Bradshaw of the Black Jesuits. Do you mind if I ask you a few questions?" That surprised me; so that was his interest in this.

"Elwood, I'm tired."

"Hush up down there, Lucille, else I'll fetch you a slap up side your head." He looked down at Reverend Bradshaw. "No, go on."

"Elwood, I'm tired."

The father turned to his wife. "Woman, can't you keep that child's mouth closed? You go on now, Reverend . . . what was your name?"

"Bradshaw. I just wanted to ask you where you're going."

"We're going to Boston, I reckon. Got some people live in Roxbury."

"I still thinks this is crazy, we packing up and going North. What'll we do when we gets there?" The wife leaned over and spoke to both Reverend Bradshaw and her husband.

"Quiet now, I told you we going because it's right to go." The husband looked at the woman menacingly.

"Yes, well, that's what I'd like to know. Why do you think it's right to go? Whatever gave you the notion?" We moved on as the man thought of his answer. I noticed from time to time small knots of whites standing along the edges of the crowd, their hands in their pockets. They didn't look like city people; they must have come in from the small towns in the country. They looked dazed, realizing, I imagine, there was nothing they could do to stop the Negroes.

They may have been afraid to try, for anything they might have done could be turned violently against them by the quiet, steadily moving crowd of dark faces.

Finally the man we had been talking to spoke. "Well, now, I reckon I don't know where I got the notion. Yesterday, I was coming from work—I sweep up in the Marsails Market, you know—and I meets a cousin of mine. 'How do, Hilton,' I says.

"'How do, Elton,' he says. 'When you leaving?'

"'Leaving where, man?' I says.

"'Why, ain't you heard?' he says.

"'Heard what?' I says.

"'MAN,' he says, 'Man, don't you know what's happening? All us black folk is moving out. We all leaving, all over the state we just a-rising up and going away.'

"Well, you know, I reckoned he was fooling, so I just looks at him for a while, but I sees he ain't busting out all smiles; he's serious as a naked man sitting in a barrel of razor blades, so I says, 'Say, Hilton, what's this all about?'

"'Well, it all started Thursday or Wednesday, I ain't sure, but it seems like all the black folks up in Sutton got it into their heads they just won't stand for it no more. It ain't worth fighting because things ain't getting any better for us here. Even the colored folks in Mississippi got it better and that's going some. Seems like if this state had really got its ass whipped in the War Between the States we colored folk'd be better off. But this state was the only one in the Confederacy what the Yankees didn't beat up on.' At least that's what Hilton told me this colored man up Sutton way said. He, Hilton that is, he says that there was this colored man up in Sutton who told the Negroes all about it, all about history and all that stuff, and that he said besides that the only way for things to be better was for all the colored folks to move out, to turn their backs on everything we knowed and start new."

Reverend Bradshaw turned slightly to me. "Thus begins a legend, Mister Willson."

I understood.

"So anyways, after I talks to Hilton, I runs on home, and tells my wife here to pack up because we leaving tomorrow, that is today, and I don't want no fooling." He turned to his wife, forgetting completely about us. "Don't you see, baby? We got to go. It's the only way because if . . ."

"We've seen enough, Mister Willson." Reverend Bradshaw took my arm and we cut diagonally through the crowd until we had reached the sidewalk. Then we started back toward the car, past a group of whites. I could hear them whispering about me. "He's a mulatto, that blond one. Why else he with a nigger? He ain't white, that one, he's got to be a nigger. But he could sure fool me." I flushed all over, and then, strangely enough, I felt a bit proud.

When we made our way back to the roadblock, through which Negroes still streamed, Reverend Bradshaw said, "Well, Mister Willson, it's unbelievable, but true." He couldn't stop shaking his head. "I never would have . . ." He let it die away. We reached the car, got in, and Reverend Bradshaw bent to the microphone. "Clement, take us back to Sutton."

The chauffeur started the car, moved slowly until he found a small alley, took it, cruising cautiously past the garbage cans and debris, until at the other end we could see the darkening sky. We followed small alleys and streets north until the crowds thinned, and by that time were in the Northside, about to turn out onto the Highway and the black bridge.

Driving now, past those same flat-faced, shingle-roofed, two-window dwellings we'd seen before, which came into view for a second in the headlights of the car, I leaned back, feeling good. "Reverend Bradshaw, do you realize how amazing this all is? Tucker Caliban! who taught me how to ride a bike. Wow! I can just see my sister. When Bethrah said she was marrying Tucker, my sister couldn't understand it, she thought Bethrah was too good for him. What a coup!" I smiled and shook my head, glanced at Reverend Bradshaw, and to my surprise, found him sitting sadly, his face gloomy, his head on his chest. "Don't you think so?"

"Yes, Mister Willson, indeed a coup. It's wonderful." He didn't mean it at all. "You haven't lived long enough, Mister Willson, to grind away your life for some cause, and then see someone else succeed where you've failed."

"What difference can it possibly make who did it? It was the thing to do; it might have happened anyway. They didn't even need Tucker to show them. They could have just got up one day and gone about it. So what difference does it make?" We were climbing to Harmon's Draw.

"I'll tell you the difference." He pulled slowly forward, looking very tired; when he spoke he took me by surprise with the sadness and resentment in his voice. "You spoke of the Tuckers not needing you, not needing their leaders. Did you ever think that a person like myself, a so-called religious leader needs the Tuckers to justify his existence? The day is fast coming, Mister Willson, when people will realize there isn't any need for me and people like me. Perhaps for me that day has come already. Your Tuckers will get up and say: I can do anything I want; I don't need to wait for someone to GIVE me freedom; I can take it myself. I don't need Mister Leader, Mister Boss, Mister President, Mister Priest, or Mister Minister, or Reverend Bradshaw. I don't need anyone. I can do whatever I want for myself by myself."

I was still too enthralled by it all to realize I couldn't ever convince him. "But this is what you always wanted, what you Negro leaders worked for. These are your people and they're freeing themselves."

"Yes, and they've made me obsolete. How would you like to

awake to find yourself obsolete? It's not particularly heartening or pretty, Mister Willson. Not pretty in the least."

I could only stare at him, seeing his eyes lighted sad by the reflection of the head lamps, his fist clenched.

Then I couldn't look at him any more. I turned away and found we were hooking down into Sutton, that already the car lamps were lighting the fronts of the stores on the western side of the street. I could see the yellow band that the bulb in Mister Thomason's store laid out across the Highway.

And when, after a few seconds, I turned back to Reverend Bradshaw, he was even more sad, his eyes glassy and faraway.

CAMILLE
WILLSON

Last night was almost like twenty years ago. We didn't have that wonderfully open feeling we used to have, but we talked; and we haven't done that in a long time. And today, walking down the platform, going to meet Dewey's train, I felt his hand on my elbow, then sliding down my arm until he was holding my hand. He was almost like the David I loved so much, not young again of course —we won't ever make up the years we lost—but that David I married aged twenty years in the same way THAT David would have aged. And I felt a little of the same things, like when we were first married, and I couldn't hardly wait to get him in bed with me. If he got anywhere near me, I'd be putting my arms around him, getting real close to him or rubbing up against him so only the points of my breasts touched him. I'd squirm around until I knew he could feel them on his chest. And then I'd let him go and act like nothing had happened, like I didn't know what I was doing. I guess that was all silly, but I loved him so much I couldn't get enough of being near him.

CAMILLE WILLSON

Sometimes, even in the middle of the afternoon, I'd get more bold and I'd write him a note:

Dear David:
You have ten minutes to finish what you're doing. Because I'm coming to get you. I love you,

Camille

I'd go into where he was reading the newspaper or writing and say, "This note came for you."

"Oh?" he'd say.

"Yes, sir. And she was VERY pretty, too." Then I'd just turn around and go out and I'd hear him laugh and say, shouting to me, "What am I going to do with you?"

And I'd say: "You know the answer to that. Come in ten minutes." And then I'd get everything cooking just right, so I wouldn't have to worry about it, and set the table. I'd run into the bedroom and get undressed and douse perfume all over me and everything else. By that time, ten minutes would be up and he'd come in unbuttoning his shirt and say, "Where's the girl who left that note?"

I'd be in bed with the covers up to my chin and I'd say in a tiny voice, "Here she is, David."

He'd come over to me and sit down on the edge of the bed, and look at me so tenderly that sometimes I'd start to cry. I'd start to cry just like a little girl. He'd be so kind to me and would sit me up and take me in his arms and kiss me so sweetly that I thought I would just dissolve—he was so sweet. And he'd say, "I love you, Camille."

"Oh God, David," I'd say, "I love you so much." And then he'd get undressed and we'd make love for hours.

But it wasn't just the making love that was so wonderful; I don't want you to think that. And it wasn't only that we'd just gotten

137

married. Sometimes we acted like people who'd been married fifty years. I imagine that it was mostly that we understood each other so well—at least David understood me, and I trusted him and so didn't really have to understand him.

Anyway, THAT was how it was when we first got married. We were living in New Marsails then and David was working for the A-T, that's the *New Marsails Evening Almanac-Telegraph*.

I had met him at a party on the Northside. My father had sent me away to a school in Atlanta, where they were supposed to teach me to be a lady, and where I was supposed to meet a nice, young southern gentleman. But I had managed to survive it, and came back to New Marsails without a husband.

When I got back, I discovered some of my friends had fallen in with a kind of Bohemian group who were studying art at the museum or writing and who sat on the floor talking about Marx. So they took me to one of their parties. I wanted very much to go because it would be such a relief from my exile in Atlanta. And I met David there.

We started to go out a lot, only it wasn't exactly what my Mama would've called COURTING, because we didn't really have dates; I just went with David when he had an assignment. But I didn't care where he took me just as long as I was with him.

But there'd be times when we were supposed to see each other that he'd call and say, "Camille, I can't come for you; you can't meet me. I can't see you tonight. I have to finish something." Of course, I'd wonder what was so special and why he seemed so hard. I knew he loved me; I knew I wasn't just fooling myself about that. And he knew I loved him. But still there were those times and the strange tone he'd get in his voice, faraway and evasive and short. He wouldn't even let me come and sit with him.

You can guess what I'd think: it was another girl, and I'd get sad and convince myself, even though I knew better, that he was just playing with me. But really, way down deep that wasn't it at all. It started to come out a little when I met his father.

One Sunday he picked me up for a ride and we started north up toward Sutton. He didn't say very much; he was thinking seriously about something. When we got to the Square in Sutton, instead of going straight he turned left, and before I realized I should have been a little nervous, I was standing in front of his father, Demetrius, who was a thin, hard-looking man with white hair. David went for some drinks. Mister Willson looked at me for a long time. "You love him, don't you?" he said.

"Yes, sir."

"He loves you too. Apt to want to marry you soon. You want to marry him?"

"Yes, Mister Willson," I answered.

"That's fine with me. But you got to know what you're getting into. You won't ever be able to leave him. He'll need you one of these days, more than you imagine he does. He's bit off a good deal more than he can chew. He doesn't know I really know about it. But I do." David came then, and Mister Willson stopped, but I don't think he would have said any more anyway.

I don't know if what David's father said made me feel any better about those nights David acted so strange; I don't know if what anyone said would've made any real difference in how I felt about him, because I was very much in love with him, and if someone had told me something bad about him, I wouldn't have believed it, and if someone had told me something good, I would've felt that of course he was wonderful.

At any rate, it wasn't long before he asked me to marry him. I married him and we were very happy. We lived in New Marsails and went to the parties on the Northside, and I went with David on his assignments. And when we came home to our place, we made love and laughed and really enjoyed being with each other. But still, there were those nights he didn't want me around, when he'd ship me off to the movies. Those evenings didn't worry me as much as they had before we were married, and even if I had worried, I wouldn't have said anything because I trusted him and didn't want to nag him. And sometimes he would say to me, "Camille, thank you for not asking me about what I'm doing. The less you know about it, the better."

Then I got pregnant with Dewey, and David got fired and everything came out into the open.

Besides writing for the A-T, David had been sending pieces to some communistic magazines in New York. He'd used a pen name, but the A-T had found out and they'd fired him, mainly because he had been taking a very radical stand on race issues. I didn't understand much more than that, but if he thought he was doing the right thing, it didn't matter to me what he was doing. I tried to tell him it was all right and if he wanted to go to New York and work full time on those magazines, we would go to New York. But when I told him about the baby coming—and I couldn't very well keep it from him—he said No, we couldn't go to New York because newspaper work was too unsteady and we might get stranded there. He tried and tried to get a job, and couldn't, and he started to get panicky and there wasn't anything I could do about it. Each day he'd change more and more.

The way he acted may have had something to do with the letters he was getting from up North. I never read them; he never told me what they said, but each time one came he'd get more distant. They all came in unmarked envelopes; they all had New York post marks. I got so I could recognize the typewriter, an elite with a broken "I." Every time the "I" was punched, the typewriter would skip automatically, so that Willson was spelled W-I-space-L-L-S-O-N. I'd fetch the mail from the box and scan the fronts and I'd come to a

letter addressed: "Mr. Davi d Wi llson"—and I'd know that whatever was inside would make David more unhappy, more unfriendly
than he already was. It got so I'd take a letter from the box and see
that typewriter and hope that one day I would meet the person who
was using it and kill him with my bare hands. Well, of course that
was just a daydream and nothing ever happened, but whoever was
writing the letters, whoever David would sit up late trying to
answer, whoever it was never came and I never saw him. Even when
the letters stopped, it was too late. The damage had all been done.

The last letter was delivered one morning after David had left for
the day. It was longer than any letter before it; I knew this because
it came in a business envelope instead of a personal one like the
others, and it seemed to weigh more. But it was the same person;
I recognized the typewriter. I carried it up from the mailbox, up
to our apartment, and thought for a long time about opening it.
But I didn't. I just sat on the bed for half the morning weighing
it in my hands, feeling how heavy it was, and wondering whether
or not, because it was so long, it would be even worse than the
others before it. And then I decided if David wanted to tell me
about it, he would, and if I could help him, I would, but if I
couldn't help him, I'd love him just the same. Then I put the letter
on top of the dresser and left the room.

David came home very late. I was already undressed, in bed
reading, when he came in and closed the door behind him. He
smiled at me, then saw the letter on the dresser; he knew who it
was from as well as I did. He looked down at me for a long time.
Then he went to the dresser, opened it, neatly at one end, rather
than across the top, sat down on the edge of the bed and read it.
It seemed to take him hours. I sat and watched him as he read one
page after another, putting each page at the back. When he was
done, he sat and stared at the floor, holding it between his knees.

Then he folded it and slid it back in the envelope and said, "Well, that's the last one. He's promised. Perhaps I'll have some peace now."

For a second I felt very warm and good inside because I was listening to his words, and not the way he'd said them.

I watched him, saying nothing as he undressed. I put out the light and we lay awake not touching each other for a long time. I knew he was awake because he was on his back; he can't fall asleep on his back. Finally he sighed and although I knew he might think I was prying, I said, "David, isn't there anything at all I can do? Anything at all?"

He was quiet for a long time, then sighed again. "You have a great deal of faith in me, don't you."

"Yes, David."

"How did you ever come to have faith in me?" He didn't ask that like he felt I shouldn't have faith in him; it was rather like he wanted a factual answer. He always wanted me to put some feeling I had into words, and I always found it hard to do, but I tried.

"I don't know. I just did. You never did anything to me that ever made me not want to. I liked you and then I loved you, and I always had faith you would never hurt me on purpose."

"But suppose I did something to hurt you? Suppose I went out of here one morning, supposedly looking for a job, and that night you read in the paper that David Willson and some married woman, both naked and in bed, had been shot to death by the woman's husband? Suppose this article said I'd been seeing this woman for two or three years? Would you still have faith in me; would you still love me then?"

While he was talking a sick feeling traveled up my spine. But then I realized he was only giving me a for-instance, that nothing like that was really going on, that he was trying to find out something else altogether. "David, don't say things like that."

"Why?" He shot up to a sitting position. "You wouldn't have faith in me then, would you?"

"It isn't that, David." I reached out my hand and put it on his arm; he didn't move away. "It isn't that. I'd want you alive, no matter what. But it isn't that I wouldn't have faith in you. You may be doing those things, but the reason I'd have faith in you is that I don't THINK you are. And if what you say did happen, I guess, after I'd been hurt, I'd think you had a good reason. Maybe I'd hate you, too. But then I'd say to myself that maybe you had to do it because of something I didn't know about or couldn't help you with or maybe even because you'd found something with her that you couldn't find with me. I guess I'd still have faith that you did the best thing as you saw it."

He didn't say anything to that.

"Well then, what if I did something like that and then found out I was wrong and felt guilty about it, and felt I'd betrayed you and, most of all, myself? Who could get me to have faith in MYSELF again?" He stopped. "Could you do it? Could you say anything to me that would make any difference in how I felt about myself?"

"I don't know, David. I'd try. I'd accept the fact that you'd done it and try to make you accept it." I could see him better now, sitting up in bed, his body leaning slightly forward, his fists clenched.

"What if I hadn't done something that perhaps I should have done? Suppose I was a coward when I should have, when I COULD have been brave? Because, Camille, that's what I am. I'm a coward when I don't have to be. And that's even worse than being a coward when you have to be, when you can't be anything else."

I wanted so much for him to tell me. "What about?"

"That isn't even important now."

"But it is!"

"Not the particular thing. Just that I was supposed to have

believed very strongly in something and when the time came to stand up for it, I didn't. I retreated."

I should have thought more carefully about what I said then. "Well, maybe you shouldn't have believed in it at all. Maybe it wasn't any good to start with."

He turned to me; I'd hurt him. "But it was good! It still is!"

"But maybe not for you. Maybe it isn't the right thing at all for you." I shouldn't have pressed him.

"Oh, for God's sake, you don't understand at all." He fell back onto his pillow, staring at the ceiling.

"I try, David. I want to. I'm sorry if I don't." Oh . . . and I didn't want to, I tried to stop and felt very ashamed of myself, but I could feel myself starting to cry. Not much, just small drops off the sides of my cheeks.

"Camille? Camille, don't. It's not your fault; it isn't, any of it, your fault." He reached out his hand to me under the covers and held my arm. And I turned toward him and he put his arms around me and kissed my eyes.

"David, I wish I could help you. I wish I could do something, but I'm not . . . I'm so . . . stupid." He kissed me again and I could feel his body and mine start to want each other and I held him to me as tight as I could and he reached down and started to pull up the hem of my nightgown. Then he stopped kissing me and I tried to pull him closer to me because making love was the only thing I could do really well, and all at once I felt on my cheek what at first I thought were my own tears, but they were his. He rolled away from me. "It's no use. I don't even feel human any more."

That was the last time we were ever really romantic; after that things never got any better between us; after that we moved to Sutton, and David started working with his father on the family businesses. His family was very nice to us, but I knew David hated being there; I knew it was the last thing he ever wanted to do because he hated the idea of people making money just because they happened to own land that other, poorer people needed to live on. He hated the idea of collecting rents and all the other things landlords do. Because he was so unhappy, we had less and less to say to each other and we never went into New Marsails to the people on the Northside. Sometimes I'd ask him about it and he'd say that we had to grow up; we couldn't do those childish things any more. We made love, from time to time, and I got pregnant again, with Dymphna, and David seemed very happy about it, but I think mainly he was happy because he didn't have to make love any more.

When we moved to Sutton I saw Tucker for the first time. He was just a baby then, about two years old, thin and very dark with a bloated stomach and a huge head. He'd sit in his playpen, surrounded by blocks. He'd stack them one by one into giant shapes. I remember once he'd built something even bigger than himself and had only one block left. He placed it on the very top and leaned back against the bars of the pen, looking at what he'd built, long and hard. Then he crawled back to it, balled up his fist and punched at it just once and destroyed it completely. He cut his hand doing it, but didn't cry at all. You had the idea, the way he did it, that he wasn't playing.

The war started and David was sent out to the West Coast. He never even left the United States. I know this must sound strange, but I was sorry about that. I wish he'd been sent somewhere into the real war, because it might have been better if he had been able to fire a gun and do something he thought was useful. He worked in an office in San Diego; it was like going to work, collecting rents, every day.

I hoped that maybe being away from home and me and the

children would do him some good, but when he came back to us, he was even worse. When he was in the house he usually stayed in his study.

That's when the loneliness started to get me. It wasn't only that I was just realizing that my marriage was turning cold. I imagine I had known and accepted that. It was being in Sutton and feeling like an outsider. There wasn't anyone I could talk to. I felt that everyone I turned to was a stranger, a Willson, and I was the only non-Willson. My children were Willsons, and besides I wanted to keep the situation from them as long as possible. They learned soon enough as it was. Even the Calibans were Willsons because they had been with the family so long. And I was a stranger in a house which was supposed to be my home.

So I did something I have been quite ashamed of until just recently.

When Dewey was young, he loved Tucker so very much that he insisted that Tucker sleep in his room. We moved a cot into the room and Tucker slept there every night. I would always tell them a story at bedtime.

This one time I had come through a very depressing day and after I'd tucked them in, I started my story: "Once there was a princess who—"

"Was she beautiful, Mama?" Dewey said. He was lying on his back.

"Sure she was beautiful. All princesses is beautiful." Tucker looked at him and scowled. He was sitting up.

"Well, I don't know. That isn't important, really. She met a prince charming one day at a ball . . . for the painters. These people were picture-painting painters." I can remember thinking that I was just taking a writer's license, using an autobiographical basis.

"What kind of pictures they paint, Mama?"

"Oh, of people and the countryside and such things."

It was dark, except for the moon, and I could see the outline of Tucker sitting up in bed. Dewey's covers were up to his chin.

"Well, the princess fell in love with prince charming and pretty soon they got married."

"Mama, is THAT the end, AL-ready?" Dewey was disappointed.

"No, dear, there's more to it. This is a story that goes on after the ending." That's when I realized what I was doing. But I couldn't seem to stop myself.

"How come?" Dewey didn't understand.

Tucker shifted a bit, and the moonlight caught his tiny glasses. "Dewey, listen at the story and she'll tell you how come."

"But how can a story go on past the end?"

"It's your mama's story. She can tell it like she wants it."

"Oh," Dewey said.

I went on. "Pretty soon they got married and the prince took her to the nicest castle you ever saw, high on a hill. They were very happy for a while until one day the prince went out to a war and came back hurt very badly."

Dewey started to breathe heavily then and I knew he was falling off to sleep. But Tucker was still interested. And even if he had fallen asleep, I think I would've continued, just to be able to say these things out loud, even this way.

"The prince was very sad because he'd lost the battle and so the princess was sad too. But she found she couldn't do anything for the prince. He even stopped talking to her after a while, and they had always talked a lot. So it got very lonely in the castle. Because the princess didn't have anyone to talk to." When I think about this I feel quite ashamed of myself. There I was, a grown woman, disguising my own story as a fairy tale and telling it to a small child, confessing, confiding in him. But that wasn't the worst of it. "She didn't have anyone to talk to, or to be happy with and so she got very lonely. Every so often she'd think about running away, about going back to her father's castle, but she really didn't want to do that because she loved the prince charming very much and she didn't want to leave him. But she began to think more and more about running away. She even, one time, told the prince what she was thinking, but he didn't seem to care. He said to her: 'Cam——' " I almost said my own name. I blushed and got warm, in the dark. I stopped then because I knew I was doing wrong. I had thought I was talking to myself, but when I looked up, I could see Tucker's tiny glasses sparkling. He was still sitting bolt straight in bed. I could feel myself beginning to cry way down deep somewhere. "Well, Tucker, it's about time you went to sleep, dear."

"Ain't you finishing, Missus Willson?"

"That isn't a very good story. No excitement or fireworks in it. You don't want to hear the end."

"Yes, ma'am, I do. I like that story."

"You do? Why?"

"It's about really living people. Like I know."

"Wouldn't a story about dragons and war be better?"

"No, ma'am. I can't believe in them kind."

"Well, dear, the story doesn't have an ending. You end it. How would you do it?"

"Me?"

"Yes, go on. What do you think the princess should do?" I thought I was playing. I couldn't really be asking him. He was only nine years old.

I looked across at him. I could see him thinking, there in the moonlight, his covers around his waist like he was standing in waist-deep, white water. He was looking toward the window, and then at me. "I think the princess should wait. She shouldn't run away."

"Why?" I wasn't playing.

He looked straight at me, like an old friend who knew about

David and me and was telling me what to do. "Because the prince, he'll wake up one of these days and he'll make it all right."

It made me feel nervous, and stupid, and a little crazy. He couldn't know; he was only nine. But I felt nervous anyway.

I did wait, living from day to day, promising myself that if nothing happened that next day, I'd go in and see my brother, a lawyer, and tell him to start divorce proceedings. But each night I'd convince myself to wait still another day.

So I waited the years by, until this last March, and then I decided I couldn't go on any longer, not like that, until I decided I owed myself a little more than I was getting, that twenty years of this kind of marriage was enough for anyone.

And so one Monday night I told Tucker I wanted him to drive me to New Marsails and to please have the car ready at ten the next morning. I got up and dressed in something dark—that was the way I felt, like I was attending a funeral—and had a cup of coffee, and got my purse and went out and climbed in the car. I started to cry then, and kept on crying all the way down the hill into Sutton and up and over the Ridge through Harmon's Draw. I could see from the top of the Ridge New Marsails in the distance, shifting and blurry. We went all the way into the city and Tucker pulled up in front of my brother's office. I told him if anything happened to contact me in the law offices of R. W. DeVillet.

That's when he said it. That's when he got out of the car and opened the back door for me, when I slid across the seat and he looked straight at me through those thick-rimmed glasses and said it, so softly, so quietly that I couldn't hear it at first over the roaring of the passing cars and the dull chatter of people, and I asked him to repeat it. Or perhaps I heard him, but hadn't wanted to believe my ears, because it was impossible that he could remember, or that he had known that long ago, known then when I told him the fairy tale. I looked up, startled, and said, "Excuse me, Tucker?"

And he said it, again: "I think the princess should wait, Missus Willson. Leastways, now when her waiting is almost over."

I told him to take me to the nearest movie. That's where I spent the day.

Each day these past several months, I've gotten up and tried to convince myself this will be the day the waiting will end, that by nighttime it will all be over. But nothing happened until yesterday. And then I'm not sure anything happened. Last night David came in, stood at the foot of my bed, looking down at me for a long time, looked down at me in the strangest way and said: "Camille, I've made a million mistakes. How'd you take it so long?" I couldn't say anything. "Camille? . . ." But he didn't go on. That's all he said. Not that he loved me, or he hoped that I could still love him. That's all he said. But it was something.

DAVID
WILLSON

Friday, May 31, 1957:

Today started the same as many others, but veered into a triumphant day for me. I feel almost as if I have a new start! as if all these years of waste (I suddenly realize how thoroughly I have wasted them) have been given back to me to live over again. I have always felt what I needed and lacked most twenty years ago was courage and faith, and that I had neither. Not the slightest particle. Of course, I have excuses; I could always say I did the responsible thing, but that rationale never for an instant convinced me.

At times I have vainly (or so I thought) wished someone could have helped me, given me faith in myself and courage to do what I so wanted to do. But I have always believed too that no one person really gives another courage; the leaders of revolutions actually help their followers to find the courage already within themselves. If these followers did not already possess that courage, the leaders' efforts would be in vain. Courage cannot be given like a

Christmas present. But it seems I am wrong—and so thankful to be wrong!—because today I have been given courage I am certain I never possessed before. Or perhaps I DID possess the courage, but in what deep abyss of my soul had it dwelt so many years? I despaired of ever finding it. Well, it has now been found, or given, or whatever.

Today, as usual, I left the house to walk to the Thomason Grocery Company and pick up my copy of the A-T. (I do not know why I have to read that particular paper every day, except that it brings back memories of better times. I enjoy reading it, looking for mistakes, errors of make-up; I enjoy seeing, every so often, names of men who started there about the same time as I did; I enjoy it, I imagine, because it is the best paper New Marsails offers and always has those stories, those tiny fillers that start small and work their way slowly toward the front page until they are important news.)

I walked downhill and into the Square and across to the store. (There were two or three men and a boy there this morning, unusual for that hour: about 7:30. I did not speak to them of course; I do not know any of them. None work my land.)

When I returned home with the paper, just as USUAL, I went into the study and began to read and then, all at once, there it was, something I now realize I have been waiting to see (I hasten to add I did not ever think I would see it, or know what it would look like, but seeing it once was knowing it), tucked high on the twentieth page above advertisements for women's summer suits and girdles, to the managing editor only one step above a filler, but to me, had I made up the paper today, important enough for page one-column eight, heralded perhaps with type as large as was used to headline the Pearl Harbor Attack. I have clipped it and pasted it below:

DAVID WILLSON

FIRE DESTROYS FARM
Set By Owner?

Sutton, May 30—A fire razed the house of farmer Tucker Caliban,
two miles north of here—and none of the thirty-odd spectators made any
effort to extinguish it. Witnesses stated the fire was started deliberately
by Caliban, a Negro, himself.

Those interviewed said they had watched Caliban most of the day
as he salted his own land, shot his animals, destroyed several pieces
of furniture, and then, at eight in the evening, went inside and set
his own house ablaze. Then, they asserted, he walked away without
explanation.

Caliban was not available for comment.

I am sure this article meant very little to anyone else. But in
light of what Tucker told me, the feelings he expressed, this is very
meaningful at least to him, and to myself. He HAS freed himself;
this had been very important to him. But somehow, he has freed
me too. He is only one man, and this, of course, does not make a
reality all the things I had dreamed of doing twenty years ago. But
it is something. And I contributed to it. I sold him the land and
the house. I doubt if he knew what he was going to do when he
bought it that night last summer, but that does not matter. Yesterday, his act of renunciation was the first blow against my twenty
misspent years, twenty years I have wasted feeling sorry for myself.
Who would have thought such a humble, primitive act could teach
something to a so-called educated man like myself?

Anyone, anyone can break loose from his chains. That courage,
no matter how deeply buried, is always waiting to be called out.
All it needs is the right coaxing, the right voice to do that coaxing,
and it will come roaring like a tiger.

A DIFFERENT DRUMMER

This is the first entry in this diary even though my father gave it to me on my last birthday (July 17). At the time, he said something about its being time, son, you started to keep a daily record of things you have seen and learned, especially since you will be going up to Massachusetts in September. I did not think too much of that. I reasoned a person would remember the really important things anyway and would forget the rest. But I have been thinking about it and perhaps he is right. It is possible something will happen to you and you will think it unimportant when it happens, and a year later it could go off like a time bomb and be very important after all.

So it might be a good thing to keep a diary.

I decided to start writing here today (this particular day) because tomorrow I will be leaving for Massachusetts to begin four (if I do not flunk out) years at college. This is the time to start things. I'm not quite sure why, that is to say, I cannot quite put it into words and perhaps putting it here will help me, but going to Cambridge is very important to me. Not for the name or the prestige but because from everything my father has told me about it (he went too) and from everything I have heard or read about it, this seems to be the place where I can start some of the things I want to start.

I look around at the South and all I can see is poverty, misery, inequality, and unhappiness. I love the South so dearly and even though it sounds sentimental as all hell, I feel like crying whenever I see what it is and compare it to my concept of what it could be. Even in times as hard as these, what with the Wall Street Crash and the Depression, the South, which was in a worse condition than the rest of the country already, is even worse off now. But that COULD BE can only come about if the people here find and try some new concept to live by. We must get away from the old patterns, must stop worshiping the past and turn to the future. (God, this sounds like a bad speech!) And I hope to discover in Cambridge some ideas, some principles that, in four years, I can bring back here to help pull the South up off its behind and into the twentieth century. I don't even know what I'm looking for; I can only hope I recognize it WHEN I see it.

Well, that's all. I have to do some more packing.

Friday, October 23, 1931:

I met an amazing fellow tonight. A negro, Bennett Bradshaw. It is the first time in my life I carried on an intelligent conversation with a negro, and the first time I felt intellectually inferior to a negro. I might resent it except that I learned too much.

I went to a socialist meeting, hoping I might hear something important; I was even considering joining—before I went! But when I arrived I found nothing but a bunch of fellows showing each other how much they knew about Marx.

Just after I got there and found a seat, a negro came in and sat next to me. That's something I will have to go into at length one of these nights: the absence of segregation. At first, I was disturbed by it, not that I mind its absence so much as when you sit somewhere you usually do not take too much notice of who sits next to you. If you are sitting on a trolley and someone sits next to you, usually you glance at him, then ignore him, that is, if he does not sit on your coattail. But when a negro sits next to me I find myself distracted from what I was reading, or from looking out of the window because I am not used to being that close to a negro in public. And so when this negro sat next to me, I noticed, and continued to notice it. He was portly, almost middle-aged looking, and wore a dark suit.

As the meeting began I tried not to stare at him. (I am trying to get over bugging my eyes out each time a negro gets near me.) But as the meeting continued, and these fellows kept trying to impress everybody, I began to squirm and wanted to leave; I do not have that brand of courage. He must have noticed, must have been looking at me because he leaned over and said, in a voice that seemed quite British (later he told me his family was from the West Indies): "These chaps have nothing to say. Would you like to join me for a cup of tea?"

I turned to him and he was smiling slightly, his eyes twinkling.

I do not yet know why I left with him, why I braved the slight offended silence which accompanied our exit; I suppose it was a combination of the following: (1) that he seemed to feel exactly as I felt about the uselessness of the meeting, (2) that he, a negro, should lean over and speak to me so brazenly, so openly, so friendly, (3) or that he was such an (this word may not be exactly right) exotic figure with his British accent. But I did go with him.

We went through the Yard into the Square, not speaking, walking side by side. I noticed him take out a cigarette, put it into a holder and light up, shielding the wind with his pudgy hands. He walked as if to some music, a march, his arms swinging at his sides. We found a restaurant; he ordered tea; I, coffee.

When we were seated he reached out his hand. "Bennett Bradshaw." I took his hand and told him my name, the first words I had spoken.

He began to laugh. "My word! A southerner. A kindred soul and yet a southerner."

At first I was a bit embarrassed, but then I was glad he had commented on the strangeness of the situation, the circumstances, and I began to laugh myself. He asked me what part of the South I was from; I told him and the mind which was to impress me more and more as we talked made a quick conclusion. "You're related to General Dewey Willson, aren't you?"

For an instant I was going to "confess" to it, but then I decided I would test him. "Why do you think so?"

"Well, first of all, you're from his state and your name is Willson."

"But many people took his name after the war. A lot of folks that weren't related to him."

"Yes, but they couldn't afford to come here, could they? They wouldn't have inherited his intelligence, would they? Besides that—"

"You win; you've got me pigeonholed. He was my great-grandfather." I chuckled, shook my head.

"And might I add, although I can't WHOLLY agree with what he fought for, he fought and led admirably. But tell me, David—I may call you David, mayn't I?" He did not wait for an answer; I would have consented. "Why were you, of all people, at such a meeting?"

I told him how I felt about my poor, lost South and what I hoped I could do for it and some of the things I had already looked into. He seemed quite pleased and when I had finished, began to explain his own reasons. He was pretty much chain-smoking.

"My people, too, need something new, something vital. In my opinion, their leadership has followed in the footsteps of the negro overseers of plantation times. Each is out for himself and money is the thing. I've done a great deal of reading since I graduated from high school." (It seems he is twenty-one years old and has worked four years to save money to come to school, and is now working in a cleaning and dyeing shop over in Boston.) "But I could find nothing. I had hoped I could find it here. Perhaps socialism or communism holds the answer, but certainly not that hollow variety we witnessed tonight—a new kind—that and trade unionism and other things."

We continued to talk, through seven cups of coffee, continued to exchange ideas. He suggested a great many books I might read; my pockets are stuffed full of little notes to myself.

He is from New York, comes from a large family, is the oldest. Tomorrow I am going to meet him at the Union for lunch.

A DIFFERENT DRUMMER

Monday, October 26, 1931:
Met Bennett for dinner. We walked until 3 A.M. God, he knows so much. I'm learning a great deal from him. Even things I did not know about my South.

Wednesday, October 28, 1931:
Bennett dropped by tonight about 9. We talked way late into the night.

Saturday, October 31, 1931:
I went to a Halloween party at the Pudding; they had asked me to come. I met a very nice-looking girl, named Elaine Howe. She is from Roanoke, Virginia. She is about five feet, three and perhaps 125 pounds. I find her very attractive and very nice. She has a wonderful going-in-all-directions walk—it could be described as aimless, meandering. But I think it is her voice that makes me feel so good—it is like "home," like a sparrow with a cough—not really high, but seeming to crack a little and soft, and aristocratic. She has light brown hair, longish, and nice eyes. I cannot help it; I have to say it; southern girls are the best in the world!

Monday, November 2, 1931:
Bennett and I lunched together; we talked all afternoon. He said—this is as much as he has ever talked about himself—that he wants to join the staff of the NATIONAL SOCIETY FOR COLORED AFFAIRS when he graduates. He does not feel it is doing all it can for the negro people, but he thinks it is a good start. What the hell am I going to be? to do? How and where am I going to situate myself to do what little I can? At least I KNOW one thing; I do not want to go home and collect rents for my father.

DAVID WILLSON

Tuesday, November 3, 1931:

I am still thinking about a profession. The *Crimson* will be holding a competition soon. I may go out for it. I saw Bennett tonight for a short while. We both have studying to do.

Saturday, November 14, 1931:

I took Elaine to a party; actually she took me. Everybody was from "home." It was wonderful hearing the southern way of speaking all at once, and again. I met a lot of nice people, especially girls.

Monday, November 16, 1931:

Sometimes I think Bennett and I are not really friends; that is, we hardly ever talk about personal things: clothes, girls, subjects (except where they enter into our future plans), or anything friends usually talk about. We talk always of politics, theories of government, communism vs. capitalism, the race problem. But then, these ARE the things which truly interest us and—why not?

The reason I express the doubt is because we can never double-date or go to the same parties. I am, I must confess, even with my liberal feelings, a clubbie, and more, a southerner. I had to come to the cold and bleak of New England to find that out. I walk through the Square and find myself comparing things, always comparing things: "The people seem sadder here than at home," I will say. Or "The houses are not as pretty," or "The people are less friendly," or, and finally and what I am getting at, "The girls are not as nice." This I always say and my feelings about this, more than anything else, keep Bennett and me apart socially. Because though we know girls here, girls who are in the liberal groups, I have yet to find one among them I would want to take out.

The reason this comes up is that I asked Bennett whether he would like to go double with me to The Game. He looked at me, shocked. "My dear fellow, have you gone completely insane?"

"Why?"

"Why indeed. Think of the girls you've been dating here. Why, it's as if you never left the South. And how do you think they would take to me? Like kittens to water. You certainly couldn't go to any of your friends' parties."

I continued to defend the idea though I could see now it was a bad one. "Well, we wouldn't have to go; we could just have a foursome. That might be nicer. Big parties are always sloppy and too noisy anyway."

He put his hand on my shoulder and smiled sadly. "David, it's better the way it is. We can't push our friendship into places where it's not wanted. Our friendship need not be all-encompassing; it need not include all of the trivial things that make up life. In our hearts we believe in the same things and what we're trying to do is work for the day when we CAN, indeed, go to a Pudding gathering together. Don't you agree? Now don't worry about me. I have parties to go to and friends to see in Boston. If we try to push this too far, too soon, we won't have anything."

I know he is right but—God damn!

Tuesday, February 9, 1932:

Bennett and I have decided to room together next year. We hope to get into Adams House, B-entry, which is the old Gold Coast, built for millionaires, gaudy, and Victorian as all hell.

Thursday, March 10, 1932:

Today (the last minute) we handed in our application to room with one another in Adams, Winthrop, and Lowell Houses in that order of choice. I have quite gotten over my awareness that he is a negro, but still I have not told my family. Of course, I have told them all about him (how could I avoid it?), even how he looks with his portly build, but always omitting the color of his skin. I know

I must tell them because they will find out sooner or later and I do not want them to think I kept it from them because I am ashamed of him. I do not, however, want to write it to them. Perhaps I will do it when I go home for spring vacation. I hope they do not make a huge thing of it because I will have to make a stand, and to be honest (I know no one will see this record), I need them, at least to send me through school. I am not as diligent and hard-working as Bennett, who is working thirty hours a week in his cleaning shop and still doing fine enough work to be in the top fifth of our class.

Monday, April 25, 1932:

I forgot to take this journal home and have not had time since I returned to write here, but now I will try to catch up.

The most important thing that happened at home was that I told my parents about Bennett.

I had waited until just before they went to bed, when they were in their room and the Calibans would not hear or come in. (I did that just in case my parents got a little heated and said derogatory things about negroes that perhaps they would not have ordinarily said.)

Mother was sitting up in bed, looking very pretty and feminine in a nightgown. The warm light caught her gray hair and made it twinkle. Father was sitting in the chair, scanning the paper.

I decided not to hem and haw. "Bennett Bradshaw is a negro," I said, just like that. "He's the boy I want to—"

"He's a WHAT?" I was quite sure Father would have said this, but he was just looking up very calmly over the tops of his glasses and his newspaper. Mother had spoken, her hands planted firmly at her sides holding her body stiff and straight from the waist. Under the covers I could see her legs moving excitedly.

"He's a negro, Mother. The boy I'm going to—"

"And you're actually going to LIVE with him for three years? Why . . . why . . . you must be joking, David."

"No, I'm not, Mama." I had not called her that in a long time. "He's my best friend at school—"

"I don't care what he is! You're not going to LIVE with him. You're not even going to speak to him, ever again. Do you hear me, David?" There was a funny quality to her voice; she should have been yelling, but instead she seemed almost to be whispering.

I nodded, but just to tell her I had heard her, and turned to Father, who was still peering over the paper, his face as lifeless as mud; I could not tell at all what he might be thinking.

"David!" Mother was talking again. "Do you realize what you're doing? Do you actually realize? Why I wouldn't be surprised if you were never invited to another respectable party in your life. Rooming with a negro—why that's the most insane thing I've ever heard."

"And you are unbelievably bigoted." I had wanted to stay calm, but all of a sudden I had blurted THAT out and saw my mother's face turn pink, and her mouth drop open. And then she started to sputter.

"You shouldn't show that kind of disrespect to your mother, son, even if you're thinking such things." Father FINALLY spoke and folded the paper in his lap and leaned forward.

But I certainly could not call the words back down my throat, and although my head was not too clear at the time—my ears were filling up with a buzzing sound; pictures and words were popping like cannons—I am not at all sure I wanted to call them back. I just turned on him too.

"It isn't fair of you to send me to a place like that and expect me to remain a good, aristocratic, southern white boy!" Only the sentence was not that clear. "There are some fellows there that don't even believe in God! And you expect—"

"I don't expect anything." Mother had recovered. She turned to Father, who returned her look. "Demetrius? I TOLD you he would be better off at State. I TOLD you that ages ago. NOW it's gone too far. Next September David will go to the State University at Willson City."

Father did not say anything; I could not see his face too well and thought I saw him nod, as if in agreement, and that was too much. The buzzing in my ears got louder and I started to cry. I have not cried in so long I forgot what it feels like; it is like vomiting. You start sobbing and you cannot see, and your stomach feels like hell. God, it was bad. They were both looking at me and I could not face them. "Awh, shit!" I said and turned and grabbed at the knob, missing it a few times, finally got the door open, ran down the hall and locked myself in the bathroom. I felt like a seven-year-old girl!

I was running the water, mopping my face and trying to stop crying, which I did pretty quick, though I was still sobbing, sitting on the edge of the bathtub, when I heard someone knocking at the door and my father's voice, calling, "David. Unlock the door, son."

I told him to go away, not so much because I was mad at him as I did not want anyone to see me, especially him. He is a hard little man; I mean, I have never seen anything upset him like that. But he kept talking through the door and finally I let him in.

He is small, at least a half-head shorter than I am and has iron-gray hair and clear gray eyes and here I was, looking down at him and sobbing. I felt foolish. He did not say anything, just came in, not looking at me, went to the toilet, put down the top, and sat.

I sat on the tub and kept swabbing my face with cold water, and drank some. Then I turned off both me (the sobbing) and the water.

We sat in silence for a few more minutes, then he looked at me. "You're right, boy. Can't expect you to come back and be the same as you always were. You got to change some. In my day this wouldn't have happened because everybody had to shift for himself, find his own room and the more money you had, the better place you'd live in and you'd be living with boys of your own level and type. They'd be your friends. But what with this new system, they take the money out of it and so you get a cross-cut. Right?"

I nodded.

He smiled, looking at the tile. "The old place has really got you by the toe, and it's not letting go soon, is it?"

"No, sir."

"Well, don't worry. You're not leaving until you get put out one way or the other: flunking or graduating. I'll see to that." He looked at me squarely; I could have run a thousand miles and never got out of his gaze. "Now tell me something. Why's it you want to room with this colored boy?"

I thought, but did not know what to say, and finally mumbled: "Because I like him and I learn a hell of a lot from him. But I guess it's mostly that I like him."

He leaned back and put his hands into the pockets of his bathrobe. "That's what I wanted to hear you say. If you'd said something silly about the equality of man, or that you were trying to make your blow for a better world, I would have told you that you're making a mistake. You don't make friends with folks because it's right, you make friends because you like them and can't help liking them." He paused. "Don't worry. I'll square it with your mother somehow." He got up, even before I could thank him, and went out the door.

So that is the way it was. God, what a showing!

Before I left, I apologized to Mother; she did not look at me.

Sunday, May 1, 1932:

Elaine Howe got engaged to, of all people, a fellow from Bangor, Maine.

Saturday, May 28, 1932:

Bennett took his last exam yesterday and left this morning. He has to start work in New York on Monday. He certainly has strength of purpose; he will not have a vacation for a long time. As for me, I have been stuffing knowledge frantically and am almost completely exhausted. I shall miss talking to him, but we will write this summer and of course room together next year in Adams House.

Friday, November 23, 1934:

When I got home from my classes (about noon) there were two telegrams for Bennett under the door. I was supposed to have lunch with him at one, was to meet him in the dining room, so I took them with me.

I was sitting at the end near the windows looking out on the old gray buildings across Bow Street, starting my meal with a cup of coffee, when he came in, took off his overcoat, put down his books. I waved to attract his attention and after he got his food, he came and sat down. "These came for you." I handed him the yellow envelopes. "I hate the God-damn things. They always bring some kind of disturbing news and they're so damned impersonal about it." I laughed.

"I agree." He smiled, picked up his knife and slit open the first one.

I was watching him, hoping the news was good, but could not tell from his face. He handed the telegram across to me:

MOTHER PASSED AWAY TEN-TWENTY

AMELIA

I did not know what to say. He was reading the other telegram but mumbled to me, knowing I was looking at him. "Amelia's my sister." Then he handed me the other telegram:

MOTHER SUDDENLY ILL COME QUICK

AMELIA

He was watching me when I looked up from the second telegram. "God, Bennett, I really don't . . ."

"She was quite a young woman—thirty-eight. It was hard work." He looked down at his plate.

I almost asked him WHAT was hard work, but then realized that had he finished the sentence it would have been: that killed her. I did not say anything. I was looking at him intently, not realizing for a moment I was searching almost sadistically for some show of emotion. I did not expect him to burst into tears before me; I wanted to see, though, just exactly what he would do. I found myself thinking: *All right, Bennett Bradshaw. You can cope with anything; nothing upsets you. Well, let us see how you handle this one. Let us see if you can be so damned smug about this.* I felt ashamed when I realized what was going through my mind.

But he showed no sign of cracking and I was glad. I guess I simply wanted to see if he was human (he is, very; I mean in this situation) and hoped he would prove to be. As many times as I have written here about him, it must be obvious I idealize him quite a bit.

He was looking at me. I hope he could not read my thoughts. "I'll have to go to New York today." He stood up. "I'll go and try to get in touch with them. Have you got a timetable?"

I shook my head.

"No matter. I'll call the station." And then he was gone, striding to the other end of the dining room where he had left his things.

I saw him again for a few minutes in the room, but he was in a hurry and I did not get a chance to talk to him.

Tuesday, November 27, 1934:

Bennett got back from New York this morning—with very bad news. His father is not alive and so he has three sisters and two brothers, all under eighteen, to care for all by himself. He can farm them out to various relatives, but he wants to keep the family together and that means he will have to leave school almost immediately and get a full-time job. He is going to try his best to finish the term, but he is not sure he can. I so wanted to tell him I would wire my father and get him enough to last until February, but I think maybe he would have declined my offer and may even have been hurt and insulted. God, with just over a half year to go, this had to happen to him. And he deserves to get his degree, would do so much with it.

Thursday, December 20, 1934:

I am writing this on the train now, going home for Christmas vacation. Bennett and I came down from Cambridge together in a truck he borrowed from his uncle, some kind of junk dealer, to bring his belongings, especially his books (he could not bring himself to sell them) to New York. He (Bennett) drove me right to Penn Station.

Driving down, we tried to keep our minds off the realization we would not see each other for a long time, and talked rather of those things that will keep us together in spirit and thought, if not in body: our common aspirations for social betterment, our common hatred of ignorance, poverty, disease, and misery, what we hope to do about it. Bennett did most of the talking, his voice resonant and eloquent, like he was addressing a thousand people, using only his voice, which has always been enough to captivate me, when we were going through a village or town, or when the road twisted dangerously through the trees, and using his hands when the snow-banked road was straight. "After you graduate, you go back South and get that writing job. We'll need your articles; you'll be our 'agent.' You can let us know what's going on. You can write articles about the situation and I'll get them published in New York. We'll shame them, persuade them, bombard them into a better way of doing things. And everybody will benefit. Think of what we can accomplish if we work hard!"

A DIFFERENT DRUMMER

We rattled on closer to the city in the unheated cab of the truck, not noticing we were cold, not having or wanting to give time to think about that.

We reached the city early in the evening and moved downtown toward Pennsylvania Station.

Bennett parked the truck on a side street and I climbed down from the cab and went around to the bed to throw back a stiff, gray tarp and lift down my suitcase.

"Redcap, sir?" Bennett came up next to me and smiled. A taxi swished by through the black slush, and sprayed his legs.

"No, thanks. I'll carry it." I hefted it in my right hand. My books made it heavy. (I hope THIS TIME I can study at home.)

He looked at me squarely. "No, let me. The purpose of friends is to do such things."

So I handed him the bag and we climbed over a low bank of dirty snow and headed toward the avenue where pink and green lights shone and we could see the high stone columns of the station.

"Do you think you'll get to finish up? School, I mean." I did not turn my head to look at him.

"I think so. Amelia will graduate from high school in June and doesn't want to continue her education; perhaps she isn't equipped to do so. She'll get a job and keep the others until I can finish."

We stopped at the corner and watched for a second, even after the light changed, the cruising taxis, and brightly painted delivery trucks, and the people, many of them carrying suitcases and trudging toward the station. We crossed the street.

"You think you'll be able to get a decent job?" This was the only way I could express it, my concern. I wanted to say so much more, but did not want to be embarrassing or sentimental. Still, in some veiled way, I wanted Bennett to know I was sorry he did not have the means to finish school immediately. I realize such things are almost a normal, expected part of a negro's life, that negroes are conditioned, almost resigned, to dashed, or at least delayed, dreams; I wanted him to know I regretted the delay, not just out of pity for the deprived ones, but because I, myself, would be deprived of Bennett's companionship.

"Yes. I wrote the SOCIETY and they said they could probably find SOMETHING for me with them." We were on the steps leading to the marble hall, overseen by a fortlike information desk.

"You won't be doing that long. They'll give you something important to do in no time."

"I certainly hope so. Forty years is a relatively short time to work miracles." We both laughed at our idealism. I realize now we wanted to laugh desperately.

Redcaps, most of them without uniforms or badges, carried luggage or pulled iron carts along the shadowy platform. Here and there stood groups of denim-clad mechanics; blue-suited conductors, with gold stars on their sleeves, checked schedules or waited, like party hostesses, in train doorways. Besides these, there were people. A family was crying good-bys to an old woman peering at them through a window. Bennett and I walked until, far down the platform, we came to an empty doorway. Bennett handed me my bag. "Well now, write, will you?" He paused, then added, "I'll be waiting for those reports."

"They won't start coming until I'm home for good, but I'll let you know if anything interesting happens in Cambridge." I put down the bag and, with my foot, pushed it up against the wall of the doorway. I was standing in the vestibule.

"Well . . ." Bennett stretched out his hand.

But I just looked at it; I did not take it, did not want to say good-by so soon, and grabbed for something to say: "Let me know what you think of that Federal aid idea I talked about."

"All right, I will. But I can say now I don't think it will work. In the first place . . . yes, well . . ." He reached out his hand again; this time I had to take it.

"Take care of yourself, Bennett."

"Certainly . . . I will." We shook hands. "Good-by, David."

Steam was beginning to rise into our faces from under the car. Down the platform, working his way toward us, a conductor was slamming doors and flipping switches.

"Good-by, Bennett." We shook hands again and he turned away just as the conductor arrived and closed the bottom half of the door. I turned into the car, then back, but Bennett had disappeared behind a bank of people. I saw him once again walking away, short, stocky, and determined, his arms swinging like marching at his sides. Then he disappeared for good as the train began to move slowly out.

Wednesday, January 2, 1935:

I arrived in Cambridge at about 9:30 P.M. A letter was waiting for me from Bennett. He started at the NATIONAL SOCIETY FOR COLORED AFFAIRS on Monday. He seems to enjoy it and says it is not just a clerical job. I did not do any studying at home (who ever does?), so I will have to get to it.

Tuesday, January 8, 1935:

I received a letter from Bennett today. He says he will try his best to write every week. I find myself almost completely friendless with him absent. At least I will get some studying done.

Thursday, June 20, 1935:

Well, I made it through. I graduated today. This week has been very hectic and I have not had a chance to write here. My parents came up, seemed to enjoy it all very much. Bennett could not make it. He thought he might. I looked forward to seeing him; I have not seen him since before Christmas. The weekly letters have helped to make our separation a bit easier. Perhaps I will get to New York in August.

Tomorrow we go home and Monday I start at the *Almanac-Telegraph* as a cub reporter. I hope I like it; I think I will. The four years on the *Crimson* gave me a great deal of enjoyment and excitement and I learned something too.

Monday, August 26, 1935:

I did not get to New York last week as I had planned. I was assigned a long piece on the Governor and had to go to Willson instead.

I sent Bennett a piece, *Trade Unionism and the Southern Negro* today. He will try to get it published up there. As he recommended I used a pseudonym: Warren Dennis. I have ideas for several others, but let us wait and see how this one does.

Monday, September 2, 1935:

I received a letter from Bennett. He liked the article "very much." He said: "It shows great insight. More of the same, dear friend." He got me forty dollars for it. I am just glad someone wanted it. I told him to accept the money as a donation to the Society. Well, I will start on those others now. I guess articles are not anything special, but at least I am doing what I can to help out—and it is far better than collecting my father's rents.

Friday, July 10, 1936:

I met—well, I did not actually meet her; I do not know her name, but I will find out somehow—the nicest, prettiest girl tonight at a party on the Northside. A pretty girl with dark brown eyes and brown hair; she was wearing a blue dress, which was a little too good for her to be a part of that wild bunch. She did not look like she belonged there at all, but there she was swilling—I first noticed her at the sink mixing a drink—with the rest of them. She was not like the others there at all, not noisy or a Bohemian. She hardly opened her mouth. She made me a couple of drinks, and sat next to me when I asked her to, but when the party broke up she had already gone. I did not see the boy she came with. I hope she is not married to someone. Anyway, I will find out.

Thursday, August 20, 1936:

I found out her name: Camille DeVillet. But when Howard told me, it was too late to call; I will try tomorrow after work.

Sunday, February 7, 1937:

I got married today; what more is there to say?

Monday, February 7, 1938:

Today is my first anniversary: one happy, good, sweet year. If, a year and three quarters ago, someone, anyone had said, "Willson, there will be a year in your life filled with nothing but happiness. You will not be so nervous; you will not smoke so much; you will eat right and sleep soundly and warm at night, and you will not, not once during that year, be lonely," I would not have believed him; I would have thought him incurably insane. But wonder of wonders, it is all true. This last year has been the happiest of my life. And the thing is, the miraculous, glorious thing is that the next fifty or so will be just as happy, just as dear, just as good.

This is no storybook, fairy tale, ever-after, never-never-land marriage. We have our squabbles. She will clean up my desk and I will not be able to find anything and will call her down for it. I will get peevish and snappy with her when I cannot seem to get a story out on paper. She will get a backache once every twenty-eight days and blame it on me as if I had anything to do with THAT. But those are tiny things, nothing compared to the days, the weeks on end when we'll just enjoy being with each other. I love her more every day; every day I learn more about her to love, and what is more, I like her. If she was not a girl, a woman (and what a woman), if she was a man, she would most certainly be my best friend.

The only thing we lack is children, a child, and this is because right now we just make ends meet. I ought to get a raise soon and then we can "git to gitting 'at young'un."

We got a card from Bennett today. He also enclosed a note saying he had sold the article I wrote: *The Corrosive Effects of Segregation on Southern Society*. The magazine, he said, is way, way, Left, but if they are the people who want what I have to say, I imagine that is all right.

Saturday, March 5, 1938:
Camille told me her period is overdue by two weeks. She did not mention it because she thought it could be that tennis we played last Sunday.

Actually she did not out and tell me; I forced it from her. There is a high shelf in the closet, where we keep some junk, some boxes of summer clothes. The boxes are quite heavy; last fall when I put them up there I had trouble with them myself. When I came in last night, she was just getting up on a chair to lug them down. I asked what she was doing.

"I'm looking for something."

I took off my coat. "Here, let me help you. They're heavy."

She looked down at me. "That's all right. I can manage. I'll do it. You sit down and rest."

"What do you mean you can manage? I could hardly manage those boxes myself. Come on, get off the chair."

Those brown eyes of hers glazed over; when she gets mad, they go flat and hard like bits of tree bark. "You DON'T have to help me. I can MANAGE."

For an instant I was going to joke with her, but then I decided to let her alone. I forgot about it (I did not even mention it here yesterday). But this morning I got up late and heard the water in the kitchen whistling and went in to say hello and she was on the floor, on her back, her legs lifted about six inches off the floor, her face red with strain, her whole body quaking, talking to herself: "Come on, come on, come on, come on!" She dropped her legs, waited a few seconds, lifted them those same six inches, held them, threw them apart, pulled them together, apart, together.

I was standing behind her; she could not see me. The kettle was whistling and I had not worn any shoes; she could not hear me, but finally I said: "Hey, Camille, the Olympics aren't until 1940, if then, what with the situation in Europe. What are you doing?"

She sat up startled, looking at me, a little afraid.

"What are you doing?"

And then she told me she was two weeks behind. "And that's strange because if watches had never been invented, I would have been able to keep track of time since I was thirteen. First the backache, then the headache, then the cramps, and then the rest. Just like that, like a train schedule or the phases of the moon."

I told her not to worry; it would come. And if it did not—so what? Maybe it is wrong for us to wait because we might wait too long. It is not of course that we do not want children; we want huge numbers of them; we want to fill a house with them. But we DID want to wait until we had some money in the bank. But anyway, I will be getting that raise soon. So there is no need to worry. Of course, we do not know for certain she is pregnant, but being a father does not seem like a bad idea at all to me. If I am going to be a Daddy, I think I will break with Willson tradition, will not give the child a name beginning with "D." And if it is a boy, I would like to name him Bennett Bradshaw Willson.

Saturday, March 12, 1938:

No sign of anything yet and Camille is no longer doing those foolish exercises. It looks like I am going to be a father. My God! How can I be so calm. I am actually going to be a father!

Monday, March 14, 1938:

I went into the office today, expecting to get a raise and got fired instead. Someone, I do not know who, read the article on the corrosive effect of segregation, found out I wrote it, I do not know how, and I got fired for it. Well, hell! I am glad it is out in the open. Now I can write them under my own name. There is no reason for me to be ashamed of the truth. I will go around to other papers starting tomorrow. I have been doing good work and people know it. I do not think it will be too hard to get another job.

Monday, March 21, 1938:

Camille went to the doctor. He says it is a bit too soon to tell, but he is pretty sure she is pregnant. He will know more in two or three weeks.

I have been to three of the seven papers here. No soap. If anything, they are more conservative than the A-T.

Thursday, April 14, 1938:

Camille is quite definitely pregnant.

Tuesday, April 26, 1938:

No paper in New Marsails will touch me. I have been blackballed. What the hell am I going to do?

I got a letter from Bennett. I had told him it looked like I would not be able to get work. He said to come on to New York. But I cannot pack up Camille now and make a total move. Suppose I could not get anything in New York. We would be even worse off. I have to find something here. Perhaps this will all die down, and someone will take a chance on me. God damn it! I am a capable journalist.

Thursday, May 5, 1938:

Nothing! Nothing!

I got a letter from Bennett. "Be brave, my friend. Come to New York. Your writing has made an impression here. You will definitely, I promise, find work. But if you can't, I am working, and thus, you are working too."

I asked Camille about it. She did not hesitate a second. "I can have everything packed in . . . let me see . . . four days."

But I suspect this is just her concept of stoic and unworldly southern womanhood. I do not think she really wants to go. I think she is more afraid than I am, if this is possible.

As much as I hate the idea, we may have to move back to Sutton, back to the Swells and my family and the collecting of rents.

But I'm not defeated yet; perhaps something will open up here.

Wednesday, June 1, 1938:

I had another talk with Camille. She still maintains she would go to New York. "I love you, David. We'll go. The baby has to go because I go." She laughed. "And I want to go because you do. If you move back to Sutton, you won't get over it. It'll never be the same. So come on now, let's go to New York. I'll follow you anywhere."

I do not believe her. She tries so hard to do the right thing, but she does not want to go. I can see it plainly.

I wrote a letter to Bennett telling him I would definitely be moving back to my family.

DAVID WILLSON

Tuesday, June 7, 1938:

I received Bennett's answer: "Now that you have made your decision, I will attempt in every way I know, fair or foul, to make you rededicate yourself and come to New York."

I am afraid it is no use, Bennett. My rebuttals to you will not be adequate to convince you, or even myself. I am watching a parade and I know I should be marching proudly, but I am shackled to the curb. I have to do what I feel is my first responsibility. There is nothing else I can do.

Wednesday, June 29, 1938:

I received a final long letter from Bennett yesterday, his last attempt to get me to change my mind. It ended:

Together, you and I planned a great deal, arrived at some remarkable conclusions about things—I thank you for your part in all this—and I hoped we could use these together to lead our peoples to the things we felt were right for them, but now you will not be with me. The enthusiasm we shared for our futures can no longer be shared. One of the important touchstones of our friendship has disappeared! All this is to say that I cannot see any reason for us to communicate with each other from this day on. This will certainly be my loss.

Of course, I will never forget you completely. You may not be a part of my future, but you will remain a part of my past.

> *Good-by, David, and Luck to you,*
> *Bennett*

Monday, August 15, 1938:

We moved to the Swells. My family is understanding. But I know they are patronizing me. All of them! Camille too.

A DIFFERENT DRUMMER

Thursday, September 1, 1938:
I collected rents for my father.

Wednesday, October 20, 1954:
I clipped this article from a national magazine today:

RELIGION

"Jesus is Black!"

As the torchlight glinted off his six-inch, watch-fob crucifix, and cries of "Jesus is black!" died in the packed hall, The Rev. Bennett T. Bradshaw, founder of the Resurrected Church of the Black Jesus Christ of America, Inc., harangued his flock in a not quite legitimate English accent: "We have declared war on the white man! To the white world and all it stands for, we vow death!"

The group, known as the Black Jesuits, founded in 1951 by New York-born, Ivy-educated, red-dipped Bradshaw, claims 20,000 members. ("And growing all the time.")

The Man . . .

Bitten by a Redhumbug early in his dear, old, incomplete (he left after 3½ years) college days, Bradshaw joined the staff of the National Society for Colored Affairs in 1935, was purged from that organization in 1950 when his communist affiliations hustled him before various congressional committees.

After the NSCA gave him the gate, finding all other gates closed to him, Bradshaw decided to sneak in by the back door of race relations: religion. Says he: "It's true that I received my calling soon after my forced resignation from the Society, but I assure you, one thing has nothing to do with the other."

Bradshaw, a bachelor, lives alone on the top floor of the Harlem building which houses his church, prowls the area in a new, black, chauffeur-driven limousine donated by a devout, brick-laying follower. ("I couldn't very well refuse it; the man saved three years to give it to me.")

. . . And the Movement

Organized like the Marines, the Black Jesuits have a doctrine which is a mixture of Mein Kampf, Das Kapital, and the Bible. The group is anti-Semitic. ("The Jews do most of the exploitation for the white man; look at the people who hold the leases on Harlem tenements.") The Black Jesuits believe only those parts of the Bible which support black supremacy, believe Jesus to have been a Negro. ("The rest was added or changed to keep the dark-skinned people in place; the Romans had their race problem too.") But even this line is not fixed. What Bradshaw preaches, the Black Jesuits believe. And though his bulls are not always consistent, Bradshaw claims they are direct-from-heaven, revised revelation.

As concern grows over the adverse effect the Black Jesuits have had on New York race relations, says Bradshaw in his best Bible-pounding style: "We have them running scared now. They know we'll take our rights, if they don't give them to us."

Bennett, Bennett, now we are both lost.

Saturday, June 23, 1956:
John Caliban, who worked for our family over fifty years, died today on the bus carrying him to New Marsails.

Saturday, August 18, 1956, 7:30 A.M. (of the past seven hours):
I have not yet been to sleep, having just returned from a ride with Tucker. We went out to look at some of my property north of town, where, years ago, before my time even, the Willsons had

179

their plantation. I sold Tucker seven acres of that land at the south-west corner.

It has been a strange evening. I do not at all understand why, but I have a feeling something special has happened; I imagine this feeling, however, is simply an overdramatization of my own experience which has not been particularly important to anyone. (I suppose I wish it had been.) Well, I might as well set it down as best as I can remember:

I was alone in the study reading. It was hot and quiet tonight —actually last night—and I had just gotten up to open the window wider, when there was a knock at the door—a quiet knock, almost timid, as if the person outside was afraid to ball his fist, not wanting to be the least bit aggressive, and instead knocked with the back of an open hand, a scraping sound. I called out: "Yes, who is it?"

"Tucker, Mister Willson." That high-pitched nasal voice of his!

I returned to the desk. "What is it, Tucker?"

"I'd like to see you a minute, sir."

"Come in."

I watched the door open, and saw him, small, dark, in his chauffeur's suit, white shirt, and black tie. He looked a child pretending to be an undertaker. He was holding his black cap in front of him in both hands. The desk lamp reflected in his glasses so his eyes looked like giant, flat, golden circles.

I was already reaching into my pocket for my wallet, taking it for granted he wanted cash to buy gas, oil, or whatever he thought the cars needed—I usually do not waste time asking him; he simply tells me how much he wants. "Yes, Tucker, what is it?" I had the wallet out, pried open to the billfold, and was ready to start counting with my thumb.

"I want seven acres of your land." He was almost rude, but that is his way. He had taken only a few steps into the room, enough to close the door behind him, and stood, looking out of those shining disks, his eyes and the expression in them hidden from me. "Seven acres up on the plantation."

I looked up surprised. "What on earth for?" I replaced the wallet in my pocket and leaned back in the chair, intent on the two small suns embedded in his face, trying to pierce through them to his eyes.

Tucker did not move; he seemed a small black statue, seven-eighths life-size. "I want to farm some." I know, knew then, this was simply an answer, but somehow it did not seem to matter. It did not seem right to baldly call him to task for lying, but I DID want to know what he was up to.

I decided to ridicule him; perhaps he would come out with it. "You farm? You've never farmed in your life. You don't know anything about it."

He nodded his head just once, acknowledging the truth of my statement. "I'm planning to try." He had not moved; he hardly seemed alive he was so still and erect.

My ridicule had not worked so I decided to be a bit more paternalistic. "Sit down, Tucker."

He did not hesitate; walked—marched really—toward the desk, sat in the chair beside it, his back still straight.

"Where did you get the money?" I leaned on my elbows, knit my hands, and rested my chin.

"I saved it. My grandpap left me some." He was annoyed by the question, did not want to be fathered. "Will you sell me the land?"

"I don't know." Perhaps I could have answered just then—Yes or No—but suddenly I had the feeling I was in a play; I had certain lines to speak, and he too, and we had to say them so the play would proceed in a predestined order. "That's the land Dewitt Willson staked out. No one has ever owned an inch of it. And I'm not sure you're the right person to be the first."

He nodded and started to get up; this too was a kind of act. "All right, sir."

It was my "aim" now to stop him. I did. "Wait a minute, Tucker. Perhaps I'm being too hasty. What do you plan to do?" Again I leaned back in the chair, still watching him. I could see his eyes now, but they were as emotionless as the disks of light had been.

"Plan? I don't understand, sir."

"Plan. What exactly are you planning to do with the land? Why do you want OUR land? Why can't you buy someone else's land?"

"I just wants to do some farming, is all."

"What kind of farming?"

"Just farming. Corn, cotton, just farming."

"But WHY come to me?" I leaned forward and balled my fists. And this is strange. I found I was taken up very much in this mock drama, found myself caring a great deal. "You must know we've never sold that land to anyone. Why should we start now?" He just stared at me. "And why must it be on the plantation? We have land to the south of town. It's better land anyway."

His lips hardly moved. "I don't want that land. Now will you sell me some land on the plantation?" The tone of his voice was almost irritated, almost angry.

Perhaps I'm a southerner after all because his almost surly attitude got to me and I snapped at him. "You shouldn't speak that way, Tucker. It can get you into serious trouble."

And he came right back at me, made me feel ashamed of myself. "We ain't white and black now, Mister Willson. We ain't here for that."

I felt very tired now, and dropped all my defenses. "But don't you see, Tucker, if I'm to sell you our land, there has to be a concrete reason. You know I can't just give it to you. I suspect you wouldn't even take it if I did. You want to pay for it." I resorted to finance and added, "And I have to know you can meet the payments on it."

"I ain't making no payments. I got enough right now."

"How do you know? I haven't told you the price yet."

"I have enough money to buy twenty acres, and besides, you know whatever I got to offer is enough." We stared at each other for what seemed like a long time.

"I know, but say it so I can hear it, Tucker. It's important that I hear it." I found myself almost pleading with him.

He nodded. "I want that land on the plantation because it's where the first Caliban worked, and now it's time we owned it ourselves."

"What else?" I was leaning forward now, anxious.

But he disappointed me. "I don't know. When I'm there I'll know. Now all I can say is my new baby ain't working for you-all. He'll be his own boss. We worked for you long enough, Mister Willson. You tried to free us once, but we didn't go and now we got to free ourselves."

I straightened up and looked down at my papers. "How much do you want to pay, Tucker?"

And so we talked cost. Tucker told me how much he had, which, as he had said, was enough for at least twenty acres. I showed him a map of the area and pointed out where the seven acres were.

Tucker nodded. "That's where I wanted it."

"Why?" We were closer now than we had ever been. We had come to a very strange kind of agreement that I don't quite understand except that I was doing something I realize I had always wanted to do, and also because it was almost like those things I wanted to see done twenty years ago. And Tucker, he had realized something was wrong with his life and was trying to set it straight. What each of us wanted so much individually we helped each other to do.

"Something special there," he answered, "something my grandpa told me was out there." He did not go on.

"Well, it's yours now. I'll have a deed drawn up tomorrow."

He continued to surprise me. "You draw it up and keep it. I

don't want no deeds. It's mine and besides, you don't want it enough to cheat me out of it." He said that with a smile in his voice, but not on his face.

It was a nice moment, one of those moments of communication I had experienced so seldom and I wanted to prolong it. I asked him if he wanted to go out there to see the property. "Now, I mean. I'd like to drive you out there."

He did not answer; he just stood and started toward the door. I followed him, and then remembered something my father had given me when I first came back to live here. He had gone into his desk and got it out and handed it to me. "This isn't yours," he had said. "It belongs to the Calibans. But they're not ready to have it yet. You give it to them when you think they should have it." He did not tell me what it was, but I knew as soon as I saw it because I knew the old tall story as well as anyone else; everyone knew it, and enjoyed it, but I doubt if anyone thought it was any more than a story. When my father gave it to me, I was not sure any more. So I went back to the desk and pulled open the drawer and found it under a pile of papers, and a bit dusty, and walking to Tucker, pulled out my handkerchief and it started to shine in the single lamp light. I handed it to him.

He took it from me, and I watched his eyes closely and saw them cloud a bit, the closest I had ever seen him come to tears or, in fact, to any other emotion. He put the white stone in his pocket, turned abruptly and went out the door.

On the way out there with Tucker beside me in the front seat, I realized this was the closest I had been physically and alone with a negro in almost twenty years, since the beginning of the Christmas vacation of my senior year. On that time, Bennett was driving, and talking, talking, as I sat beside him worrying that he would not watch where he was going, would not be able to see even an elephant in time through the dark glasses he had suddenly begun to wear for

no apparent reason and we would crack up and not even get a chance
to start all the things we planned. Both of us shivering like wet
kittens in the cab of that truck. The closest I have been to a negro,
yes! in more ways than one.

Perhaps it would have been better if I had not survived that trip.
As it turns out, I never accomplished anything anyway. I do not
mean, of course, I wish now, at this very second, to be dead. That
is a little too melodramatic. I mean only that I have made so many
people I loved so unhappy because I did not have the courage to go
ahead with my plans. Because I was a coward, I made them all
cowards, made them worse than cowards because they waited for a
coward to take action.

Especially Camille, waiting, patient, faithful Camille. She made
her stand so much better than I did, told me she would go to New
York just as long as I was happy. And I can see now she meant it.
But I did not believe her. She had the faith in me I needed, and
because I would not accept that faith, she lost faith in her faith too;
I cheapened it. It was too late when I realized that, after all, she
was actually a human being capable of thought, not just a slave or
a pet or a southern woman. I betrayed us both.

This was one of the things I asked Tucker tonight. I turned to
him and found him sitting there staring far out down the road,
thinking, as engrossed in his thoughts as I had been in mine, and
I asked him what Bethrah thought about all this, about his buying
the land.

"She's worrying, Mister Willson. I reckon she thinks I gone
crazy." He does not even have it as easy as I had it. Bethrah is a
lot more independent than Camille ever was.

"Doesn't that bother you at all? Doesn't that make you want to
stop?"

"No, sir. It's something I got to do."

"Doesn't she want you to think about it? Buying a farm is a big step, especially since you've never farmed before. Does she want you to do it?"

"No, sir."

"How can you then? Don't you think she has some say in the matter? I mean, you know she's a very intelligent girl. And she may be right."

"Don't matter if she is right. It don't even matter if I'm wrong. I got to do it, even if it's all wrong. If I don't do it, ain't none of these things going to stop. We'll go on working for you forever. And that has got to stop."

"Yes, it does, doesn't it."

"Yes, sir."

We drove on. To our right, above Eastern Ridge, the sky began to get gray, the black lifted, and the country took on the blue color of a stained-glass window, seeming to possess light but not to give it off. We had come almost to the farm. I turned once more to him. "Could anything make you give this up?"

He did not hesitate. "No, sir."

"I don't imagine anything could, if owning that farm means so much to you."

He looked at me. "You only gets one chance. That's when you can and when you feels like it. When one of them things is missing, ain't no use trying. If you can do it, but don't feel like it, why do it? And when you feels like it, and ain't no opportunity, you just knocking your head against the front of a car going a hundred miles an hour. There ain't no use in thinking about it if you ain't got both. And if you HAD both and missed out, you might as well forget about it; your chance is gone for good."

I nodded; I know all about that.

THE MEN
ON THE
PORCH

They had not gone home.

They sat now at nine o'clock Saturday evening as the last carloads of Negroes passed by Mister Thomason's porch through Sutton going north. All afternoon the cars had been moving by in caravan, with the frequency of those in a funeral procession. Now the flow was thinning, not appearing over the Ridge in bunches, but singly like lone vacationing families. There were still more automobiles than usual, but not as many as before. To himself, each man sitting on the porch wondered whether the slackening numbers of vehicles laden with children, old people, adults, and babies, mattresses, blankets, and suitcases meant that New Marsails was vacant of Negroes.

They knew for certain no Negroes remained in Sutton, for after two that afternoon, only a straggling few had lined Thomason's porch waiting for the buses, and from where the men sat on the porch, looking toward the Square, they could no longer see any cars coming from where the Negroes lived at the northern edge of town.

A DIFFERENT DRUMMER

After Mister Harper left at six, some of the men went home to supper, though most bought something from Thomason, and continued to sit, munching on crackerjack, peanuts, candy, or apples. After they had balled the wrappers and tossed them into the street, some of them had stood and gone up to the Negro section to look around.

They had found nothing, no houses lit; the Negroes had felt no need even to set lights in the windows as people do to keep burglars away, for they had taken anything they really valued, had left the rest for burglars, making it easy for them by leaving the doors swung open. Some had even left keys in the locks, an invitation to anyone who might want to occupy the house for good. The men from the porch could not bring themselves to enter the houses, retained that respect for house and property that is southern, that kept them from setting foot on Tucker Caliban's land on Thursday, but they did peer over the thresholds into the darkness and found a great many things inside: chairs, tables, sofas, rugs, brooms, beds, and trash. Most of the walls were empty of the pictures of stern grandparents, or soldiering sons or married daughters, and crucifixes, those things without which people do not feel able to start a new home. If the men had gone inside and looked under beds, they would have found the dustless rectangles where, only a few days before, suitcases had rested. There were no Negroes at all.

So they came back to the porch. They did not discuss what they had seen, for each man had seen it himself. They sat silently, thinking, trying to figure out what all this had to do with each of them, how tomorrow, next week, or next month would be different from what yesterday, last week, last month, or all their lives had been up to this time. None was able to think it through. It was like attempting to picture Nothing, something no one had ever considered. None of them had a reference point on which to fix the concept of a Negro-less world.

THE MEN ON THE PORCH

Then Stewart came, driving up in his wagon, a jug as squat as he was himself sitting beside him on the seat; they passed it around, each man wiping the nozzle with his sleeve in the old, useless rite of purification and cleanliness.

That was when they began to get angry, quietly fighting mad, like a bride left at the church, wanting revenge, but having no one on whom to avenge herself, angered by her own frustration more than anything else. They disguised their loss by maintaining it was no loss at all, just as the Governor had done that morning.

Stewart took another healthy swallow. "Sure! What we need them for anyways? Look what's happening in Mississippi or over in Alabama. We don't have to worry about THAT no more. We got us a new start, like the fellow says. Now we can live like we always lived and don't have to worry about no nigger come a-knocking at the door, wanting to sit at our supper tables." He was sitting on the porch steps next to Bobby-Joe, who had been very quiet since Mister Harper left.

"Look-it, there'll be plenty of work, plenty land—all the work and all the land them niggers was taking up. We'll be doing right well soon as we get arranged." Stewart was sweating now, as he always did, drinking or no, hot weather or cold, and pulled his handkerchief from his pocket.

"But there might be too much work and too much land." Loomis pushed his hat forward on his brow and tilted his chair back against the wall of the building. "We might not have enough folks to do it all. That's some economics I learned upstate. That means we won't have enough food. There'll be a parcel of land nobody can use. There's always been enough land for everybody, leastways enough to break your back on. This ain't JAP-an; you don't see nobody planting up on the sides of the Ridge, using a rope to keep him from falling off."

"We'll still be better off." Stewart turned around, squinting to

189

make out Loomis in the shadows of the porch. "Take Thomason there. He's running the only store in Sutton now. Before, there was two; that nigger up there, he had a store. Now Thomason's got all the business."

Loomis shook his head. "Yes, but there's LESS than half the customers."

He could not stop Stewart. "And look at Undertaker Hagaman. He's the only undertaker around now. We all got to get buried one day. I hear tell how even some white folks in Sutton used that nigger undertaker."

"I just ain't sure it's all to the good. You never had no WHITE folks sweeping around in stores, only colored. You getting a job sweeping now, Stewart? That's the only job you really good for."

Some of the men laughed.

Bobby-Joe snapped his fingers; the sound carried, echoed. "That's it!"

They all turned toward him. He had not been talking, though he had taken a few drinks. He sat with his feet planted at the edge of the Highway, resting one elbow on the naked knee showing through a hole in his coveralls. "I told you-all there was more to it than that."

"Look there, Loomis. Bobby-Joe's talking to hisself already and he ain't had but a couple swallows." Thomason was sitting on a chair he had carried out of the store. "Son, you shouldn't drink if you can't hold your liquor no better than that."

"Shut up!" Bobby-Joe was savage. "You too drunk or stupid to see what's really going on around here." He paused. "Now, what you suppose he doing down here if it ain't to carry in all this trouble? That's it! I knowed there was more to it than that."

They stared at him, blinking, squinting, trying to see him better, as if seeing him better would help them to better understand what he was talking about. "Who's doing what?" Thomason leaned over his stomach toward the boy. Stewart mopped his face nervously, as he did when he thought he was too dense to understand something that was supposedly easy to understand.

Bobby-Joe twisted around. "That nigger preacher come driving by here and we just sat here watching him like he was the President. We should-a knowed; we could-a done something about it." More excited now, he jumped to his feet, turned to face and lecture them. "We could-a stopped him; that was like having a naked girl in arm's reach and not doing nothing about it but blush."

"Now, hold on, Bobby-Joe." Thomason turned to Stewart for an instant: "No more for him," then back to the boy. "We'll listen to you, son, but you got to make yourself plain. Now, why don't you just settle down and start all over again."

But Bobby-Joe just went on. "God damn! if we ain't a stupid bunch of bastards! We could-a done something when we was a-gazing at that car, and at that driver, and all that money he was tossing around. We could-a done something, YESTERDAY, instead of just sitting there and looking, and then we wouldn't be crying now because they's all gone. We could-a DONE something!"

All at once Thomason understood. "You talking about that nigger from the Resurrected Church, ain't you." It was not a question, rather a realization, as if the idea had suddenly popped into his head without Bobby-Joe's help: about Friday and the Negro in the limousine.

"Yeah. That's what I'm talking about. That northern nigger preacher what came down here and started all the trouble. God damn! And we had him right here and didn't do nothing about it, just stood around watching him flash all that money."

"Now hold on, boy. That man didn't show up here until AFTER Tucker Caliban did all his business. He asked Mister Leland what he knew. He couldn't-a knowed nothing about it."

"Did you believe that? Did you really believe that? You REALLY think Tucker Caliban was smart enough to start all of what we got on our hands? I bet you did." He spoke as if he believed Thomason had committed a crime. "Well, I didn't believe it for a minute. I knew what that northern nigger was up to all the time." Bobby-Joe was waving his arms now, striding up and down before them as if they were a jury, and he was a lawyer. "That African and his blood coming down to Tucker Caliban. That's bull if I ever heard it!"

Stewart, weaving a little from the waist, pointed a finger up at the boy. "Oh, sure you knowed all the time." He smiled. "That's why you said so MUCH yesterday! Boy, don't lie to me; you didn't know nothing more about it than we did. So don't lie to me because I'm apt to take it personal."

Bobby-Joe backed up a step. "Well, all right, so I didn't know yesterday, but you-all heard me when I said I didn't believe that blood business Mister Harper was trying to feed us. I didn't believe that crap, and that's what it was too: crap! How the hell can something what happened a hundred fifty years ago—if it happened at all—how can that have something to do with what happened this week? That ain't nothing but tripe. No sir, it was that northern nigger, that agi . . . agi . . . what they call fellows what come in and stir up trouble?"

"Agitators." Loomis stuck in his answer though Bobby-Joe had hardly paused.

"That's right, Mister Loomis, them agi-TAT-ors. He came down here, him in that big black car, and got all the niggers to move off, go somewhere else instead of staying here where they belongs."

"But he didn't know nothing about it, Bobby-Joe." Thomason did not know why he kept resisting an idea that seemed so easy to accept. Perhaps it was his store-keeping mentality, the numbers and figures he had to tally and carry, keeping him from believing something he probably wanted to believe. "Or else why did he come back here? Ain't no man dumb enough to come calling on you after he raped your wife or knocked up your daughter. He'll leave you alone, or run, or hide, but he won't come knocking on your door."

Bobby-Joe put one foot on the porch and leaned forward. "I always thought you was plenty smart, Mister Thomason. You been smart enough to fool folks into thinking your prices is fair, but you ain't smart enough to see he'd come back here just out of ordinary, everyday meanness to crow over us, and see how his plans worked out. That's why he come back."

"Say now, maybe the boy's got something." Stewart turned his head to look up at Thomason, nodding.

Thomason was speaking to them all, trying to bring some reason into the conversation. He was beginning to sense, almost smell in the air, that they were listening and believing Bobby-Joe. "But we ain't seen him today, boy. He ain't drove by here at all after yesterday; he ain't been hanging around the colored section helping them pack. And there ain't been no other fellows around here making sure they all had a way to travel." He was losing them, like grain between his fingers and wished Mister Harper was there to keep reason, or Harry to slow them down.

"He didn't have to see that," Bobby-Joe went on. "Why should he? Them northern niggers don't really care about the niggers down here. They just want to give us white folks trouble and make us all, white and black, unhappy. His job was over when he started them off. Then all he had to do was sit in the back of that car and laugh his ass off, all he had to do was watch the fun. What he care about how they got away? They all traveled without any help from anybody anyways."

Thomason sighed. "Well, all right then. So what? So he caused it. Can't do nothing about it now."

This silenced them all for a moment. Bobby-Joe sat again and lit a cigarette. The rest stared off above the roof tops at a few bright stars. Someone asked for a match. Someone else gave it to him.

"It's all over now." Thomason went on. "There ain't no reason to get all bothered about it. If he did it, I reckon he did himself a good job. There ain't nothing more to say." Give a little to get a little, Thomason was thinking.

The men nodded, murmured agreement.

"Boy, if I could get my hands on him, I'd surely have something to do." Bobby-Joe pounded his fist into his hand. "I'd punch that smile right off his face."

Had they been sitting across the Highway, they might have seen the car come over the Ridge, its lights tilted upward as it climbed through Harmon's Draw, illuminating a small rim of the horizon like a tiny, cold rising moon. Then it gained the crest, tipped downward like a delicately balanced scale, bathed the road in front of it in one long stream. The light was visible and the car behind it dark, so had they been looking, they would have seen only the shaft swooping toward town, until they would no longer have seen the shaft either, just one ball of light made up of the lamps and the grill. Then as it got closer, they would have seen, not the one ball, but two distinct head lamps and finally the lamps and above them the faint patch of green with a light-skinned Negro's face in the right corner. It was that close when they noticed the stream in the street in front of them, lighting the buildings across the way, and they turned toward its source to count, as the car sped by, the number of Negroes they expected to find inside, not that they were tallying any totals, just counting individual carloads only to forget them almost immediately. But there was only the light-skinned Negro in front of the limousine, and in back, two figures, the nearer, a Negro with long graying hair and dark circles for eyes, sunglasses, reclining as if in a beach chair. Then Bobby-Joe hopped to his feet, rushed into the middle of the Highway in enough time to be obscured by the dust and exhaust and the shadows, and the men on the porch could hear him screaming out of the veil of dirt: "Hey you, you God-damn preaching son of a black bitch, stop that car! You hear me, nigger? STOP THAT CAR! I WANT TO TALK TO YOU! STOP THAT CAR!"

When they passed Thomason's store, Dewey did not see the boy, close to his own age, his hair hanging shaggy and straight around his ears, lunge into the street behind them, waving his fist at the car, but the chauffeur saw, and heard the boy yelling after them, and smashed the brakes so the car came to a skidding, screeching halt just under the General's gaze. Bradshaw bent to his microphone. "What's wrong, Clement?"

"Someone back there was yelling at us. I didn't see anyone, Reverend. I don't think I hit anything." Before he finished the men from the porch pounded down the street to them, surrounded the car, tore at the handles, opened the doors, and a young face, that Dewey recognized, but could not name, was peering in at them through the open back door nearest Bradshaw. Even across the seat, Dewey could smell the stench of stale liquor.

"Well, look-a-here. We got him. It's him. Look, Mister Stewart."

Another face joined the boy's, an older face, with red, flabby, sagging jowls which almost obscured a thick-lipped mouth. "Well, God damn! Is this him, Bobby-Joe? So that's the nigger what started all the trouble." He smiled.

The boy nodded. "It surely is. What'd I say? You remember? I wanted to get my hands on this one, didn't I? And some angel must-a heard me, because here he is."

Dewey leaned across Bradshaw up into the boy's face. "Wait just a minute. What's wrong with you?"

The boy grinned down at him; his teeth were uneven, several front ones chipped and broken off short. "If it ain't one of them nigger-loving Willsons what let Tucker Caliban work for them until he was rich enough to start this trouble. Did you help your nigger friend plan this, MISTER WILLSON, SIR?"

"Plan what?" Dewey could feel his body beginning to shake; he tried to steady his voice.

"Plan WHAT?" The boy nudged the fat man with his elbow. "Plan what, Mister Stewart? What he talking about? You reckon he's talking about all the niggers running off? Yes, I reckon that's what he's talking about."

The fat man grinned. "Must be what he talking about, Bobby-Joe."

Behind these two, Dewey saw two or three others, then four and then five materializing out of the shadows, standing quietly, listening, their faces alike, unfriendly, in the leftover light of the head lamps.

"He didn't have anything to do with that." Dewey tried to remain calm, hoping that his own calmness would calm them, as he would try to remain calm when approaching a cornered animal. "It wasn't planned at all."

"How do you know? You been talking to somebody? You been talking to your nigger friends, MISTER WILLSON?"

"This man didn't have anything to do with it. It was completely spontaneous."

"Oh, it was spon-TAN-eous, was it?" The boy turned to the fat man. "You hear that, Mister Stewart. They sent him North to learn some big words and I reckon he come back with a carload. What's spon-TAN-eous mean—planned?"

"No, not planned. It means it just happened all by itself." Dewey reached out and tried to pull the door shut. The boy punched his hand away from the upholstered handle.

"You better watch yourself, MISTER Willson, unless you want a piece of this nigger's pie."

"Come on, don't be ridiculous. He didn't have a thing to do with any of this."

"He tell YOU that?" The boy leaned into the car; the liquor smell became stronger, intoxicating.

"Yes, of course. He doesn't even know Tucker Caliban. He told me he didn't have anything to do with it." He looked into the boy's eyes. In the eight months he had been away, he had almost forgotten the gaze he found there, the gaze which came in moments like this, for it was not one of the looks that New Englanders use or have ever used to express a turn of mind or heart; it was a gaze more cold, more mean, more cruel even than the gaze a Vermont farmer gives a stranger asking directions; more cold, more mean, more cruel because it was completely blank, that very blankness a sign of the renunciation of alternatives, of tenderness or brutality, of pleasure or pain, of understanding or ignorance, of belief or disbelief, of compassion or intolerance, of reason or unswerving fanaticism; it was a gaze which signals the flicking off of the switch which controls the mechanism making man a human being; it said: Now we must fight. There is no more time or need for talking; violence is already with us, part of us.

"He didn't have anything to do with it." Dewey tried one last time, softly. "Reverend Bradshaw, tell them." He grabbed the Negro's arm, looked into his face and found not fear was keeping him silent, but disillusionment. He was not thinking of the present danger at all, only of the Negroes, his Cause, riding out from under him. If anything, Dewey realized, Reverend Bradshaw wishes he could say he had been the instigator, wishes he could say he planned it by himself, got Tucker to buy the farm and destroy it, told the Negroes this was their example, exhorted them to follow. But he could not. And this was no time for disillusionment and self-pity. "God damn it, tell them!"

The fat man too was leaning into the car. "Why don't he say something?"

The boy chuckled. "Could be he's too honest to tell no lies." He grabbed the collar of Bradshaw's shirt. "Tell the truth, nigger! Did you have anything to do with it?" He lifted him partly off the seat.

"No! I'm sorry to say I did not."

It was as if the second had swelled, and was about to burst. All seemed to solidify into an instant of violence like a statue depicting the moment a warrior's blade enters the body of his adversary, and the stricken man is about to fall but has not yet fallen, is lying flat out on the air itself, defying balance. And then the moment burst, and the boy took a firmer hold on the shirt—"You're a liar!"— pulled Bradshaw forward, dragged him from the car, out of Dewey's vainly reaching arms, and onto the pavement. Five men surrounded him quickly all flailing, punching, kicking.

Dewey slid across the seat, looked down, and saw Bradshaw lying face up, a strange, twisted, fearful smile on his face; he did not seem to be struggling or resisting, as if he realized it was no use. His eyes were open, watching, active, looking up almost disinterestedly into the dark and grotesque faces of his assailants, following the punches as they came down from high above him and broke on his face and body, seeming to possess no more concern for them and whatever pain they caused than a man sitting in a warm room watching snow fall by his window. But Dewey was screaming, trying to pull the men away. "It was Tucker Caliban! It was Tucker Caliban!" He was silenced by an elbow which swung back at him, stung his mouth, and made blood ooze from a cut on the inside of his cheek.

"Get him away from the car!" someone yelled. "Give me some punching room too! Get him over here!" The man who yelled reached down into the midst of the flying fists, grabbed Bradshaw by his legs, dragged him toward the sidewalk. The rest, not to be cheated, followed their target.

Dewey followed the mob, still clutching at arms and backs, then saw the boy turn to him, his jagged mouth grinning, saw, but could not duck the blow which landed flush on his temple, saw then the blackness broken into flecks of white and red. An instant after, he found himself on the pavement, his hands in the same defensive position he had thrown up against the oncoming blow. The boy stood over him for a second, then turned away to where the men had gathered around Bradshaw, driving their fists into his face, and kicking him as one kicks a tin can down a dark street, with absent-minded savagery.

"Hey, hold it! Hold on for a second, fellows!" The boy was running toward the men, waving his arms. "Hold it!"

Dewey, still sitting on the ground, saw some of the men turn around. "Why? What?"

He pulled himself to his knees, still groggy; perhaps the boy, who seemed to be their leader, did believe him after all. Perhaps he would persuade them to stop now.

"Hold it, fellows. I just thought of something." All of the men had stopped now, were standing up straight, listening. Bradshaw lay groaning softly at their feet. "You fellows know this is our last nigger? Just think on that. Our last nigger, ever. There won't be no more after this, and no more singing and dancing and laughing. The only niggers we'll ever see, unless we go over into Mississippi or Alabama, will be on the television and they don't sing none of the old songs, or do the old dances no more. They's high-class niggers with white wives and big cars. I been thinking that while we still got one, we ought to get him to do one of the old songs for us."

The men stood blankly, not quite understanding what the boy

was talking about, trying to decide if he was serious or not. A few, who wanted to get on with what they had started, looked down at Bradshaw.

Then the fat man spoke up. "I get your meaning, Bobby-Joe. I get your meaning." He started to laugh uproariously. "Our last nigger! That's good. He weren't really ours when he come down in his big car, but he is now, and we can have him do anything we want him to do."

"That's right, Mister Stewart." He joined the fat man in laughter. One by one, so did the other men: "I get his meaning."

The boy pushed his way through the gathering and with the fat man's help, tugged Bradshaw to his feet.

Dewey was on his feet too, realizing they were not stopping, but rather drawing out the ritual. "You can't do that to him!" He rushed into the mob, his head down, his fists swinging, but was caught tight just short of the boy by two or three men.

The boy looked up. "Somebody get a rope from Thomason's and tie up this nigger-lover. If we hurt him we WILL be in trouble. His pa'll put us off his land." Several men held Dewey while someone ran for the rope, returned; they bound him hand and foot and pushed him down to the pavement.

"Now let's get on with our show. What can you do, nigger? All you niggers can do something."

Bradshaw stood dazed and bleeding between the boy and the fat man, his clothes ripped and rumpled, his glasses, miraculously still on his nose, a bit crooked. He did not answer.

"Talk now! What do you know?"

The fat man balled his fist. "I'll make him talk."

"No, Mister Stewart, there'll be time enough for that. Right now, he's being good enough to entertain us. What do you know? Do you know 'Curly-Headed Pickaninny Boy'?"

Dewey saw Bradshaw nod; of course he knew, everybody knew

it; it was a song liberal-minded third-grade music teachers in New York, Chicago, Des Moines, San Francisco, and all the towns in between had their pupils sing to acquaint them with Negro culture; in Cambridge it was sung whenever anyone with a guitar who prided himself as a folk singer got together with a group of people who considered themselves folklorists; it was known all over the country, had been sung for a long time. And Dewey realized that Bradshaw's nod had signified a knowledge of something else; he knew now and could understand why the Negroes had left without waiting or needing any organizations or leadership.

"Well then," the boy started and then his eyes narrowed. "Sing it."

Bradshaw sang softly in an off-key, near monotone:

> *Come, come, come to your mammy,*
> *My curly-headed pickaninny boy.*
> *Come, come tell me your troubles*
> *And mammy will give you joy.*
> *I know what you need is a kiss on the cheek,*
> *To sooth all the bad dreams that on you sneak—*
> > *So,*
> *Come, come, come to your mammy,*
> *My curly-headed pickaninny boy.*

It was a fast song, with a cakewalk beat, and sounded strange coming from Bradshaw because, with his British accent, he pronounced all the words correctly without a trace of a Negro accent. The men did not like it that way and began to grumble. "He ain't very good."

The boy gripped him by the throat. "This time sing it like a nigger, nigger."

The fat man wanted something else: "Yeah, and dance too!"

"And sing loud so I can hear it," shouted someone at the edge of the crowd.

Dewey sat straining against the ropes, but could not free himself. He had been yelling for them to stop, but no one paid any attention.

Bradshaw started again, this time hopping comically from one foot to the other, his stomach jouncing. He had half-finished when the boy stepped in front of him and punched him full in the face. "You stink! Get him in the car. We might as well use HIS car to take him. It's bigger. More of us can go." The boy and the fat man grabbed Bradshaw by the shoulders, half carried, half dragged him, almost over Dewey, back to the car, tossed him in.

"He didn't have anything to do with it!" Dewey twisted toward the car; the chauffeur had fled, no one had seen him go. Someone climbed into the driver's seat, found the keys, started the motor, making more noise revving it up than was necessary. The driver was calling to the others to climb in, and Dewey heard the doors slam, one—two—three—four. He tried to scramble to his feet, still yelling after them, but he had not even gained his knees when it sped off, up the Highway in the direction of Tucker Caliban's farm. Even when he could no longer see it, he could still hear the motor.

"But he didn't have anything to do with it." He slumped, like a baby sitting down, and began to cry.

The street was empty; peaceful like a spot where a rock has been newly turned, after the bugs have scampered away and there is no sign of bugs ever having been there. Dewey was sitting almost on top of the white line, crying in the stillness.

Then he heard the squeaking wheels, the constant, piercing scream of the unoiled joints; saw the chair and the erect, limp-haired woman and the old man coming out of the shadows. He said nothing and they did not see him at first. Then they were close enough to hear his quiet crying and started toward him. "Who they got, Mister Willson?" Before Dewey could answer, the old man turned to his daughter. "Untie him, honey."

She let go the back of the chair and came around behind him. He felt her soft hands on the coarse ropes; the pain stopped as his bonds loosened. "Reverend Bradshaw. They think he did it . . . started the Negroes off. I have to hurry. Maybe I can save him." He jumped to his feet as soon as she untied them.

"You might as well not try, son. You won't get there in time. And they'll be worse after they've done it. None of them'll come to town tomorrow . . . won't be able to face each other for a while." The old man looked sad.

"You actually feel sorry for those bastards! Well, maybe you won't do anything, but I have to do what I can." He took a step away from them.

"You can't do anything, boy." The old man raised his voice. It rang quietly down the empty street.

The lights of an oncoming car shone on the buildings. The old man's daughter rushed to the chair and wheeled it closer to the curb.

"Boy! Look at this car!" The old man swiveled and shouted at him. "Study it!"

Dewey turned and watched the car. There was a fat Negro driving. His wife sat peacefully beside him, her eyes awake and bright. In her arms was a small child, a girl with many tiny parts in her hair; she was sleeping. The back seat was piled high with luggage.

"Yes, I feel sorry for my men. They ain't got what those colored folks have."

Dewey was still watching the car. It had reached the outskirts of town and then was gone. He approached the old man.

"If it'll make you feel any better, Mister Willson, that's the last time. And I'll tell you something else." The old man looked up at him and smiled. "The General wouldn't have approved." He turned to his daughter. "We still got some coffee in the pot, honey?"

"Yes, Papa."

"Mister Willson, how'd you like some coffee? You better not go home just yet. You better clean up first."

Dewey nodded and they started up the street together.

Mister Leland did not know what woke him. At first he thought it was Walter shifting, recoiling from a many-headed monster in his dreams, but when he looked over at his brother, he found him in the same position into which he had wriggled just after their mother had kissed them good night. And then he heard it again: a scream.

It came from the direction of the Highway, maybe up near Tucker's, came through the muffling trees separating their two farms. Maybe Tucker was back and having a party. But where? Tucker did not have a house. But he could be having it outside, it was warm enough, and besides, no one else would be at Tucker's farm.

He started to shake Walter to tell him Tucker was back and having a party. Now he could hear other voices, other men laughing, and he knew they must all be Tucker's friends, slapping him on the back, happy to see him again, especially since they thought he had left for good. He stopped shaking Walter because the shaking and nudging had done no good, and even if Walter were to wake up, he would be too groggy to understand anything.

Mister Leland lay on his back, listening to the faint laughter and to someone who had started to sing and thought about the party. They might have popcorn there, and candy, and soda. It would be a good party, with people happy to see each other like the reunions his people had at his grandfather's house in Willson City. He had been to only one of those reunions himself and even though he had been very small, he could remember it very well. He had been lying in bed, and could hear the grown-ups laughing and singing and when he got up in the morning, they were all asleep, even his grandfather who was a farmer like his own father and usually started work while it was still dark. He had gotten up, the only person awake in the house, had gone into the parlor and found they had left some of the candy and popcorn from the night before. When everybody finally woke up, red-eyed and wrinkled, his uncles and aunts, he had already eaten enough of the leftover party food not to be hungry any more.

He lay on his back and thought about that, and then he knew what he would do when morning came. It would be Sunday and first they would eat and go to church, where his mother taught Sunday school, and then they would come home. He would take Walter by the hand and they would go back through the woods and come out on Tucker's field. Tucker would see them and wave and they would run across the soft, gray earth of the plowed and salted field toward him. He would say hello, and would be glad to see them. Mister Leland would show him Walter.

Then Mister Leland would ask Tucker why he came back. Tucker would say he had found what he had lost, and he would smile and tell them he had something for them. He would bring out large bowls of the leftover candy and popcorn and cracker-jack and chocolate drops. And they would eat until they were full. And all the while, they would be laughing.

ABOUT THE AUTHOR

William Melvin Kelley was born in New York City and attended the Fieldston School and Harvard, where he studied under Archibald MacLeish and John Hawkes. He has taught at the New School and the State University of New York at Geneseo and is presently teaching at Sarah Lawrence College. His stories and articles have been published in a number of magazines, including *The Dial*, *Accent*, *The Harvard Advocate*, and the *New York Daily News*. Mr. Kelley has lived in Paris and Jamaica and now resides in New York City, where he is writing, teaching, and creating videos.